Following the example of Calamity Jane and Belle 'the Rebel Spy' Boyd, more of J.T.'s ladies prove that they too can play a major role in stories of action and adventure.

Annie 'Is-A-Man' Singing Bear, Rita Yarborough, Dawn Drummond-Clayton and Woman Deputy Alice Fayde all demonstrate that they *don't* need a gallant hero to solve their problems for them!

J. T. Edson

MORE J.T.'S LADIES

CORGI BOOKS

*For all the ladies who have acted as my 'minder'
and nursemaid at various Western Writers of
America Conventions and probably aroused much
speculation amongst the other members present*

MORE J.T.'s LADIES

A CORGI BOOK   0 552 12899 6

First publication in Great Britain

PRINTING HISTORY
Corgi edition published 1987

This book is set in 10/11pt Times

Corgi Books are published by Transworld Publishers Ltd.,
61–63 Uxbridge Road, Ealing, London W5 5SA,
in Australia by Transworld Publishers (Aust.) Pty. Ltd.,
15–23 Helles Avenue, Moorebank, NSW 2170, and in New
Zealand by Transworld Publishers (N.Z.) Ltd., Cnr. Moselle
and Waipareira Avenues, Henderson, Auckland.

Reproduced, printed and bound in Great Britain by
Hazell Watson & Viney Limited,
Member of the BPCC Group,
Aylesbury, Bucks

Contents

Author's Note

To save our 'old hands' from repetition, but for the benefit of all new readers, we have included in the form of APPENDICES details regarding the career and background of Woman Deputy Alice Fayde and Dawn Drummond-Clayton, also an explanation of various terms about which we have frequently received requests for clarification.

We realize that, in our present 'permissive' society, we could use the actual profanities employed by various people in the narrative. However, we do not concede a spurious desire to create 'realism' is any excuse whatsoever for doing so.

Lastly, we refuse to pander to the current 'trendy' use of the metric system. Except when referring to the calibre of those weapons traditionally measured in millimetres—i.e. Walther P-38, 9mm—we will continue to employ miles, yards, feet, inches, stones, pounds and ounces, when quoting distances and weights.

J. T. EDSON,
Active Member, Western Writers of America,
MELTON MOWBRAY,
Leicestershire,
England.

PART ONE

ANNIE 'IS-A-MAN' SINGING BEAR
In
TO SEPARATE INNOCENCE FROM GUILT

'I'm sorry, Miss Singing Bear,' the bartender stated with genuine sounding contrition. 'But I can't serve *you* no liquor, not so much's a beer, even though you're only part Inj—you're here with this reverend gent.'

Business was not particularly brisk at the Lone Star Saloon in Claxton, seat of Gareth County, Texas, that Friday evening. Half a dozen soldiers were drinking beer at a table near the main entrance, the newness of their dark blue uniforms and their sun reddened faces suggesting they were recruits only recently enlisted in the United States Cavalry. There were eight cowhands wearing what was just as clearly their 'go to town' clothes who were imbibing by the side door. Maybe twice as many more local citizens formed smaller groups scattered around the rest of the bar-room. In addition to the girl accompanied by the sombrely dressed man who had just arrived at the counter, six players in a stud poker game completed the roster of customers.

In view of the comparative lack of trade, the declaration by the bartender might have struck some people as strange for one who should have his employer's profits at heart. However, although the female customer was only in her late 'teens and, as yet, no legal restrictions of that nature were enforced, it was not her age and, as suggested by the lack of rings on her hands, unmarried status which had provoked the comment. Those who possessed a greater knowledge of the West and the laws of the United States governing the prohibition of sales of liquor to Indians would have appreciated what was meant by the first part of the revised explanation.

Not more than five foot four in height, the attire and appearance of the girl gave indications that she was of mixed blood and, to those cognizant with such matters, probably of Comanche origins on one side. However her hair, instead of being black, cropped to shoulder length and parted down the middle as was usual for an Indian of her age and sex, was reddish brown and formed into two braids after the fashion of a warrior. While her pretty coppery bronze face was broad and the brown eyes were somewhat slanted, the nose was snub rather than aquiline, making the whole more Caucasian than Indian in its lines. When crossing to the bar, her movements had a light footed agility which implied she was very fit and the 'hourglass' contours of her curvaceously buxom figure were clearly comprised of firm flesh rather than produced by artificial aids such as corsets. Bareheaded, she wore an open necked, loose fitting, multi-coloured cotton shirt hanging outside faded Levi's and she wore moccasins on her feet. In further defiance of accepted Comanche female fashion, buckled around her trim waist over the shirt was a belt inscribed by the medicine symbols appropriate only to a fighting man of that race. It carried a walnut handled Colt 1860 Army revolver, with the barrel shortened by about half, in an open topped high cavalry-twist draw holster at the right and, at the left, a J. Russell & Company 'Green River' hunting knife hung in a sheath made from *wapiti* hide.

Despite the girl's companion having ordered a beer, although he had been prevented from saying anything else by the warning from the bartender, there was some justification for him having been referred to as 'the reverend gent'. Of medium height and in his late twenties, he had a black Texas-style Stetson hat tilted back on his head to show rusty-red hair. Despite a luxuriant moustache enhancing a solemn expression, his tanned face had a rugged attraction. His stocky, powerful frame was clothed in a sombre black three-piece suit, white shirt and black necktie, such as a stringently practising member of one of the more strict religious denominations might wear. While his black boots had sharp toes like those favoured by cowhands, their heels were low and suitable for one who spent much of his time on foot. Riding slightly higher than was usual on a stiff wide belt, an open fronted spring retention holster of a kind more often seen on shoulder rigs held a Rogers & Spencer Army Model revolver with bell-shaped, square bottomed black walnut grips.

'I'd serve you, was I allowed,' the bartender supplemented. Being experienced in his work, albeit newly arrived at Claxton, he was aware there were often very stringent objections when he had to refuse to make a sale. 'But it's the *law*, you know!'

'That it is,' agreed the black clad man, his tone as solemn as his appearance and his deep voice that of a native Texan. 'And, like the Good Book says, whether the law of the land be right or wrong in your opinion, verily it's still the law of the land and has to be upheld.'

'Being reared right 'n' proper on momma's milk, I've never took to beer nor nothing stronger,' the girl went on, her accent also Southron in timbre. 'A big ole glass of "sass-parilly" will do most well for me.'

'Coming right up!' the bartender declared, joviality replacing the concern he had experienced over having to refuse to serve the female customer with beer. He was relieved that she responded in such an amiable fashion. While he was reaching beneath the counter, having had a religious upbringing which had enabled him to supplement his wages by settling more than one bet on the subject, he tried to remember whether he had read the man's quotation in the "Good Book". Failing to remember it, he brought out a bottle of sarsparilla and poured its contents into a glass. 'I prefer this to liquor myself, Miss Singing Bear. Excuse me, it looks like them gents from the Wedge want serving.'

'How're you making out with that Pointin jasper,

Annie?' the sombre looking man inquired, after the bartender had walked away, curling his fingers around the glass instead of holding it by its handle, and turning to lean against the counter with an air which suggested—his appearance notwithstanding—he was at ease in such an environment.

'He's been steering clear of me just recent', I'm right pleased to say,' Annie Singing Bear replied, eyeing the man in question—who was one of the poker players—with a less than flattering gaze. 'We got on great until he started on about how Indians never slaughtered the buffalo, nor no other wild critters, promiscuous like the white folks do. Seemed he didn't take kind' to me telling him how I'd seen pappy and the other bucks of our village run more than one herd of buffalo over a cliff and leave 'em to rot 'cause getting 'em out' d've been too much of a chore. It got worse when I let on's how it wasn't only us Comanch's did it, but every other tribe—' specially the Cheyenne and Sioux—and the *Itehta'o* was give that name by the rest of us *Nemenuh* because they allus put up a whole slew more pemmican than they could figure on eating in a winter and threw away so much's'd been left over in the spring, it seemed right 'n' fitting they got known as the 'Burned Meat' band.'[1]

'His sort only want to be told what they want to hear,' the Texan declared and his scrutiny of Clivedon Pontin was no more complimentary than that of the girl.

'Ain't that the truth, Solly,' Annie seconded. 'He's the first white man's I've ever met's'd believe them secret things, like sitting 'n' sending messages to folks's a long ways off somehow,[2] like some of our medicine makers can do. He was just's willing to take's true some antics I made

---

1. 'Nemenuh', *'the People'*, *the Comanches' name for their nation.*
1a. *The spelling of all Comanche names is phonetical.*
2. *Examples of how one trained in the mysteries of Comanche 'medicine' could communicate by some form of mental telepathy with a person many miles away are given in*: GO BACK TO HELL *and* WHITE INDIANS.

up which were so magical, I figured a jasper's well schooled as he allows to be'd know they wasn't nothing 'cept tall tales. Would you reckon *anybody'd* take it as true when he was told's, after the proper medicine was made, a brave could follow a feller on a sunny day by the marks his shadow left on hard rock? Well, *he* did.'

'I'm not surprised,' the black clad man admitted in tones redolent of disgust. 'While his kind won't accept *nothing* miraculous from the Bible, nor what it's reckoned elsewhere's white folks can do, they're willing to take as gospel everything jaspers from other countries, so long's they aren't Europeans, are reckoned to be able to do, no matter how unlikely, nor even impossible.'

'He's not showing what I'd call real *good* sense sitting in a game with that lard gutted Martin Oates,' Annie declared, directing an equally distasteful glance at the other player clad in eastern style clothing, albeit of a cheaper kind and older in style, if no more cleanly. 'Which I hear him and those three college-Injuns he brought along've been losing regular in the evenings out to Oates' trading post ever since they got here.'

'The game should be straight enough tonight,' the Texan assessed, making a gesture which indicated the two Texas cowhands and the big Cavalry sergeant seated at the table. 'Leastwise, I don't reckon Oates'd be *loco* enough to chance anything crooked with Stone Hart, Waggles Harrison and Paddy Magoon in the game.'

'Just take a look here, Johnny,' a voice with a Texas' drawl requested, before the conversation could be continued. 'Would it be Calamity Jane, or maybe the lady owlhoot, Belle Starr, would you reckon?'

'It ain't not neither of them ladies, Rusty,' replied the second speaker, whose tone indicated similar origins. 'This here's Annie Singing Bear, only she's better knowed's "Is-A-Man".'

Even without having heard their accents, the pair who had come to the counter while the bartender was delivering drinks to their companions would have been identified

11

as typical Texas' cowhands. In their early twenties at most and bare headed, the taller had fiery red hair and the shorter's was of a rusty brown hue which indicated how he had acquired his sobriquet.

'Now why'd you reckon they'd call a *gal* that?' "Johnny" inquired.

'They reckon's how she's been taught as a brave, 'stead of learning right humble 'n' proper to be a gal,' "Rusty" explained, as the pair came to halt in front of the girl and black clad man. 'Now me, I don't reckon's how such should be.'

'Nor me,' Johnny asserted. 'Anyways, I don't reckon's how *any* gal can learn how to do things like a man. 'Specially something like drawing a gun, for instance. *Every* gal's I've met, which's *plenty*, would shriek, holler and have the vapours should they even *see* it being done.'

'Would you, *Is-A-Man*?' Rusty queried, his manner implying he considered her sobriquet undeserved.

'Could be *I'll* shriek, holler and have the vapours was you to draw,' Annie replied with deceptive mildness, moving a few steps away from her companion and thumb hooking her hands into her belt. Her manner was redolent of challenge as she continued, 'Anyways, being so all-fired eager to find out, why don't one of you knobheads give it a whirl and see?'

'Hot damn iffen I *don't*!' the taller cowhand accepted, stepping away from his companion and halting in front of the girl. 'Ain't *nothing* riles me *more* than an uppity woman and ain't nobody going to say's how Johnny Raybold of the Wedge was *slow* to put her in her *place*!'

Having delivered the final sentiment, the fiery haired Texan sent his right hand towards the butt of his low hanging Army Colt. While the move lacked the flashing speed which could be attained by one of the acknowledged masters of Western style gun fighting, it was performed with sufficient precision and rapidity to indicate he was reasonably well versed in such matters. Nevertheless, he did not meet with the success he had clearly anticipated.

12

Far from shrieking, hollering, or having the vapours, Annie reacted in a much more positive manner!

In one respect, Johnny might have counted himself fortunate. As was implied by Rusty, the girl had been educated to be a Comanche warrior. What was more, her sex notwithstanding, she had learned her lessons so well that she had earned the right to have the name she was given in her childhood, 'Should Be A Boy', changed to, 'Is-A-Man'.[3] However, she refrained from employing any of the more lethal methods which she had been taught. Despite having two weapons on her person which she could handle with considerable proficiency and deadly effect when necessary, she made no attempt to touch either. Instead, displaying a speed in excess to that of the cowhand, she caught his right wrist in both hands just before he could touch the butt of his revolver. With a deft notion which prevented his fingers closing on the walnut grip, she twisted his arm behind his back. Then, putting to good use the strength of her well muscled buxom body, she swung him around and, bringing her left knee against his rump, propelled him away from her with some force.

Although the girl had dealt with the attempt to draw a gun in a most competent fashion, her troubles were not over. Taking advantage of her having turned away from him when sending his companion staggering, Rusty lunged forward. However, he too did not offer to bring out a weapon. Encircling her arms with his own from behind, he pinned them against her sides. Hugging her to him, taking the precaution of twisting his face sideways so she could not seek to escape by slamming the back of her head against it, he made the most of his extra inches of height to hoist her feet from the floor. Suspended in such a fashion, she found her strength unequal to the task of breaking the powerful grip which threatened to incapacitate her.

3. *How Annie Singing Bear acquired the training which made her accepted as a warrior of the* Pahuraix—Waterhorse—*Comanche band and was granted her 'man-name' is told in*: IS-A-MAN.

13

'Hold on there, Rusty boy!' Johnny requested, having managed to bring himself to a half without falling. Striding back, he grasped the glass holding the sarsaparilla by its handle and raised it in a menacing fashion. 'I'm going to hand her *needings* like she's asked for!'

* * *   * * *

Prior to the arrival of the Wedge cowhands, it might have struck a casual acquaintance that the man who was the main subject of the discussion at the bar, was unlikely to be involved in any kind of gambling!

In his late twenties, Clivedon Pontin was tall and skinny, with greasy brown hair longer than was considered *de rigueur* by cowhands west of the Mississippi River. Not that anybody would have assumed he was engaged in such a strenuous form of employment. Nor was there even anything to indicate he was an author—even though his claim to the designation stemmed from having written two books published at the expense of his doting parents—and had come West to carry out research for a volume which, he had claimed in the 'liberal' Eastern newspapers sponsoring him, would 'expose the truth about the abused, down-trodden and mistreated Indians'. Having a day-old stubble his features—like his hands being in need of a wash, were sallow and not rendered any more prepossessing by an expression that was intended to indicate a sense of superiority to those about him, but in fact left the impression that he was smelling something unpleasant. His face was even less likeable at the moment, as he was scowling and making no attempt to conceal his bitterness over being a continual loser. With the exception of the other player dressed in a similar fashion, all the customers had taken the trouble to wash and tidy their appearance for the visit to town; but his expensive Eastern style clothing was grubby and unkempt.

Slamming down his cards and glowering balefully as Martin Oates collected the latest pot to which he had contributed not wisely but too well, Pontin and his

14

attention—like that of the other players—diverted to the bar!

If he had been more perceptive, Pontin might have thought that the response from two of the men in the game in particular was surprising. From what he had heard since it started, one was the trail boss who employed the cowhands confronting Annie Singing Bear and the other was their foreman. Yet neither offered to prevent the pair behaving in such a fashion. Nor, despite having a rugged look which implied he would be able to do so, did the black clad man with her show any sign of rendering assistance. Furthermore, although the author had he noticed would have considered it indicative of their intolerance towards anybody who was not of their race and creed, the other cowhands and local customers were registering more amusement than disapproval.

Regardless of his often stated declarations of wanting to help those of mixed blood as well as the Indians, Pontin remembered how the girl had cast doubts upon a number of his most treasured theories. What was more, she even had had the temerity to tell him what he had learned later—but not before he had made himself look foolish by repeating it—was a lie about the ability of Indians to follow tracks. Therefore, never being one to forgive and forget, also possessing a *very* strong sense of caution where possible danger to himself might be involved, he remained in his seat.

Of all the occupants in the room, only the recruits gave any indication of interfering. Nevertheless, their intentions were motivated more by a willingness to tangle with cowhands than the laudable desire to help a girl in distress. However, on coming to their feet, they saw her companion was striding purposefully in their direction.

'Like it says in the Good Book,' the black clad man drawled, shoving open the left side of his jacket. 'Yield not to the temptation to bill in uninvited on other folks' doings, lest you wind up in a fight and get throwed in the pokey for causing a disturbance.'

15

Delivered by a civilian who had the appearance of being some kind of preacher, albeit one who was not averse to entering a saloon and drinking beer, the comment alone might not have induced the recruits to restrain their impulse. However, the silver badge of office pinned to his vest, which had been concealed by his coat until that moment, but which was now brought into view, put a very different complexion on the affair. New they all might be to the service, but even those who did not recognize it could read the inscription stating that the wearer was a United States' deputy marshal. This discovery, plus recollecting the stringent orders regarding their conduct which they had received from Sergeant Paddy Magoon before leaving camp[4]—not to be lightly disregarded by any recently enlisted soldier who wished to have a comparatively restful life—served to bring about a change of mind. What was more, they soon realized there was no need for their intervention.

Although nobody else was offering to come to her aid, the girl proved she was still capable of defending herself more than adequately. As the taller red head was starting to bring the glass towards her, albeit more slowly than if he was meaning to thrust it into her face, she lashed up a kick which caused its contents to splash into his own. Then, bowing her body at the waist and swaying herself forward, she contrived to get her feet on the ground. Before Rusty could tighten the grip on her arms which he had inadvertently loosened and prevent her from moving further, she reached between her legs. Catching hold of his left ankle with both hands, she straightened up and lifted it. Having his balance destroyed, he toppled over and alighted with her rump coming down on to his stomach.

4. *Some information regarding the career of Sergeant Seamus Patrick 'Paddy' Magoon, United States Cavalry, can be found in*: THE RUSHERS *and* APACHE RAMPAGE.

4a. *When recording a meeting he had with Martha 'Calamity Jane' Canary, due to an error in the source from which we produced the manuscript, we referred to Sergeant Magoon as 'Muldoon'. See*: TROUBLE TRAIL.

No longer under any kind of restraint, bounding from her captor-turned-victim like a rubber ball, Annie ducked her head to charge at her other assailant. Having placed the glass on the counter so he could wipe the sarsparilla from his face, Johnny was rammed in the chest before he could clear his vision. An explosive grunt, echoing that his companion had emitted on landing, burst from him and he was driven backwards once more, this time to sit down with a thud.

'All right now, Annie-gal!' a drawling voice said from the direction of the main entrance. 'You stop abusing those two poor ole boys right now!'

* * *   * * *

Swinging his startled gaze from the bar to the speaker, a hiss of anger left Clivedon Pontin!

The man coming through the batwing doors was tall, lean, leathery-faced, grey-haired and dressed much the same way as the cowhands. However, even without seeing the badge on his calfskin vest, Pontin would have identified him as Homer Tomlinson, the sheriff of Gareth County. Having all the antipathy of his kind towards every type of peace officer, unless in need of their protection, he was always delighted when presented with an opportunity to show one of them was in the wrong. Therefore, ever eager to display his sympathy for what a later generation would call a member of a minority group, he forgot his antipathy towards the girl and came to his feet with a violence which sent his chair flying behind him.

'Is this *your* idea of *justice*?' the author demanded, stalking with what he imagined to be awesome dignity across the room. 'Those two men attacked her and, because she's a half—of mixed blood—it's her you're going to arrest.'

'Well now, *Mister* Pontin,' the sheriff drawled, showing no noticeable emotion over the accusation other than the emphasis he had placed upon the honorific. 'I don't recollect's how I said I was fixing to arrest *nobody*.'

17

'Those two abused and attacked the girl without the *slightest* provocation!' the author protested, glancing around and sensing, as he had anticipated, that he did not have the support of the crowd. 'If it hadn't been for those wrestling tricks she'd learned from the Comanches, she would have been badly hurt. I know she's only a ha—!'

'If you mean how I handled Johnny 'n' Rusty,' Annie interrupted coldly, guessing the reason why Pontin had come to her "rescue" and not caring for it. 'The Comanch' don't know spit, shit, nor piss in the bucket 'bout wrassling with their bare hands. When they fight, it's with *weapons's* can kill a whole heap easier. I was taught to fight that way by my *white* momma, who used to be a gal-wrassler in a tent show.'

'Bu—But those two attacked you witho—!' Pontin spluttered, his animosity towards the girl returning.

'The boys wasn't *attacking* me no more'n they do when they meet up with Dusty Fog 'n' try to prove they can out-wrassle him.'[5] Is-A-Man corrected, in the manner of one explaining something to a far from intelligent child. 'They'd heard tell about me and just natural' had to come on over to find out if what they'd heard was true. There wasn't no hard feelings give nor meant, 'though I'll have to 'fess up's how I'd've been tolerable riled happen Johnny's got 'round to pouring that sassparilly over my head like he was figuring on.' Swinging her attention to the cowhands, who were sitting up and showing breathless amusement rather than anger over the way they had been treated. 'How's about getting up and one of you buying me another sassparilly?'

Realizing that he had failed to achieve his purpose, the author gave a snort. Swinging around, he returned to the

5. *Two occasions when Johnny Raybold and Rusty Willis attempted to prove they could beat Captain Dustine Edward Marsden 'Dusty' Fog at wrestling are recorded in*: TRIGGER FAST *and* BUFFALO ARE COMING!

5a. *Information about the career and special abilities of Dusty Fog is given in various volumes of the* Civil War *and* Floating Outfit *series*.

table in a much more subdued fashion than he had left it. His temper was far from being improved by noticing the disdainful fashion in which the other occupants of the bar-room, with the possible exception of the man who had brought him there and been responsible for his involvement in the poker game, were looking at him. While not generally susceptible to atmosphere, he realized that he had forfeited all chance of receiving the respect which he considered was due to one of his importance as a result of his behaviour towards the well liked sheriff. Feeling more sheepish and uneasy than he would have believed was possible, he had no desire to go on playing poker. Nor was he required to do so.

'Well, that's over,' Martin Oates commented. 'Shall we get on with the game, gents?'

'I reckon that's quite enough for me tonight,' declared the trail boss, whose good looking face was marred by a livid white scar running down his right cheek.

'And me,' seconded the other Texan.

'Sure and it's enough I've had of it, too,' declared the big and burly sergeant and the shorter, Gallic looking corporal who had joined the game with him nodded concurrence. Swinging his gaze to the second civilian player, he went on in a neutral tone, 'I've *never* seed *anybody* so all-fired *lucky* as you, Mr. Oates.'

'Now me,' Waggles Harrison drawled, also studying, with a similarly inscrutable face, the bulky and untidy owner of the trading post at the *Pahuraix* Comanche Reseveration. 'I wouldn't go selling Mr. Oates short by calling it just *luck*. I ain't never seed *better* playing, 'cepting maybe by Last-Card Johnny Bryan. You mind him, Stone?'

'I surely do,' admitted Jethro Martin "Stone" Hart, then looked across the table as if considering he was imparting information which was unknown to Oates. 'They called him "Last-Card" because it was *amazing* the strength he could get from the last card when he was dealing at stud. Time after time, up would come something that turned what looked like a certain losing hand into a winner. There's no telling how far he could've gone, happen Bad Bill Longley hadn't got riled at losing to him and put a blue window in his skull.'

'I'd often heard tell's how old Last-Card might've been a *cheater*,' Magoon remarked, sounding shocked by the possibility. 'But folks are allus reckoning that about a *lucky* player. Say though, Stone, being so keen on poker 'n' all, I bet Doc Leroy'd've admired to see Mr. Oates play. He could've likely learned something.'

If the expression on the surly, unshaven face of the trader was any guide, he was far from flattered or pleased by the remarks about the way he played stud poker. Although he considered it inadvisable to mention the matter, there had been no need for the explanation of how Jonathan Bryan acquired the sobriquet 'Last Card' where he was concerned. They had worked together before he took up his present occupation and he considered himself even more adept at dealing cards from the bottom and middle of the deck. In fact, despite the comments which the black clad Texan had made to Annie Singing Bear regarding him being disinclined to take the chance in such company, the numerous pots he had won resulted from cheating and not luck. However, even though his dishonest tactics had gone unchallenged during the game, he was aware what had really been implied by the reference to the man who would have 'admired' to see him play. In addition to being a member of the Wedge trail crew and possessing medical skill which had produced his nickname, Marvin Eldridge 'Doc' Leroy was acknowledged for his ability to detect crooked gamblers.[6]

6. *How Marvin Eldridge 'Doc' Leroy acquired his medical skills and ability in the detection of crooked gambling is explained in various volumes of the* Floating Outfit' *and* Waco *series.*

6a. *The Wedge acted as a contract trail crew for groups of ranchers who had too few cattle to consider making up and delivering a herd individually as a viable prospect. They make 'guest' appearances in*: QUIET TOWN, TRIGGER FAST, BUFFALO ARE COMING!, GUN WIZARD *and* THE RIO HONDO KID.

'We'll have to get him into the next game,' Oates said with forced cheerfulness.

'There won't be a next time,' Stone Hart declared with a noticeable finality which was not softened to any great degree by him continuing, 'We've delivered the herd to the Agent out to the Reservation and been paid, so we'll be heading on comes morning.'

'And me 'n' Henri here'll be taking those Johnny Raws of our'n on our ways at sunup,' Magoon claimed, indicating the corporal. 'Anyways, on Army pay we can't afford to play with a feller's *lucky*'s you.'

'Let me stand you all a drink, then,' the trader suggested, as the winner was supposed to do at the conclusion of a game.

As Pontin listened to the Texans and soldiers decline the offer—although he did not realize it was a warning for his benefit prompted by them having heard of his previous misfortunes when playing poker with Oates—he knew enough about the West to realize that such behaviour was not usual. Although their refusal of a drink had been polite, taken with the comments they had passed, it suggested to him that they believed they had been cheated. Never a good loser, this conclusion supported suspicions he had already been harbouring about his own frequent losses.

Much as it went against the grain for the author to think well of Southrons or members of the military, he considered that if any of the four men had detected definite cheating on the part of the trader, they were tough enough to have made it known immediately. None had, so he decided he would be advised to keep his suppositions to himself. While he judged the other customers would be disinclined to exert themselves on his behalf, the sheriff was at the bar with the black dressed man and the girl. However, he felt sure that—especially after the way he had just behaved—his unsupported accusation against a local businessman would not be accepted by the peace officer.

21

Drawing these conclusions with regards to the other occupants of the bar-room, Pontin turned his thoughts to the rest of the players and could draw no consolation. Regardless of being likely to benefit financially should his disclosure be accepted, he suspected that he could not count upon any support in that direction if he should protest. Knowing he would never admit openly that somebody was more perceptive than himself, Pontin believed everybody else shared the same tendency. Therefore, should he attempt to prove Oates had been cheating, he would have to accept the consequences without aid from anybody, and he lacked the courage to face them. Much as it rankled to know that one whom he had considered would prove easy prey had made a fool of him, he decided it behoved him to keep his mouth shut until he could obtain assistance. Remembering there were others besides the players tonight who had suffered losses in stud poker games with the trader, he felt sure he could obtain support if he demanded that these losses should be made good.

* * *   * * *

'Is-a-Man!' yelled the grizzled old timer who worked for Martin Oates in the capacity of cleaner and occasional sales assistant, emerging hurriedly from the main building of the trading post which he had just entered. 'Come on over here *pronto*. Oates's been *murdered*!'

After having spent the rest of the previous evening in an enjoyable fashion at the Lone Star Saloon, albeit without having achieved their real purpose for going there, Annie Singing Bear and United States' Deputy Marshal Solomon 'Solly' Cole had come to the headquarters of the Indian Agency. This was situated on the banks of the small stream which denoted the border of the *Pahuraix* Comanche Reservation in the area. Martin Oates' recently established trading post was nearby. At the other side of the water, a group of the band's older members had set up their homes so as to benefit from the facilities which the Agent—one of the fairest and most enlightened men to

22

hold such a position—had set up to improve their lot.

On receiving a report from the girl—in her capacity as a member of the Reservation Police—that liquor was being sold to the Indians under his charge, Agent Moses H. Dillingham had been most concerned. Appreciating the danger such activities could create, although as yet there had been no problems, he had written to ask Cole to help Annie Singing Bear by making enquires outside the Reservation. Hoping to avoid the man who they believed was behind the sale of liquor from guessing that such an investigation was to be made, they had spread the word that the peace officer who was paying a visit was a kinsman of Mrs. Dillingham and, as she was unable to meet him, Annie would be collecting him from Catlett.

Instead of setting off for the Agency immediately they had met, the girl and the peace officer, having seen Oates going into the Lone Star Saloon with Clivedon Pontin, followed him in the hope that they might obtain some evidence to indicate he was implicated in the whiskey peddling. This had not happened either on the premises, or while they were continuing to keep him and the author—who had become very drunk—under observation on the way back to the trading post. Wanting to resume the investigation without delay in the morning, Cole had suggested that Is-A-Man also spent the night with the Dillinghams and she had accepted. Rising early, they had just finished breakfast and were going to collect their horses and engage upon a scouting mission in the Reservation. However, hearing the shouted news about Oates caused all thoughts of immediate departure to leave their minds.

'You *sure* he's been *murdered*, Toothless?' Annie inquired, despite knowing that age had not reduced the assistant to the point of dotage.

'Well now,' the old man replied, showing little concern and no grief whatsoever over the death of his employer. 'It just *might* be "sewer-side", 'cepting I cain't figure out whether he scalped his-self *afore* or *after* he done it.'

23

'*Scalped*?' Annie said, turning her gaze to the black clad peace officer.

'I've seen it done a whole heap *neater*,' Toothless declared, with more relish than remorse. 'But his hair's been took-en's well's him having his throat cut practical' from ear to ear.'

The last part of the comment was delivered to the backs of the girl and the peace officer. Without waiting to ask further questions, they set off side by side towards the larger of the two one storey wooden buildings which, along with a pole corral at the rear and a backhouse, Oates had had constructed as his trading post. Because it held his living quarters, it was a more substantial structure than the one to its right which was currently occupied by Pontin and his three Indian companions, Dillingham having declined to offer him accommodation in the Agency when he heard why they had come. Going through the open door, Annie and Cole found themselves in the business section. Its sole furnishings were a couple of rickety chairs and a roughly made counter. Behind the latter were several shelves holding a wide selection of cheap 'trade' goods—clothing, items of food, tobacco, kitchen untensils, gardening implements, a variety of cutlery for the home or hunting and boxes of tawdry jewellery—intended for sale to the Indians on the Reservation. In keeping with their surroundings, none of the goods were any too clean. However, paying no attention to the state of the premises, they looked for but did not see the body.

I've never seen that unlocked before,' Annie commented, pointing and leading the way to where a door between two sets of shelves was gasping open. 'Fact being, this's the first time I've ever even seen a key in it.'

Entering, the girl and Cole discovered the more spacious back room was used as a repository for stock until it could be put on display. Although there were bars at the windows, which the rest of the premises did not have, its contents appeared to be little different from those on the shelves in the trading section of the building. There were

24

several hatchets and hunting knives in sheaths on a small table at the centre. Two of the former, one of the latter and, a short distance from them, an empty sheath, lay on the floor, so it appeared they had been pushed aside to make space for a lamp which was standing on it still alight.

However, as Annie and the peace officer found that Toothless had spoken the truth, they did not give much attention to the room and its inanimate contents. Clad only in a nightshirt, with a Colt 1860 Army revolver and a bull's eye lantern lying on either side behind where it had fallen, Martin Oates' body was sprawled supine and with the blood it had shed staining the dirt floor. It was a far from pleasant sight. In addition to gore having flowed from his nostrils to spread over the lower cheeks and mouth, which the old man had not mentioned, the throat was cut almost from one ear to the other and the scalp had been removed. There was some already dried human vomit nearby and what was obviously the knife used by the killer lay a short distance away.

'Toothless called it *right*,' the girl asserted, having studied the condition of the head. 'Any *tuivitsi* on his first war trail'd've lifted the hair a whole heap neater'n this's been done.'

'I reckon *you'd* know about *that*, being a *tehnap*,'[7] Cole replied, but there was no implied rebuke nor derision in his tone. Bending down, he made a wry face as he moved the dead man's right arm. 'Been dead two or three hours, I'd say.'

'Smells that way,' Is-A-Man admitted, wrinkling her nose in distaste and glancing around. 'I'd say he must've caught somebody's'd snuck in to rob him, only they got the jump on him.'

That's how I read it.'

'I wonder what whoever done it took?'

'Whatever it was, it's not likely to be *them*,' the peace

7. *A* tuivitsi *is a young warrior, a* tehnap *one who is fully trained and experienced. An adolescent boy is called a* tuinep'.

25

officer replied, jerking his thumb towards a couple of wooden boxes inscribed 'BIBLES FOR THE ENLIGHTENMENT OF THE SAVAGE HEATHEN, Boston, Mass.' standing against the wall by other door. The lid of one had been raised and, crossing to look inside, he went on, 'Even though this's empty.'

'Hey, Toothless!' Annie called, looking around as the old man came through the connecting door. 'Who-all's been buying the bibles?'

'*Bibles*,?' Toothless repeated. 'I've never seen no *bibles* for sale in here. They're not Oates' line.'

'How about *these*?' Cole inquired.

'Damned if I've ever seen 'em afore,' the old man declared. 'Oates never let me so much as peek in here, which's how come I found him. I'd never even seen the door open and, it being, I come over to see was he up and about.'

'How'd you get into the store?' the peace officer asked. Retrieving a hatchet similar to those on the table from where it lay nearby and concluding it was brought there for the same purpose, he used it to pry open the lid of the second box. 'Was the front door unlocked?'

'Naw, Mr. Cole,' Toothless denied, having waited for the second question before speaking. 'He lets me have a key to it, but *nothing* else, so's I don't have to wake him when I get here in morning.'

'You know me?' the peace officer queried with asperity, having placed his badge in his pocket to avoid having his official status discovered.

'Shucks, I mind you from when Is-A-Man took 'n' kept her blood oath to get those greasers' raped and killed the gal on the Reservation. But I didn't say your name outside, 'case somebody's you didn't want to know who you be might hear,' Toothless replied, referring to the incident which had created the girl's man-name. Then he looked into the box and went on, 'Well I'll be switched. They don't look like no *bibles* as I've ever seen.'

'Nor me,' Cole admitted, also gazing at the two large

26

cans he had exposed. Raising the hatchet, he slammed it on to the lid of the one on the right. Liquid splashed through the gash he caused and a pungent aroma rose to drown the stench of death emanating from the corpse. Enlarging the opening, he scooped up some of the brownish fluid with his cupped left hand and tasted it. Spitting it out, he gestured downwards and went on, 'What do you reckon *this* is, Toothless?'

'Well now,' the old man said, showing his toothless gums in something close to approval after he had carried out a similar experiment but without ejecting the sample. 'It's better than no whiskey at all.'

'And you never saw it before?' the peace officer asked.

'The hell I did!' Toothless affirmed, his manner bristling with indignation. 'Hell, I know I'm nothing but an old and wored out squaw man's lives with his missus's kin across the stream 'n' booze a mite when I can get into town for some. But there's things I wouldn't do nor stand for and selling liquor to Injuns's top of the heap. Had I knowed Oates was doing it, I'd've told Agent Dillingham straight off.'

'I'll go along with you on *that*,' Annie declared, having known the old man enough years to be aware of his feelings on the matter.

'*Gracias*, Is-A-Man!' Toothless replied and there was no mistaking the gratitude in his tone. 'You reckon some of the bucks've done it?'

'I hope not,' Annie said.

'This's unfastened,' Cole commented, having accepted the girl's summation and gone to examine the exterior door. 'The lock's been forced from the outside. Damn it, the ground out here's so hard you could drive a herd of longhorns over it without them leaving so much's a hoofprint. This's when we could use one of those jaspers who can follow the sign made by a shadow on solid rock should the sun be bright enough.' Pausing and looking away from the building, he continued, 'Hello, who-all's this?'

27

'It's See,' Annie supplied, joining the peace officer and looking at the elderly Indian who was approaching across the bridge over the stream.

'Who?' Cole inquired.

'His full name in English'd be, "Can-See-Better-Than-Man-With-Eyes",' Is-A-Man explained. 'From what Grandpappy Brother-To-The-Hawk and Daddy Singing Bear told me, he was one hell of a fighting man until a trade gun bust in his face. Well, after he got used to living blind, things he could do give him the name. But it's a mite more of a mouthful than folks can manage, even in *Nemenuh*, so it's got whittled down to just "See". His lodge's just across the creek with the other old folks'. Which, seeing he's closest to the water, he's been sort of keeping an eye on Oates' doings for me.'

Tapping the ground ahead of him with a long stick as he walked, the man approaching the trading post had the taller and more slender build which differentiated between the *Pahuraix* and other bands of the Comanche nation.[8] Clad in a buckskin shirt, Levi's and moccasins, although his carriage was erect, he was clearly well advanced in years. White haired, the seamed puckering of the flesh on his cheeks and nose indicated where they had been badly burned in the accident. The most striking thing about him was his eyes. They had no lids and their iris and pupils were white. In spite of his total lack of vision, aided by his deft manipulation of the stick, he came up to the girl and peace officer with no more difficulty than if he could see them.

'Greetings,   Can-See-Better-Than-Man-With-Eyes,'

8. *According to the Comanche legend, being inveterate gamblers, the members of the* Pahuraix *band acquired their untypical builds by reaching high to pile up their bets.*

8a. *Although Annie Singing Bear's father was a typical* Pahuraix *in appearance, she had inherited the physical characteristics of the majority of Comanches from her buxomly curvaceous mother, Rebecca 'Becky' Ingraham of Surbiton, Missouri, whose name amongst the Waterhorse band had been 'Woman Of Spirit'.*

28

Annie Singing Bear said in Comanche, employing the full name as being the due of a senior and esteemed member of her band. 'You have something to tell?'

'I have,' See replied. His nostrils quivered and he directed his sightless eyes briefly at United States Deputy Marshal Cole. Although he returned his attention to the girl, he resumed speaking in Spanish, 'Early this morning, I was wakened by hearing horses being disturbed and saddled in the corral behind the trading post. Then there was a crack like metal being broken. It came from the trading post. Thinking it might be something you would want to know, I came to the edge of the stream. There was a creaking which I have heard a box's lid make when it is opened. Next the hinges of an inside door squeaked and Oates said a few words in an angry voice. Then there was the thud of a blow, his words ended and I heard a heavier bump such as a man makes when he is struck down.'

'He was more than just struck down,' the girl confirmed. Knowing how well the old man had developed his other senses after the loss of his sight, she was not surprised by the indication that he had detected Cole was with her. She concluded that, in spite of him being a stranger, See had accepted it was safe to speak in his presence. 'We've just been looking at him. He's *dead*.'

'I thought he might be,' the blind man admitted. 'He did not speak again. The others talked, but more quietly and, after they had taken two cans from what must have been the box they opened, they came out and closed the door, then went to the corral, walking like men who had been drinking firewater. Then they rode off. Do you find it strange that I can tell so much, friend of Is-A-Man?

'The fame of Can-See-Better-Than-Man-With-Eyes has come to me,' Cole replied formally, in equally fluent Spanish, speaking the truth, although he had not remembered what he had heard until Annie said the name. He was impressed by the amount of information which was supplied and did not doubt it was accurate. Nevertheless, he hesitated a moment before asking, 'Were they *Pahuraix*?'

29

'They wore moccasins,' See answered. 'But they weren't of the *Nemenuh* and their horses were shod.'

'Then they weren't Indians?' the peace officer suggested, sensing the girl was relieved by the implication that members of the *Pahuraix* band were not involved.

'That I couldn't say,' See admitted. 'They spoke what sounded like *your* language, but I don't understand it, and they didn't move as quietly as would any brave-hearts from the tribes I know, even when drunk on firewater. There was another wearing moccasins who came later, but he wasn't of the People either. He went in and came out after a shorter while than the others stayed. I heard a few noises, but couldn't say what caused them.'

'Did he leave on a horse?' Is-A-Man inquired.

'No,' the blind man replied, pointing towards the house which Pontin and his Indian companions had rented from Oates. 'He went in there.'

* * *   * * *

'Hot damn, Solly!' Annie Singing Bear whispered, coming to a halt and gesturing with the Winchester Model of 1866 carbine—its woodwork decorated by patterns made from brass thumb-tacks—in her hands. 'I'm right pleased those three sons-of-bitches *aren't Pahuraix.*

'How come?' the peace officer inquired just as quietly.

'I'd hate to think any *Nemnuh* and one of *us* in particular wasn't a whole heap better taught than they show signs of being,' the girl replied. 'A *tuinep*' fresh started at hoss herding could've trailed 'em with one eye shut and now they've let us come this close without showing a sign of knowing we're around.'

Despite having had faith in the summations made by See, Solly Cole had warned Is-A-Man that they would need corroboration before they were acceptable in a court of law. The investigation he had carried out in the storeroom of the trading post, after hearing what the blind man had to say, was thorough, but inconclusive. There was nothing to indicate who had killed Martin Oates. The girl had conceded that the way in which the scalp had been removed was far from being decisive enough to prove it had been done by Clivedon Pontin. In her estimation, the three Indians, belonging to tribes living further East and having had such a long association with white men that they had not received the training in the skills of warrriors taught to earlier generations, would probably have displayed an equal lack of ability.

Conferring with Agent Dillingham, Cole had suggested a plan of campaign which it was hoped would establish the required proof. Taking advantage of the fact that the killing had not taken place on the Reservation, which would have rendered it a Federal rather than local matter, a message would be sent for Sheriff Tomlinson to come and give the impression he was handling the investigation. On his arrival, everybody having been confident he would co-operate, he would be given instructions not to let it be known that the author was under suspicion. If Pontin should show curiosity, he was to be told that his companions were considered the guilty parties. While the sheriff was playing his part in the deception, the deputy marshal and Annie would follow and try to bring back the Indians alive so they could be interrogated and the truth of the affair established. Before leaving, Is-A-Man had suggested a contingency plan should other ways of obtaining the required result fail, and had asked Dillingham to ensure everything was ready to put it into effect when they returned.

During her training to become accepted as a Comanche warrior, an important part of Annie's instruction had been in reading tracks. Nor, despite opportunies to ride the war trail, thus gaining the acclaim every brave-heart seeks, being curtailed by her decision to live on a reservation,[9] had she lost any of her ability. In fact, watching her as she guided him in the direction taken by the three

9. *Why the decision to go on to a reservation was reached is described in*: SIDEWINDER.

Indians, Cole had been willing to admit she was the equal of anybody with whom he had worked during his career as a peace officer. At no time had she needed to dismount from her wiry little paint pony, saddled for her by See while Toothless was preparing Cole's bigger dun gelding, to make a closer examination of the ground. Before they had gone far, she had declared that everything pointed to the fact that the men they were pursuing had been drunk when setting out and, noticing the undulating path they were taking, he had agreed. However, although there were times when he had not been able to discern the slightest trace of the trio's passing, she had continued to lead him in an easterly direction until more positive evidence came into view.

After having covered about six miles, the pair had seen the tracks disappear into a fair sized clump of woodland. Circling around it, they had been unable to discover any indication that the men they were following had come out. Cole suspected that Is-A-Man's suggestion that they should continue on foot was prompted by a lack of faith in his ability to pass through the trees without making a noise, but he did not raise the point and he continued to be guided by her. Although he was wearing his gunbelt, he had no intention of relying upon his Rogers & Spencer Army revolver in the event of trouble. Having been informed that the Indians had brought firearms with them, and acting as would any competent peace officer envisaging the possibility of armed resistance when making an arrest, he had drawn the Winchester Model of 1866 rifle from his saddleboot.

Leaving the horses tethered at the edge of the woodland, the girl soon realised her precautions were justified. Although Cole moved as quietly as any other white man she had known, regardless of his sombre apperance and generally dour manner of speech—which she realized was employed to lessen the chances of his official status being suspected and which in fact covered a lively sense of humour she could admire—he did not match the silence every *Pehnane tuinep'* was taught to acquire before being allowed to be considered even a *tuivitsi*. In fact, if they had been up against any other kind of Indians, she would have expected warning of their presence to be detected before they came into view of their quarry. As it was when she saw the men they were after, her suppositions about the trio were proved justified and provoked her comments.

From their appearance Annie concluded that the trio's drunken condition had been responsible for their decision to halt and rest on the banks of a stream in a clearing. They were bare headed as usual, but she noticed that since she had seen them the previous afternoon they had cropped their black hair raggedly to something closer to the fashion of white men. Lined with obvious suffering as they were getting to their feet, their faces looked greyish under the deep bronze. As both cans of whiskey they had stolen at the trading post were standing unopened, it seemed they had been too far gone in intoxication to have sampled the contents during the journey or after they had arrived. Furthermore, not one of the horses—which she recognized as being those that Oates kept in his corral, renting to anybody who wished to use them—had had its saddle and bridle removed. In fact, only having been trained to stand still when the split-ended reins were dangling free had prevented them from straying.

The girl also felt that the way in which the three were dressed was significant. When travelling around the Reservation, in addition to supplying names they translated as 'Plunging Eagle', 'Swift Runner' and 'Bold As Puma'—which she suspected had been selected by themselves as sounding impressive rather than being genuinely earned man-names—they had always worn what they claimed was the traditional attire for their respective tribes.[10] Although they still retained the moccasins, in addition to having cut their hair so that it no longer suggested their

10. *The documents from which we produced this narrative did not supply the name of the tribe to which the three Indians belonged.*

33

Indian upbringing, they had changed the rest of their clothing. The expensive Eastern style suits they wore were badly rumpled as a result of having been slept in, and their collarless white shirts were as stained and grubby as the rest of their garments. While she had never seen them armed in any way, there was a Colt 1860 Army revolver in each waist band.

'How do we play it?' Cole inquired, estimating the distance to the trio and envisaging the problems involved in issuing a demand to surrender from where he and the girl had halted. 'Soon's we shout, they're likely to be up and running. Or maybe go to throwing lead.'

'Could down 'em all *real* easy from here,' Is-A-Man commented with a glance from her carbine to the rifle her companion was holding, but refraining from mentioning she considered the former line of action was more likely to be taken.

'We *could*,' the deputy marshal replied. ''Cepting I'm not Wyatt Earp, nor one of his Kansas trail-end town fighting pimps. And, even if I was—may the Good Lord forbid—we need 'em alive and talking.'

'Momma allus allowed white folks never do *nothing* the easy way,' Annie commented dryly. 'Tell you what, seeing's they for sure ain't *Nemenuh*, let's snuck around until we're closer to where they're standing. Happen we get there and bust out on 'em unexpected like, could be they'll be too hung-over from that liquor they had last night to be able to get away.'

'I'm game to give it a whirl,' Cole agreed and, although his voice remained solemn, a twinkle of amusement came into his eyes. 'Only, me being white and all, you don't reckon it'd work was they *Nemenuh*.'

'Was they *Nemenuh*,' the girl answered with a grin. 'I wouldn't count on either me or *Cuchilo* being able to snuck up on 'em.'

'Anyways,' the peace officer drawled, being amused rather than annoyed by the insinuation. ' 'Less we snuck up on the other side of the clearing, which wouldn't bring

34

us much nearer to them, we're still going to have to cross the water before we're close enough to make those jaspers stay put instead of trying to fight us off, or light a shuck for the tall and uncut piney woods.'

'Well I'll be switched if I hadn't forgotten that lil ole stream was there,' Is-A-Man declared, sounding so contrite this might have been the case. 'But, should you be willing to *bet* we couldn't, I'd reckon *one* of us at least could jump it and be among' 'em afore they was up 'n' running.'

'The Ysabel Kid was *right*,' Cole claimed, using the name by which the man to whom Annie had referred was better known to members of his race.[11] 'You blasted *Pahuraix* will bet on *anything*. And I'm not so old's I can't figure out which one of us you figure it'll be can't make the jump.'

'Happen you want to odds on it, I'll match you at no less'n *five* to one?' Annie offered, but did not wait for a reply. 'Anyways, let's up 'n' give it a whirl.'

'Go to it,' the peace officer assented. 'And, *when* they get away on account of all this fooling, I'll tell my boss's, like the Good Book says, "Pity the poor yahoo's gets led astray, 'cause he knoweth not what damned fool thing he'd got led into".'

Realizing that her suggestion had been accepted, although doubting whether such a quotation appeared in the white man's Bible, Annie led the way through the bushes towards where the three Indians had halted the night before. Once more, she was grateful that they were not Comanche or members of any other warrior race west of the Mississippi River. Her companion, as had been the case when coming through the woodland to the edge of the clearing, moved with commendable silence, despite his

11. 'Cuchilo', *the Spanish word for 'knife' and granted in honour of his ability at wielding one as a weapon, was the man-name earned by the Ysabel Kid while he was growing up amongst the Comanche. How he received it is told in*: COMANCHE. *Further details of his family background and adventures are given in the* Floating Outfit *series.*

footwear being far less suitable than moccasins. Nevertheless, she considered that any competent brave, especially of the *Nemenuh*, would have heard enough to detect him approaching. However, as they were what she referred to in a derogatory fashion as 'college Indians', she felt sure his stalking would prove adequate.

The supposition proved accurate until the girl and the peace officer were level with the Indians. However, while they were carrying out the stalk, Plunging Eagle and Bold As Puma had come to the edge of the stream. Both were down on one knee at the bank and splashing water onto their faces. Such a posture should have been advantageous for the stalkers. Unfortunately, either through some instinct or because bending forward added to the throbbing ache in his head, Plunging Eagle raised it. He could hardly have chosen a more auspicious moment, or less, depending upon one's point of view. Seeing Annie, although Cole was still concealed by the bushes, he let out a howl of alarm which caused his companion to duplicate his action of rapidly straightening up.

* * *   * * *

Annoyed at having been the one to be detected, being sure Deputy U.S. Marshal Cole would hooraw her about it later, Is-A-Man responded with the speed of a Comanche *tehnap*. Thrusting herself forward as if propelled by a coiled spring, to the accompaniment of an ear-splitting and awesome *Nemenuh* war yell, she hurdled the six foot width of water as if it was not there. Starting to follow her, the peace officer felt his right foot slip on the slick grass. Although he retained his balance and was able to keep going, he realized he would be too late to help. In a continuation of the movements which brought them erect, while each was starting to grab at the butt of his Army Colt, the two Indians staggered backwards a couple of paces and away from one another. Their actions were involuntary, rather than as a result of any conscious thought on either's part. However, the separation did not

36

prove as beneficial as it might have been under different circumstances.

Alighting on the opposite bank, the girl's response would have gladdened the heart of any Army sergeant giving instruction in using a bayonet. Although she had never seen such a style of fighting, the way in which she lunged with her Winchester carbine was a perfect example of how to deliver a thrust from that weapon. Its muzzle took Plunging Eagle in the pit of his stomach with the full power of her hard muscled buxom body behind it. Being so addicted to eating that one of the *Pahuraix* had suggested the reason the eagle plunged was because it was too fat to fly upwards, his body was ill prepared to accept such treatment. An explosive belching croak burst from him. His right hand left the revolver it had been tugging at and joined the left in clutching the point of impact. Winded and helpless, he folded at the waist. Then, with the weapon slipping unheeded from his waist band as he went, he blundered to the rear a few steps before toppling sideways to the ground.

Nor did Bold As Puma fare any better, even though he was able to liberate the Colt from his waist band. In a continuation of the jab she delivered with the carbine, striding onwards, Is-A-Man removed her left hand and swung it with the right in a sweeping arc. The round twenty inch long barrel struck the Indian at the back of the head before he could turn his own weapon into alignment. Although the blow was not as hard as would have been the case if both hands were employed, it proved sufficient for her needs. Sent in an uncontrollable sprawl, with his senses whirling, he dropped on to his hands and knees incapable of further resistance.

Having been on the point of joining his companions by the stream, Swift Runner changed his mind on seeing the girl at the other side. Although he too reached for his revolver, he refrained as he discovered she was accompanied by a white man wearing the insignia of a peace officer—Cole having returned it to his vest before leaving

37

the Agency—and carrying a rifle. Spinning around, although he had not shown signs of living up to his man-name since arriving at the *Pahuraix* Reservation, his movements were given an added impetus by watching the way in which she was dealing with the other two. He had never before faced any kind of danger and chance, rather than deliberate planning, caused him to react in a fundamentally sound fashion. Darting by the two nearer horses, relying upon them to shield him from the weapons of the newcomers, he snatched up the reins and started to mount the third.

Ignoring her recumbent victims, Is-A-Man took in the sight of what the third Indian was doing. While appreciating the reason for his motives, she had no intention of relying upon the carbine as a means of effecting his capture. Instead, dropping it without breaking stride, she bounded into the air. Landing with her right foot on the saddle of the closest horse, she stepped from it to the second and flung herself onwards. Just as Swift Runner swung astride his selected mount, she arrived. Her arms wrapped around his shoulders and her weight was sufficient to thrust him over the other side. Although they went down together, expecting what had happened and having an almost cat-like agility when falling, she came out of the landing far better than her captive. Slammed against the ground, he was incapable of any resistance as she straddled him with her knees. Nevertheless, thinking like the *tehnap* she had become on launching the attack, Annie brought out her Green River hunting knife and swung it upwards ready to deliver a slash which would lay his throat open to the bone.

'Is-A-Man!' Cole thundered, having leapt across the stream. '*Stop!*' Although his words prevented the blow from being struck, the knife was not lowered and the face which turned towards him was the implacable mask of a *Nemenuh* warrior on the point of counting coup. His voice continued to be commanding, if milder in timbre, as he continued, 'That jasper's no good to us *dead*!'

38

For a couple of seconds, the life of Swift Runner hung in a *very* delicate balance!

'Aw *shucks*!' Annie ejaculated at last, lowering the weapon and starting to rise. 'A gal can't *never* have no *fun* these days!'

'Tell you what, then,' Cole drawled, glancing from Plunging Eagle to Bold As Puma. He concluded that they were able to understand what he was saying, even though still incapable of trying to resume hostilities. 'Happen they don't tell us *everything* we want to know, I'll let you have your *fun* by working on them until they're so minded to speak up truthful true.'

'Y—You're a sworn officer of the law!' Bold As Puma gasped, sitting up and ensuring he did nothing which might be construed as trying to retrieve his Colt. 'You *can't* let her *torture* us!'

'I couldn't was I *here* when she was doing it,' the peace officer admitted, deciding Is-A-Man was giving a very realistic impression of being ready and willing, eager even, to carry out whatever means were required to achieve their purpose. What was more, the Indians were convinced by her performance. 'Only I'll've gone to fetch up our horses afore she starts.'

'Wh—What do you want to *know*?' Plunging Eagle gasped, moving until he was sitting huddled with his stomach still being held by his hands.

'For starters,' Cole replied, collecting the two revolvers while Annie disarmed the still prone and barely conscious Swift Runner. 'Which of you-all killed Martin Oates?'

'He isn't *dead*!' Bold As Puma claimed in tones of growing alarm. 'I only knocked him unconscious when he came in on us.'

'He was dead and scalped when we found him this morning,' Cole declared.

'*We* didn't do it!' both Indians asserted in the same breath and their manner was convincing.

'I'll keep an open mind on *that*,' the peace officer promised. 'Even though this's what I was told came off.'

Given the added inducement of the peace officer passing on what he had been told about their activities by Can-See-Better-Than-Man-With-Eyes, but having omitted all reference to the second visitor, Plunging Eagle delivered the explanation with Bold As Puma giving continual confirmation!

When Clivedon Pontin had suggested they passed the time in the evenings playing poker, the three young Indians had been motivated by the expectation of making some easy money from the owner of the trading post. However, they too had discovered that the declarations made by Oates of having little knowledge of the game, had little basis in truth. Such had been their losses, all four of them had signed i.o.u.'s for considerable sums of money without realizing how these were mounting up. Having discovered their stay in the area was almost at an end, the trader had become threatening when making his demands for payment and had hinted at painful repercussions should this not be forthcoming.

Knowing they could not obtain anywhere near the amount they owed, the trio had hatched a plot while drinking some of the liquor they had brought from Oates. On his return from Claxton, waiting until they were sure he was in bed and checking that Pontin was also in a drunken sleep, they had put their scheme into effect. Having saddled horses in the corral and fastened their belongings to the cantles, ready to seek safety in flight back East, they had used a crowbar to break open the side door of the trading post. Admitting to having been aware of how the whiskey was delivered and offering to disclose the source in return for a promise of immunity from prosecution for their actions, Plunging Eagle then had told how they had been removing two cans when the trader had arrived. Hearing him fumbling at the lock and seeing the light of his bull's eye lantern through the crack beneath the door, Bold As Puma had had time to get across and fell the trader with a pick handle as he came in.

Although admitting so much, the Indians had been

40

vociferous in the claim that Oates was still alive—albeit unconscious—when they left. In fact, they asserted it would not have suited their purpose for him to be otherwise. If he was found dead, a murder hunt would be launched and they had no wish to suffer the consequences which would follow their arrest. Instead, they had carried on with the plan of taking some of the whiskey and leaving a note threatening to tell whence it had come if the law, or anybody else, should be sent after them. None of them could offer any suggestion of why the message had not been on the table when Cole searched the room, as they insisted it was left against the lamp so Oates would be sure to see it after he recovered.

'You're *got* to believe me!' Bold As Puma declared at the conclusion of the story. 'He *was* still alive when we left!'

'I don't *have* to believe you was you to tell me Monday's the day afore Tuesday every week,' Cole corrected coldly. 'Which being, we're taking you back with us and we're going to get at the why-all of it.'

* * *   * * *

'This is Raccoon Talker, chief medicine man of the *Pahuraix*,' Annie Singing Bear said in the manner of one who was very impressed by being allowed to perform the introduction, and indicating the taller and more bulky white haired Comanche who was accompanying her. 'He has come with Can-See-Better-Than-Man-With-Eyes to separate innocence from guilt in the way the *Nemenuh* have always done.'

Having returned with the three young Indians, Deputy Marshal Cole had left them guarded by Sheriff Tomlinson and Agent Dillingham while he went to collect Clivedon Pontin. Found lying on his bed in his room, on being aroused from a sound sleep, the author claimed he had collapsed there in a drunken stupor when he returned the previous night. Everything about him had suggested he was speaking the truth. He was still dressed as he had been

41

in Claxton and his sallow, unshaven face had haggard lines which made it even less prepossessing than usual. On being taken to join his companions outside the main building of the trading post, his declaration of horror when being told of how Martin Oates was found had been brought to an end by the arrival of Is-A-Man with the two elderly *Pahuraix*.

'What do you mean?' Pontin asked, recognizing both the men without needing the introduction.

'Can-See-Better-Than-Man-With-Eyes told us those three yahoos raided the trading post last night,' Cole explained. 'And, as they'd lit a shuck when I went to ask them about it, Is-A-Man and me took out after them. Trouble is, they all allow's *they* didn't kill and scalp Mr. Oates, but'd just gone riding to clear their heads after drinking more than was seemly—or *legal*—for Injuns. Which being, I'm set on finding out whether they're lying to save their necks.'

'How?' the author inquired, with something more than just the casual interest of one who was in no way concerned.

'Raccoon Talker allows he can find out for us,' the peace officer replied, waving a hand in the pre-arranged signal for the young Indians to be brought to him. 'Which, knowing just how *effective* these Injun medicine men are, I'm fixing to let him have a whirl at it.'

'You mean you *believe* he has the power to do it?' Pontin queried, sounding surprised and not a little worried.

'Hell, *yes*,' Cole confirmed with convincing confidence. 'Don't *you*?'

'Well—!' the author began, then realized his hesitation was not in accord with his earlier and frequent declarations that the medicine men of the Indian nations possessed powers beyond the comprehension of white men. 'Y—Yes, I do.'

'That's *bueno*,' the peace officer declared. 'Which, you writing a book about such doings, I reckoned's how you'd be wanting to see how it's done.'

'I *do*,' Pontin agreed, refusing to meet the cold and

42

angry gaze of the three young Indians who had arrived under what was obviously an armed escort.

'Then we'll get to it,' Cole stated. His voice took on a polite timbre as he turned towards the elderly *Pahuraix* and continued, 'By your leave, *gentlemen*.'

'We thank you, man of the law,' Raccoon Talker answered in good English and See nodded as if he had understood what was said.

'You have *everything* you need?' the peace officer inquired.

'We have, except water freshly drawn from the stream,' Raccoon Talker replied. Gesturing from the three blankets decorated by medicine symbols hanging over his left arm to the items Annie was carrying, he continued, 'Give me the magic pouch and bucket, Is-A-Man. Then help Can-See-Better-Than-Man-With-Eyes to put these over the windows of the room where Trader Oates died.'

'Can I do anything?' Cole offered, as the girl was exchanging the wooden bucket and box, each having been painted with the medicine decorations, for the blankets.

'No, man of the law,' Raccoon Talker denied. 'While the medicine works for white men as well as red, none but those of Indian blood and trained in such things may help me make ready.'

While the medicine man walked away with the bucket and box, Annie accompanied See into the storeroom of the trading post. Commenting that the body had been taken away and ordering them not to do any talking, Tomlinson allowed young Indians to join Pontin in watching from the doorway. Although they darted glances which were less than friendly at the author, and he refrained from even looking their way, the instructions were obeyed. Looking inside the building, they listened to the blind man and the girl chanting in their native language while she followed what were clearly his directions by fixing two of the blankets so they hung over the windows. After she had removed the now unlit lamp, hatchets and knives from the table, he placed the other on it and they came outside.

Returning from the stream, Raccoon Talker entered the building and set the bucket on the floor. Placing the box on the table, he raised its lid and took out an earthenware bowl about a foot in diameter and depth and with similar decorations. Beginning to chant in Comanche, which none of the quartet most interested could understand—having relied upon an interpreter when talking to the people on the Reservation—he filled this to just below the brim with some of the water he had collected. Continuing to chant and going to where the body had been lying, he knelt and made a circular motion over the position with the bowl. Having completed this ritual, he returned it to the table and covered it with the blanket.

'All is ready,' the medicine man claimed in English. 'Which of these who are to be put to the test is first?'

'Go to it, *hombre*,' Cole commanded, reaching out a hand and making the selection without waiting for a volunteer.

'W—Why *me*?' Bold As Puma gasped, noticing his companions and Pontin were backing away to leave him alone.

'You allowed's how it was you whomped Oates over the head, but'd left him alive,' the peace officer pointed out. 'So you should oughta be real eager to get it *proved* that's *all* you did.'

'I—It's a *trap*!' the young Indian gasped.

'Your Great Spirit and mine both know the *truth*,' Raccoon Talker pointed out. 'Only one who is *guilty* need fear the test.'

'Hell,' Tomlinson commented, sounding bored with the entire affair. 'Looks like this jasper's done the killing, else he'd be going in there like a shot. Might just's well haul him off to the pokey and get ready for him stretching hemp.'

'I—I'll g—*go*!' Bold As Puma declared hurriedly, feeling sure the sheriff and local white population would be all too willing to consider they had sufficient evidence for hanging an Indian no matter how much he denied the killing.

Before the young Indian could move, Raccoon Talker grasped him by the shoulders and looked into his eyes with an intensity which seemed to burn through his whole being. Removing his hands, the medicine man began a shuffling and chanting dance around Bold As Puma and, giving no indication that he was blind, See joined in. After a few seconds, Raccoon Talker stopped and extracted some white powder from a pouch on his waist belt to toss it into the young Indian's face.

'All is *ready*!' the medicine man declared dramatically, as the recipient of his attentions staggered back a pace and spluttered. 'Go into the room.'

'Wh—What do I do?' Bold As Puma inquired nervously.

'Nothing but stand by the table until I come to let you out,' Raccoon Talker replied. 'The Great Spirit knows your heart and, if you have lied, all the water will have left the bowl beneath the blanket.'

Looking distinctly perturbed, yet also somewhat relieved, Bold As Puma did as he was instructed. Closing the door, the medicine man resumed the dancing and chanting accompanied by See. After about a minute, they halted and Raccoon Talker went inside. Moving forward but obeying his order to remain outside, the other two young Indians and Pontin watched him raise the blanket.

'The bowl is still *full*!' the medicine man stated. 'You speak truly.'

'You're next!' Cole stated, as Bold As Puma came out showing satisfaction.

'*Me*?' Plunging Eagle yelped.

'*Somebody* killed him,' the peace officer pointed out. 'And, just 'cause it's been *proved* your *amigo* didn't, we want to find out who *did*.'

Accepting the statement with somewhat better grace than had Bold as Puma, Plunging Eagle was put through the same ritual before being sent into the building. An examination of the bowl by Raccoon Talker established it was still full of water. Nor did the situation change when the third of the young Indians was subjected to the test.

'Well,' Pontin said, as Swift Runner was pronounced innocent and emerged. 'That settles it.'

'It *doesn't*!' Cole denied.

'But who else could have killed poor Mr. Oates,' the author queried.

'*You*!' the peace officer replied.

* * *   * * *

'*Me*?' Cliveden Pontin yelped, his face working spamodically. 'How *dare* you accuse *me*. Don't you realize who I *am*?'

'I do,' Deputy U.S. Marshal Cole answered calmly. 'You're a suspect in a *murder*.'

'*Suspect*?' the author snorted. 'I was so drunk that I fell asleep as soon as I got in last night and you had to wake me up.'

'Then how come Can-See-Better-Than-Man-With-Eyes reckons he heard somebody come over here, after those three gents'd lit a shuck, and go into your place when he left?' the peace officer challenged.

'How could he *see* me?' Pontin demanded, despite having seen sufficient of the old man's abilities to realize such evidence could have been obtained from hearing instead of sight. 'He's *blind*.'

'He never said he *saw* you,' Cole countered. 'He allow's how he *heard* somebody do it. So I reckon we'd best let Raccoon Talker's test show us the truth.'

'You mean you *believe* that rigmarole?' the author snorted, sounding distinctly uneasy.

'We *all* believe the medicine, such having been proved to work so often afore,' the peace officer confirmed and received concurrence from the three young Indians as well as the rest of the group. 'So, happen you're *innocent* like you claim, you've got *nothing* to be scared of by going through the same's your *amigos* did.'

'I—I—!' Pontin began, his face losing what little colour it had and continuing to twitch with emotion.

'Looks to *me* like he's maybe not so all-fired innocent as

46

he let's on, Solly,' Sheriff Tomlinson declared, eyeing the author with what seemed to be malicious satisfaction. 'I'll haul him down to the pokey and see happen me and my deputies can beat—*get*—the truth out of him.'

'W—Will you accept the verdict of the test?' Pontin inquired, feeling sure the local peace officer would be only too pleased to have an excuse to carry out the threatened beating regardless of the way the statement was amended.

'It *allus* works,' Cole asserted, the question having been directed at him. 'And the result's good enough for me.'

'Then I'll do it!' the author stated, considering a U.S. deputy marshal had higher jurisdictional authority than a county sheriff and stepping forward as Raccoon Talker came from the building.

After having been subjected to the preliminary ritual, hoping he was not showing the perturbation which had assailed him while the medicine man was staring at his face, Pontin went into the room. Although the door was closed behind him, sufficient light came from around the edges of the blanket for him to be able to make out some of his surroundings. Listening to the chanting being recommenced, he walked over to the table. Staring at the blanket, he experienced a surge of relief as he felt sure he was going to ensure his safety.

On returning the previous night, the author had gone straight to bed. However, he was less drunk than he had given the impression of being. Deciding to wait until he was sure Martin Oates was asleep before telling the Indians of his suspicions that they had been cheated and explaining his plan to avoid paying their losses, he had heard the sound of hooves. Going to their room, he had discovered it was empty and even their belongings were gone. Angered by what he had believed was no more than their desertion, he had left the building with the intention of arousing the trader and having them fetched back. On entering the storeroom and finding Oates lying on the floor and showing signs of recovering consciousness, he had thought of what he considered would offer a better and safer way out of his indebtedness. What was more, he was still drunk enough to have the nerve required to put his scheme into effect.

Taking and removing the sheath from one of the knives on the table, Pontin had cut the trader's throat. The sight of the blood gushing from the wound had inflicted him with such nausea that he had become sober while vomiting. On the point of leaving, he had seen the note left by the Indians and realized how he might suggest that they had been responsible for the murder. Driven by fear of the consequences should he fail to convince the local peace officers that the trio were guilty, despite finding the task less easy than he anticipated, he had removed the scalp from the body. Discarding the knife and taking the gory trophy and the note with him, he had returned to his room. Washing the blood from his hands and off his clothes, he had gone to bed. Once there, he had spent several restless hours before exhaustion and the reaction to what he had done made him fall asleep, and he had not come back to sentinence until being roused by Cole. Much to his alarm, as he had expected they would be shot on sight and prevented from making an explanation, he was informed that the trio were prisoners. Protesting they must be innocent, as he had guessed would be expected of him, he had accepted an invitation to come and witness the truth of the matter established.

What the author had not anticipated was that he too would be subjected to the test!

However, Pontin had drawn consolation from having been informed by the deputy marshal that the result would be considered as accurate!

For his part, his claim to believe in the mystic powers of Indian medicine men notwithstanding, the author was convinced he had nothing to fear. Although those ignorant country bumpkins outside accepted the test would work, he regarded himself as far too well educated and mentally superior to do so. Knowing he did not possess such abilities, his ego refused to accept anybody else could have attained them. That was why he had yielded to the demand that he should be subjected to the test. Confronted with what they would consider to be the innocence of himself and the Indians, the peace officers would have to direct their search for the culprit elsewhere and, by announcing his research in the area was completed, he would be able to return to his home while they were conducting their fruitless enquiries.

Smiling smugly at the thought of how he had solved his problem and outwitted the stupid Southron peace officers, Pontin could not resist lifting the blanket!

What the author saw drove all the satisfaction from him!

The bowl was empty!

Shock numbed Pontin, but only for a moment. Realizing that the discovery he had made—inexplicable as it was—would be regarded as having established the proof of his guilt, a sense of self-preservation goaded him to think. Looking around the room and wondering whether to try to escape through another part of the building, he saw what offered a more satisfactory solution. Taking the bowl to the bucket, he filled it with water and returned it to the table. Nor had he moved a moment too soon. Just as he had replaced the blanket and was stepping away, the door opened. Slipping his right hand into the outside pocket of his jacket, he watched Raccoon Talker come in followed by the deputy and the girl.

'Well,' Pontin said, reminding himself not to let his relief be too obvious as the medicine man was lifting the edge of the blanket. 'Is the water still there?'

'The bowl is full,' Raccoon Talker replied.

'Then the Great Spirit knows I'm innocent,' the author claimed.

'The bowl being full proves you killed Oates,' Annie Singing Bear corrected. 'Because, while you were arguing outside, Raccoon Talker tipped the water he'd put in it on to the floor.'

A surge of anger filled Pontin as he realized how he had

fallen into a trap. By employing what he did not doubt was genuine Comanche ritual to separate guilt from innocence, the presence of the medicine man and the behaviour of the sheriff had been arranged to bring him to a receptive frame of mind. Even if his companions had doubted the potency of the test, which he suspected had not been the case, the information given by the blind man had established they were speaking the truth when claiming to have left Oates alive. Therefore, any examination they might have carried out would have established that the bowl still held water. However, it was emptied while his attention was diverted and, having failed to notice that the floor beyond the table was wet, he had responded as was anticipated by refilling it.

'You *bastards*!' Pontin screeched, being grateful for the precaution he had taken, in spite of believing he had nothing further to fear.

Saying the words, the author responded with the spurious courage of a cornered rat. Ever since coming West, he had taken to carrying a Remington Double Derringer in his jacket's right side pocket. Driven by the speed of desperation, he snatched it out faster than he had ever managed to do in practice.

Having detected and suspected what was making the slight bulge in the pocket caused by the weapon, but refraining from commenting about it, Annie and Cole responded to the movement as soon as it was commenced. Once again, the girl proved to be the faster of them. Although satisfied that Cole could have coped with Pontin, her movements were further fueled by having learned, while bringing the Indians back, what was the real purpose behind his visit to the West. Aware of the suffering it could have caused to both races, should he have succeeded, she was disinclined to let him be taken alive to stand trial and, possibly—aided by the influential people who were behind the foul plot—evade the full penalty for what he had done.

Gliding forward until she was between the author and

the peace officer, preventing the latter from using the Rogers & Spencer he was drawing in the belief that the sight of it would end the attempt at resistance, Annie once more swept the Green River knife from its sheath. Whipped around with the skill acquired by long training, its razor sharp blade tore into and ripped across Pontin's stomach. Blood and intestines gushed from the awesome gash she made. As he stumbled back, the little pistol slipping from his grasp, her left hand rose to give him a push which helped send him dying to the floor.

'*A:he*!' Is-A-Man ejaculated, responding instinctively as a *tehnap* of the *Nemenuh* by giving the traditional Comanche declaration of, "I claim it!", and having achieved the highest form of coup.[12] Watching Pontin writhing and gasping from the pain of the mortal wound, she went on in English, 'You and those college Injuns of your'n won't stir up no reservations and fuss 'tween the white 'n' red folk like you planned.'[13]

---

12. *The Comanches considered a coup counted by laying a hand on a living enemy was superior to any other kind.*

13. *Another plot by Eastern 'liberals' and 'college' Indians to cause hostilities between the whites population and various tribes is described in*: BUFFALO ARE COMING!

PART TWO

RITA YARBOROUGH, COMPANY 'Z'
In
BEHIND A LOCKED AND BOLTED DOOR

'All right, you bitch, what the hell do you find so god-damned *interesting* about a certain good friend of ours?'

In less disturbing circumstances, Rita Yarborough might have conceded there was justification for the question spat at her by the shorter of the two men who had dragged her into the darkness of an alley between two closed and unlit business premises!

The alarm Rita was experiencing was increased by suspecting who the 'certain good friend' might be, but she had not expected the matter to be raised!

When she had first felt her arms grasped and a hand clapped over her mouth to prevent her crying out, Rita had believed theft was the intention of her assailants. Although she did not have the kind of physique to suggest she would prove a weak and easily cowed victim, the way she was dressed, which was intended for a very different purpose, could have given the impression that robbing her might prove lucrative. Everything about her implied she was a wealthy 'flapper' who had chosen to walk somewhere instead of travelling in a vehicle.

Not long past her twenty-fifth birthday, Rita was around five foot six in height. Pretty, without being excessively beautiful, she had applied more makeup than usual to add to the appearance she was seeking to create. Cut in a shortish, tousled, curly 'wind blown bob', her reddish-brown hair was all but concealed beneath the felt cloche hat with a velvet band which enveloped her head to the neck at the back and came to just above her eyebrows at the front. Although the current trend of fashion called for a slim and boyish figure, even if attaining it required the use of such a device as a Poiret-designed 'flattening brassiere', her shapely body only just fell short of the Junoesque 'hourglass' contours which had been all the rage a few decades earlier. The swell of her full and firm bosom, her trim waist and well rounded hips were shown to their best advantage by the shiny form fitting black satin dress—cut daringly low at front and rear and leaving her arms bare—she had on. Adorned by a fringe of slightly longer tassels of the same material, its slightly flared skirt ended about three inches over knee level, the better to display shapely legs in black stockings, their calf muscles being set off in bold relief by her very high heeled red pumps. She had an elegant black and white trimmed Chantilly lace *mantilla* dangling around her shoulders instead of being taken up over a comb on top of the head. In addition to what was an almost mandatory long string of pearls dangling to waist level, she had an apparently diamond studded black velvet 'choker' necklace about her throat. Giving further indications of potential wealth, long pendant earrings, several bracelets on each wrist and the lumpy rings gracing her fingers also had the sparkle of precious stones. What was more, not only was the vanity bag she had dropped when being grabbed made from gold lamé, it was bulging in a way which suggested it held a considerable sum of money.

However, while Rita had been born into a class of society which produced many wealthy and pleasure seeking 'flappers' such as she gave the appearance of being, she was dressed in such a fashion for a serious purpose!

What was more, if the 'certain good friend' was who the girl suspected he was, the reason for the attire she was wearing had to do with him!

Much to her annoyance and disappointment, being accepted as an 'unofficial official' member of Company 'Z' of the Texas Rangers, Rita had for once found there was no part in the current assignments of this little known—yet elite—group which called for her specialized services.[1] With all the men of the Company away on assignments, wanting to ensure she would be readily available should she be needed, she had elected to stay at the ranch not far from Fort Worth which served as their headquarters instead of finding temporary accommodation in that or some other city. Being active by nature, despite helping with the chores around the property and working as secretary for their commanding officer, she had found time hanging heavily on her hands. Therefore, she had been delighted when a report which arrived for Major Benson Tragg—who was in Austin attending a meeting called by the Governor—had offered her a chance of doing something more active than dealing with correspondence, no matter how interesting some of the contents might be.

Generally, the fact that an English author was making a lecture tour around major cities in the United States would have aroused little interest on the part of the authorities. Nor, on the surface, should Philip Redmond have been the exception which by tradition proved the rule. Although his work had acquired a reputation in some circles for its 'highly intellectual' quality, it was unknown to the vast majority of the reading public, even in the country of his birth. Being even less of a celebrity in America, where his books failed to attract more than minimal sales in spite of receiving acclaim from a few supposedly influential literary critics, his presence was not expected to attract such vast crowds that the local police department would be required to employ an inordinate number of officers to keep them under control. Even had this been the case, despite Austin being an unlikely location for him to select for a longer stay than anywhere else on his itinerary, his intention to spend over a week there

1. *Why Company 'Z' of the Texas Rangers was formed and some information regarding Rita Yarborough's connection with it is told in*: APPENDIX THREE.

would not normally have caused him to be considered a suitable candidate for the specialized attention of Company 'Z'.

It was not as a tribute to Redmond's literary efforts, nor even to supply protection against those who objected strongly to his derision and vilification of everything they held dear, that Major Tragg had become involved in his affairs. In every city he had visited, there had been at least one political assassination or bombing incident which a group of anarchists calling themselves the 'Brothers of the Red International' had publicly announced, via letters to newspapers and the fast growing radio networks, were committed by their members to 'strike a blow against Capitalist tyranny'. An official source in England had reported he was known to be sympathetic to similar organizations in Europe and it had been decided, at a high level, to act upon the suggestion of the man who supplied the information and keep Redmond under surveillance. Special Agents of the Federal Bureau of Investigation— still a few years from acquiring the sobriquet 'G-Men'[2]— were already trying to obtain evidence against the Brothers of the Red International. While they were unable to prove any involvement on his part, what had come to light was that the organization was in alliance with and engaged in collecting funds to supply arms to certain revolutionary factors in Mexico. Therefore, as Austin was the closest point to the Mexican border on Redmond's itinerary, the length of his stay had aroused considerable speculation. John Edgar Hoover—soon to become known as 'Mr. F.B.I.', as a tribute to his excellent work as its Director—had admitted frankly that, having only comparatively recently been completely reorganized, his own agency had neither sufficient men nor the local connections

2. When cornered by Special Agents of the Federal Bureau of Investigation in the early hours of September 26th, 1933, the notorious criminal George 'Machine Gun' Kelly is recorded as having pleaded, 'Don't shoot, G-Men, don't shoot!'.

to keep Redmond under surveillance during the visit.[3]

Wanting to avoid the diplomatic repercussions which would arise should a revolution south of the Rio Grande be proved to have had its origins in, and support from, the United States, the State Department had insisted that some other law enforcement agency must be employed to try and discover whether the author—being less likely to arouse suspicion than any of their members—was acting as a go-between for the Brothers and the Mexican revolutionaries. Because of what was regarded in official circles as the delicacy of the situation, Redmond having associates in England who would be delighted to make political capital out of any complaint he lodged against his treatment by the civic authorities in America, it had been regarded as inadvisable to assign the duty to the Austin Police Department, the sheriff of Travis County, or even the conventional Texas Rangers. Being one of the very few people outside its members who knew of Company 'Z's' existence, the State Attorney General had considered they were the most suitable to carry out the assignment.

Although the information could have been passed to the Major by telephone, Rita, seeing what she believed to be an opportunity to play a more positive part in the duties of Company 'Z' than the routine office work, had suggested to the retired Ranger who ran the ranch that she should deliver it personally. Not only had he agreed on reading the report, but he had been able to help her make the journey to Austin far more quickly than would have been possible by car. The assignment upon which Sergeant Ranse Smith was engaged had not called for him to use the converted Douglas DT-2 two seater biplane assigned as part of the Company's means of travelling quickly around

---

3. *Founded a year earlier by United States' Attorney General Charles Bonaparte, the Federal Bureau of Investigation was given its name in 1909. It was completely reorganized in 1924 by John Edgar Hoover and under his aegis it was set upon the path to becoming the large, superbly equipped and efficient law enforcement agency it is today.*

the State and, as Buck Audley was an equally competent pilot, she had been able to go by air.[4]

The decision and being able to make the trip in such a fashion had proved fortuitous!

Although the letter read by Rita had passed him as he was on his way to Austin, Major Tragg had been given the gist of its contents verbally when he paid a courtesy call to the State Attorney General on his arrival. Knowing it would take some time to bring even one of his men from their current assignments, he had telephoned the ranch to ask the girl to join him and was informed by Mrs. Lorna Audley that she had already set out to do so. When they had met, he had acted as she hoped would be the case by telling her to commence the surveillance. Stating he was aware she could take care of herself in many conditions, he had pointed out that she would be operating alone for the first time and warned her against doing anything to arouse Redmond's suspicions.

Without waiting for Rita to join him, the Major had made arrangements for her to have the room opposite the one reserved for the author—whose repeated pronouncements of Socialistic beliefs did not preclude him from demanding accommodation of the finest kind wherever he went—at the luxurious and highly priced Capital Hotel. She was registered in her own name and the story was circulated that she was a very wealthy heiress from New Jersey taking a vacation. Knowing that all the men were engaged, and hoping she would be given the assignment, she had brought a trunk filled with such of her clothing as she had thought would help in the task. Other items, including excellently made costume jewellery and a variety of costly garments had been procured to help establish her in the character she was to play.

One thing had quickly become apparent to the girl when

4. *An occasion when Sergeant Ranse Smith displayed his skill as a pilot is recorded in*: THE RETURN OF RAPIDO CLINT AND MR. J.G. REEDER.

she watched the arrival of Redmond and his British born secretary, John Broome. Attractive to most masculine eyes as she knew herself to be, her deliberately enhanced feminine attributes were unlikely to serve as a means of making the acquaintance of the two men. Instead of trying, she had decided to adopt other methods to carry out her assignment. For the past three days, making such changes to her appearance as she had felt were needed to be acceptable in the company he was keeping, she had followed the author whenever possible. She had learned nothing more than that he was a pompous, self important, arrogant snob with delusions of grandeur and a bitter resentment of everybody who was better favoured, or more successful, than himself. Although they were far from sufficient in number as purchasers of his books to justify the considerable costs to his publisher that he was incurring, he had gathered a clique of well-to-do intellectuals and 'liberals' of similar pretensions with whom he spent a good deal of time deriding what they all considered to be the faults of materialistic Capitalist society. However, despite his obvious political point of view, there had been nothing to suggest he was doing other than giving talks about his literary efforts and, as he had claimed to a reporter from the *Austin Gazette*, recuperating for a few days before continuing his tour.

Taking advantage of the author being absent giving a lecture which would keep him occupied for a couple of hours that afternoon, Rita had attempted to do something more positive in the hope of discovering if he had an ulterior motive, connected with the Brothers of the Red International and Mexican revolutionaries, for remaining in Austin longer than at any other city on his itinerary. Her efforts had proved to be of no avail and, having learned he was spending the evening at a high class restaurant, she was on her way there to resume her surveillance. It was only a short distance from the hotel and, feeling like taking some exercise, she had elected to go on foot instead of calling for a cab.

What happened as she was walking along the apparently deserted street about halfway to her destination warned the girl that she had made an unwise decision!

'Talk up, god-damn you!' demanded the shorter of the two men, twisting the arm he was grasping behind Rita's back.

'I—I don't know wh—what you mean!' the girl gasped, restraining her inclination to struggle and realizing the hand which had been removed from her mouth would quickly be replaced if she attempted to shout for help.

'She don't know what you mean, Tex!' asserted the taller captor in a mocking tone. 'The hell you *don't*! You've been following him, dressed a whole heap different than you are now, ever since he got here, and this afternoon you paid a maid to let you use her clothes and go into his room while he was away from it.'

'Why'd you do *that*?' demanded the shorter man, forcing the arm he was holding even further upwards.

'I didn—!' Rita began and the pain which tinged her voice was not simulated. 'S—Stop i—!'

'Then tell Leory what he asked you,' the one addressed as "Tex" commanded, loosening his grip slightly.

'I—!' the girl gasped and, as the twisting was resumed, went on hurriedly, 'I'm a reporter for th—!'

'Like hell you are!' denied the taller man, digging his fingers and thumb into the girl's cheeks. 'No god-damned sob-sister for a lousy rag in this crumby town could afford to dress like you do and have rooms at the Capital.'

'M—My father owns the p—paper!' Rita gasped as the grip was relaxed, using the excuse she had planned if she should be questioned on the subject. 'D—Daddy said he'd let me work full time if I could come up with a good story about Re—*Mr.* Redmond.'

'So you're snooping to get a writing job on *daddy's* god-damned newspaper, are you?' Leroy demanded. 'You don't sound like a *Texan*!'

'I'm *not*, daddy owns the *Trenton Herald*!' Rita answered, in a manner implying she expected the name of a newspaper published in the State capital of New Jersey to frighten away her captors.

'I don't give a damn if it was the *New York American*!' Leroy declared, his voice charged with menace. 'When we've finished with you, you're going to wish you'd never come here and you'll not go sneaking and spying on him again!'

'Ar—Are you going to h—*hurt* me?' Rita asked and the concern in her voice was not entirely assumed.

'Not where it'll *show*,' Tex replied, moving until he was standing behind the girl and transferring his grip so he was holding her by the biceps. Giving no indication of having discovered they were much firmer than he might have expected from one of her appearance, he went on, 'But what we're going to do will cure you of poking your nose into places where it isn't *wanted*!'

* * *　　　* * *

'I'll tell you something else now, because you won't be able to listen when we're through,' the man who had been called "Leroy" stated, drawing back his right fist. 'If you either tell the police, or write in your god-damned *daddy's* newspaper why we did it, we'll do something even *worse* next time!'

While the conversation with her captors was taking place, Rita Yarborough was thinking fast!

Every instinct the girl possessed warned her that she was in as desperate a predicament as she had ever faced!

Instinctively, Rita had been studying the pair with the dual purpose of ascertaining just how great a threat they posed, and also being able to identify them later. The one in front of her was about six foot and—despite possessing a far from impressive build—he would be strong enough to administer a severe beating, especially as her arms were held to prevent her from being able to defend herself. The other, although only a couple of inches taller than she was, had a thickset physique and the grip he had upon her biceps warned that he too was no weakling. From what she had been able to discern when her eyes had become accustomed to the gloom of the alley, they had on open necked shirts, sleeveless leather vests and Levi's pants such as cowhands still wore in Texas. However, their bare heads and the flat heels of their footwear suggested such was not their occupation. Nor, regardless of addressing one another as 'Tex' and 'Leroy', were their accents those of the Lone Star State. Rather their speech gave a clear indication of origins further to the north-east and, despite the coarse timbre each put into his voice, she concluded they were better educated than they were trying to appear. In fact, although she could not recall having heard their names, she believed that she had seen them among the wealthy intellectuals and 'liberals' attending the lectures given by Philip Redmond.

In addition to having reached her conclusions with regards to the two men, the girl was also thinking now she might avoid what they had in mind. Even before she had been told what was planned, unlike the heroines of movies and the books of the day—whose response in similar circumstances would have been to swoon or wait passively to be rescued by the conveniently available hero—she had no intention of submitting meekly to her capture. She did not minimize the risks she would be facing, but she was also aware there was something in her favour unsuspected by the men. Since being accepted as an unofficial member of Company 'Z', she had been taught a very effective system of self defence to supplement the more rough and tumble skills acquired during her tomboy childhood. However, competent as she knew herself to be, she was not unmindful of the difficulties in adopting any course of action.

Beneficial as doing so might be, enabling them to be arrested and questioned, Rita accepted that she would not need to render them both *hors de combat* to make her escape. If she could get free and reach the street from which she had been dragged, although she had not seen anybody while walking from the Capital Hotel, she felt

61

sure she could make enough noise to attract attention, and they would run away instead of trying to recapture her. The problem to be solved was how make her escape. Given an opportunity, or rather making one for herself, she believed she could bring this about. Provided she liberated herself from 'Tex's' grip in a suitable manner, she was confident that a charging butt into 'Leroy's' chest would leave the way clear for her to dash from the alley. Nevertheless, she was equally aware that releasing herself from 'Tex' would be far from easy.

A quick study of her surroundings informed Rita that they could be helpful in her bid to escape. Although there were several trash cans on each side of the alley, it was sufficiently wide to give her room to manoeuvre. Nevertheless, under the prevailing conditions, she would have difficulty in compelling the man behind her to release his hold. While the application of some of the fighting tricks she had learned from Sergeant Alvin Dustine Fog would have achieved the desired effect,[5] especially with the advantage of being delivered unexpectedly, the way she was being held rendered those requiring the use of her hands impossible. The concrete underfoot was level enough to offer a close to ideal surface for kicking, but the very high heels created a serious impediment to the mobility she would require and the otherwise less than sturdy construction of her shoes made them practically useless as an aid to inflicting sufficient pain to cause her arms to be released.

Rita was just reaching the latter unpalatable conclusions when the shorter of her captors began to tell her just they intended to do with her!

'Excuse me, young lady,' said a masculine voice from the mouth of the alley, before the threatened beating could be commenced. It continued with the somewhat

5. What the 'fighting tricks' were and how Rita Yarborough's instructor learned and put them into effect himself is told in various volumes of the Alvin Dustine 'Cap' Fog series.

sing-song inflection sometimes employed by people of Nordic birthright. 'But are them two fellows ban annoying you?'

Looking past the taller of her would-be assailants as he swung his gaze in the same direction, the girl felt a sensation of relief. Not only had the speaker approached until quite close before speaking, but he was a match in size and weight for 'Leroy'. Given his support in diverting the man in front of her, she was hoping to be able to deal with the other in spite of the way she was being held. Unfortunately, there was a factor which threatened to prevent his intervention from providing the required assistance. Having remained there unsuspected by her, a masculine figure dressed in much the same way as her attackers appeared from recessed side entrance to the building at the left. That he was not merely an innocent by-stander was evident from the way in which he was moving swiftly towards the newcomer.

'Behind you!' Rita shrieked as 'Leroy' swung around.

Before the girl had said the second word, the newcomer responded to the danger with a speed which suggested it was not entirely unexpected. Coming to a halt, he pivoted on his forward foot and his other leg lashed around in a kick much like she had been taught to deliver by Alvin Fog. The speed with which he did so took the approaching man unawares. Caught in the ribs, he let out a startled and pain filled gasp as he was propelled at a tangent. However, making the most of the opportunity, 'Leroy' covered the intervening distance in a bound and threw his arms around those of the rescuer. Colliding with the right side wall and rebounding, the man from the doorway rushed forward to resume the thwarted attack.

Until the newcomer had arrived, it had been Rita's intention to alleviate the impediment they might present by slipping off her shoes as a prelude to seeking liberation from the hold on her biceps. Seeing what was happening, she did not take the brief time which would be required to do so. Instead, moving back her right foot until it located

63

its target, she bent her leg and stamped it down hard. Unsuitable as the high heel would have proved for further agile movement, it was most effective when used in such a fashion. Spiking into the top of her captor's shoe, it elicited a yell of pain and caused his hands to relax their grip. Giving him no chance to tighten his grasp, shrugging the *mantilla* from her shoulders, she twisted herself clear of his clutching fingers. Instead of taking flight, she spun around with the intention of trying to keep 'Tex' from further participation. However, the vigour of her movement caused the other heel to snap.

Some people might have considered that, instead of coming into the alley when he saw the girl's predicament, the newcomer should have yelled to summon help. Or, having elected to make a rescue attempt himself, he was ill-advised to have announced his arrival by speaking. However, having protected himself against the third of their party, he continued to show how capable he was of defending himself. Bracing his back against 'Leroy' and being supported by the encircling arms intended to render him unable to resist, he swung up his legs until his feet reached the chest of his intended attacker. The thrust which was delivered not only turned the third man's charge into an involuntary retreat, it made his companion stagger and release the newcomer. Nevertheless, as the man with the Nordic accent alighted, 'Leroy' caught him by the shoulder and pulled him around to launch a punch which sent him reeling.

Being thrown off balance by the loss of the heel, Rita only partially achieved the effect she sought when the back of her clenched hand caught 'Tex' on the side of the jaw. He was hurt, but not as much as would have been the case if she had been able to hit with her full power. Spitting out a profanity, he grabbed her by the shoulders and flung her so she stumbled and almost fell between two of the trash cans. Seeing him following, she snatched the lid from one of them and interposed it like a shield against the blow he was directing her way. Before he could stop it, his fist met metal instead of human flash and a howl of pain burst from him. Nor were his troubles at an end. Retaining her grip on the handle with her left hand, she caught the side of the lid with her right and swung it in a horizontal arc. Clasping his throbbing knuckles to his mouth in an involuntary gesture, he received a jab in the stomach from the rounded edge and stumbled backwards with both hands transferring to clutch at the point of impact.

Brought to a halt by the opposite wall, the third of the attackers felt his foot strike something alongside a trash can which made a glassy tinkle and he decided it would provide him with a useful weapon. Snatching up the bottle, which was half full of some kind of liquor, he began to move towards where 'Leroy' and the newcomer were struggling together. Raising his improvised club, he was prevented from putting it to use. Yelling a warning, the girl flung the lid she had used so effectively against 'Tex' and it proved equally efficacious. Struck on the shin by the edge, the man released the bottle. Although it burst on the ground to spray its contents over the right trouser leg and shoe of its intended target, it had no other effect.

Seeing his intended victim had thown away her extemptorized protective device, 'Tex' was impelled by his suffering to try and seek revenge. Removing his hands from his aching stomach, he rushed at her with them reaching out like the talons of a hawk. Watching the menacing way in which he was approaching, Rita considered he was still dangerous. Kicking off the pump with its heel intact, to allow a greater and safer mobility, she stepped aside an instant before his claw-like fingers could close upon her. Allowing him to blunder by, she pivoted at the waist and slammed her left elbow into the centre of his back. Not only did his attack come to nothing, once again he was sent into a helpless sprawl away from her.

Giving no sign of being aware of his narrow escape, the newcomer continued to display his capability. More by chance than deliberate intent, 'Leroy' had clutched him by the throat and was squeezing savagely. Thrusting his hands between his attacker's arms, he snapped them outwards with a power sufficient to break the choking grip. Then, in what was clearly a continuation of his actions, he drove his clenched left fist with an equal force against 'Leroy's' jaw. Having done so, sending his victim in a reeling plunge across the alley, he swung his attention to his second intended assailant. However, his preparedness to deal with further hostilities was unnecessary.

'Get out of here!' yelled the man from the doorway, swinging around and taking his departure in a hurried, albeit limping, run towards the entrance to the alley.

Whether inspired by their companion's advice and actions, or because they realized that the affair had gone completely wrong, the other two men wasted no time in following his example. Shoving away from the wall against which he had once more been driven, 'Leroy' went just as quickly in the direction from which he had helped bring their intended victim. On the point of resuming his attack upon the girl, 'Tex' proved he too considered discretion the better part of valour. However, concluding that to go after the fleeing pair meant passing her very competent rescuer, he extricated himself from between the trash cans where he had come to a halt and raced towards the rear end of the alley.

Meaning to tackle and hold 'Tex' until her rescuer could come and lend a hand in subduing him, Rita darted on a converging course. However, her hope of taking a prisoner who might supply information when subjected to interrogation by Major Tragg came to nothing. Catching a glimpse of her approaching from the corner of his eye, either by luck or deliberate design, he thrust a hand against her face. The shove he gave caught her in mid-stride and caused her to lose her balance. Toppling backwards, she alighted on her rump to the accompaniment of tearing cloth as her tight black satin dress split along both its seams from top to below waist level.

Being winded, although the instincts she had acquired riding horses allowed her to reduce the effect of the impact

66

of her descent, Rita could do nothing more than sit and watch 'Tex' disappear around the corner of the right side building. Then, letting out a breathless hiss of disappointment, she looked in the opposite direction. Discovering that her other assailant and his companion had already gone from sight, she gave her attention to the man whose fortuitous arrival had saved her from being beaten up. As he was coming towards her, she took in details of his appearance which she had previously been too engrossed to observe. Bareheaded, with longish blond hair, he was wearing a stylish black tuxedo and its accoutrements. Because of the inadequate illumination, she could see little more of his face than that it had a neatly trimmed beard and moustache. Although the light was also insufficient for her to be able to hazard a guess at his age, he moved with the ease of a man in the prime of life and his ability at fighting suggested he was in excellent physical condition.

'Are you all right, young lady?' the rescuer inquired solicitously, reaching towards the girl with his right hand.

'Y—Yes!' Rita gasped and allowed herself to be helped her to her feet. Sucking in deep breaths, she went on, 'Th—Thank you!'

'It ban nothing,' the man asserted, releasing his hold. 'Were them fellows trying to rob you?'

'They said so,' the girl lied, feeling gingerly to ascertain the extent of the damage her dress had suffered and trying, without much success, to draw the parted seams together.

'Shall I go and call for a policeman?' the man offered.

'N—No,' Rita replied. Remembering the warning she had been given by Major Benson Tragg that it was inadvisable to have the involvement of Company "Z" brought to the attention of the local authorities, not all of whom would have approved, she wanted to discuss the incident with him before taking any further action, and she thought fast to select an acceptable reason for the refusal. Gesturing to where the vanity bag she had dropped on being dragged into the alley was still lying at the entrance, she continued, 'They didn't take anything and

I'm sure my family would rather not have my name and what happened mentioned in the newspapers.'

'I know how they feel,' the man claimed. 'And I'd rather my name not ban mentioned in the newspapers either. I'm Professor Arne Jorgensen, the explorer, and I've come to Austin to get away from people who ban wanting me to give them talks about my experiences.' He paused and ran his gaze over the girl. Then, looking away, he went on, 'I hope you haven't got to go too far, the way your dress ban torn by them fellows.'

'I was going to the Ambassador,' Rita admitted wryly.

'Now doesn't that ban a coincidence, so was I,' Jorgenson declared, then raised his right leg. 'But the bottle that fellow tried to hit me with put something wet over my trousers' leg and shoe.'

'I've a room at the Capital,' Rita said, wanting to learn more about her rescuer. 'Why not come with me.' She paused, trying successfully to look modestly flustered, then went on, 'Good *heavens*, how that must have *sounded* to you. I'd better tell you it has its own bathroom where you can wait while I see if I can sponge off whatever is on your trousers' leg and have a bellhop come to get your shoes cleaned.'

'I ban staying there myself,' Jorgenson replied. 'But, perhaps as we haven't neither of us eaten yet, you would like to take supper with me at the Ambassador after we've changed our clothes.'

'I'd be *delighted* to,' the girl claimed and was sincere. Not only did she feel gratitude for her rescue, but accepting the suggestion would allow her to do as she had originally intended. The threats uttered by ''Leroy'' and ''Tex'' made her more certain that the surveillance of Philip Redmond was justified and she refused to be deterred from continuing it. What was more, his reaction to her appearance without any injuries at the Ambassador Restaurant would be worth watching. 'Except—although I hope you don't think me too forward for suggesting

68

it—perhaps you'll come to the Ambassador as my guest. It's the least I can do to repay you for saving me.'

* * *   * * *

While drawing on the royal blue cotton trousers of her pyjamas, Rita Yarborough continued the train of thought which had occupied her as she was having a bath before going to bed!

Five days had passed since the incident in the alley and the girl was wondering whether she had achieved anything worthwhile on her first unsupported assignment for Company 'Z'!

Returning to the Capital Hotel on the night of the attempted assault, acting upon the advice of Professor Arne Jorgenson to go in through a side entrance to which he had acquired a key from some unspecified source and for some reason, Rita had been able to reach her suite without anybody else having seen the dishevelled state of her attire. On reaching the first floor, much to her surprise—as their paths had never crossed until that evening—she had discovered he was occupying the adjacent room. Having arranged for him to call for her when he was ready, they had parted company in the passage.

Going into the small bathroom of her luxurious quarters, having washed and renewed the makeup which was part of the character she was portraying, the girl had replaced her shoes and the stockings laddered during the struggle. Then she had changed into an undamaged dress which was just as revealing as its predecessor. Waiting to be collected by her rescuer, she called a telephone number with which she had been supplied for use in case of an emergency. After a delay while he was brought away from a dinner party he was giving, Major Benson Tragg on hearing what had happened, had stated his approval of her decision not to involve the Austin Police Department.

As the Major had pointed out, no matter whether Rita had stuck to her pretence of being a budding newspaper reporter or explained her true status when telling the local

69

peace officers—not all of whom would have approved of the involvement of the conventional Texas Rangers, much less Company 'Z'—all that had been said, there were objections to an attempt being made to bring about the arrest of her attackers. 'Leroy' and 'Tex' had not referred to Philip Redmond by name, nor had either confirmed he was the 'certain good friend' when she had mentioned him. Therefore, should he be questioned, he would have an excuse to claim he knew nothing of the incident. On the other hand, because the police had shown that much interest in him, he would behave in a more circumspect fashion and might even take the precaution of ending whatever association he might have with the Brothers of the Red International. If that happened, the authorities would have lost their possible connection between the group and the Mexican revolutionaries and, before another was discovered, whatever trouble was contemplated could have taken place.

On being informed of the girl's intention to go to the Ambassador Restaurant, Major Tragg had expressed concern over her safety. While admitting that the response elicited from the author might prove informative, he had pointed out the incident in the alley proved she was already under suspicion and, even if her explanation had been accepted, more lethal methods might be adopted to bring her surveillance to an end. She had already been aware of the possibility, but declined—on the grounds that Redmond would almost certainly learn who she was and conclude her pretence of being a hopeful reporter was false—Tragg's suggestion that he should leave his guests and join her. She had reassured him by explaining that she would be accompanied by her rescuer, who had spoken as if considering himself a person of considerable renown. If this was the case, she would take the precaution of disclosing his identity to everyone. The author and his associates would then realise that any mishap befalling Jorgensen would arouse more interest on the part of the police than was desirable for them, and so it was unlikely they would attempt any extreme measures while she was in his company. Promising her superior that she would take care, regardless of her suppositions, a knock on the sitting-room door caused the discussion to be brought to an end.

Coming into the room, Jorgenson had apologised for having taken so long. He had changed his trousers and shirt, but a glance downwards had informed Rita he was still wearing the same footwear. They were, despite having been described by him as 'shoes' suitable for semi-formal evening attire, actually a sturdily made pair of boots. However, the cleaning they had obviously been given could not remove the traces of the liquid which had splashed over the one on his right foot.

'I hope the stain doesn't show too badly,' the Professor had said, following the direction of the girl's glance. 'Trying to clean it off was what took me so long. They ban most comfortable and, anyway, they ban the only black pair I have with me!'

Assuring her rescuer that his appearance was satisfactory and accompanying him to the elevator, Rita studied him more carefully than had been possible when they first met. Despite the more adequate lighting, she still found herself unable to form any better opinion of his actual age than she had in the alley. While pleasant, his neatly bearded and moustached face could not be considered handsome. Deeply bronzed, as if from long exposure to the elements, it had slightly bulging cheeks, too prominent teeth, very bushy eyebrows and a tin jagged white scar which ran down the left cheek. Furthermore, its hirsute adornment tended to give the impression of him being somewhat older than she suspected was the case.

Except for having found her escort to be good company and an excellent dancer, even displaying an unexpected ability at the vigorous 'Charleston' which was currently very popular, and allowing her to ensure she came to Redmond's attention, the girl felt she had achieved nothing positive during the visit to the Ambassador Restaurant. If

Redmond had been surprised to see her, or was, in any way, put out over the failure of 'Leroy' and 'Tex' to inflict the threatened beating, he had shown no indication of it. In fact, he had hardly given her a glance, even when she and the Professor had been allowed a clear space by the other dancers to demonstrate their dexterity in performing the rapid and complex four-four time gyrations of the Charleston which had put them in full view of the table Redmond was occupying with several of his clique of local well-to-do intellectuals.

When the restaurant closed in the early hours of the morning, Rita had declined Jorgenson's offer of a cab on discovering that the author was returning to the hotel alone and on foot. Rita said it was such a lovely night she felt like walking. Only one thing materialised from her decision. Passing the alley into which she had been dragged by 'Leroy' and 'Tex', the Professor remarked he had overheard them saying that she was being taken there because of the interest she had shown in the author. Showing no sign of suspecting that she was other than what she had claimed to be, he had offered his assistance at keeping Redmond under observation in exchange for her assurance that she would not request he gave her information about his own activities. Even though he warned he might not be available all the time Rita had accepted his suggestion, including his proviso, as she could see he might provide physical protection if it was needed. On being informed of the development over the telephone the following morning, Major Tragg, whilst telling her that she must try to avoid putting the distinguished visitor in any danger, had given his approval of the arrangement as he still had none of his men available to act as her escort.

However, despite her hopes where Redmond was concerned having come to nothing, Rita had been able to report success in another area. Before contacting her superior, she had questioned the maid—a woman given to reacting in a most excitable fashion if anything untowards happened—whom she had bribed to supply the loan of a uniform and pass-key to gain admittance to the author's room and supposedly prepare a suprise for his birthday. Calming a close to hysterical outburst by promising she had no intention of taking the matter further, she was told it was Redmond's secretary who had learned of what she had done.

Since that morning, during the daytime when Jorgenson was not available, the girl had continued to follow the author. Instead of her revealing evening wear, she had donned spectacles with plain glass and dowdy clothing selected to give the impression that she was one of the intellectual college students who formed the majority of the audiences he attracted. Keeping to the routine of lectures and meetings with his clique, he had done nothing to even remotely suggest he was serving as a go-between for the Brothers and the revolutionaries. He was generally accompanied by John Broome, a tall, lean, poorly dressed and miserable looking young man who, despite her suspicion on first seeing them that they had a closer relationship than that of employer and secretary, occupied less costly accommodation at the hotel. However, despite being confident she could recognize them no matter how they were dressed—although the same did not apply to the third member of their party—she had never seen either 'Leroy' or 'Tex' again.

Nor, even with the assistance of the Professor, had Rita found the surveillance in the evenings any more informative. However, having Jorgenson with her at such times had proved useful in that it offered a passable reason for her to follow her quarry to the places he visited. Despite his assertion of Socialist beliefs, although they did not extend to having his secretary included in the company on such occasions, Redmond had proved to have a taste for expensive diversions after the sun went down. Behaving as if they were having a very intimate relationship, Rita and the Professor had followed him on his nightly rounds of the best restaurants and other places of entertainment.

On the second evening, seeing Redmond was taking an

unaccompanied ride in one of the open topped horse-drawn Victorias which still plied for hire in the high rent district they were frequenting, the girl and Jorgenson had decided it was such an unusual activity for him that it warranted investigation. Accordingly, indulging in behaviour more suitable for lovers than watchers, they had followed in a similar vehicle. However, nobody had contacted him as he was taken on a leisurely circular route through the area around the State Capital building and, apart from having aroused their speculation as to why he should have indulged in a solitary sight-seeing trip at such an hour, having gone after him on the ride provided no more information than anything else.

While taking the ride, Rita had had a feeling that she and the Professor were being watched. Contriving to look around, she had been unable to find out whether this was the case. No vehicle was following them, but the leisurely pace they were travelling would have allowed a watcher on foot to keep them in view and there were enough shadows on each side of the road to offer concealment from detection.

However, such was the enthusiasm displayed by Jorgenson on learning of the girl's suspicions that she had started to wonder whether he might have an ulterior motive behind his offer of assistance. Not only did he begin to exhibit such seemingly romantic behaviour towards her during their surveillance in the evenings that it had supplied a convincing reason for them being together, but he had carried it to other extremes at the hotel. When she had queried his habit of having sizeable bouquets of flowers delivered to her room each day, accompanied by notes expressing endearment in no uncertain terms, he had explained in his lilting Nordic accent, 'This ban the best fun I've had for a long time and it will well make any of them fellows he might have watching us think we ban *very* good friends. Anyways, if you ban selling a story about him to your father, you can pay me back for them from your expenses.''

74

In the days which followed, having admitted he too felt they were being kept under observation, the Professor's response to the possibility had not been confined to trying to locate the observers and supplying the bouquets. On their return to the hotel each night after following Redmond, he had insisted upon spending a few minutes indulging in what he called 'kissing and cuddling' outside the girl's door. Claiming it too was a precaution in case they were being watched by the author's henchmen, he had also intimated in a carrying voice that he would come to her room later. This had not happened, nor was it ever mentioned when they were in a position to talk without being overheard. Nevertheless, in the early hours of that morning she had received a telephone call from a woman who had asked with a slight Southern accent if he was there. Annoyed at having been woken up, Rita had replied in a tone of irritation, 'What is it to *you* if he *is*?' and hung up. Then, knowing the call must have been passed through the hotel's switchboard, she had contacted the operator and was informed that it had come after one to the Professor's room went unanswered. Pressed for further information, he said it originated over an outside line from a pay telephone and, despite having claimed the matter was one of urgency, the woman had not given any name.

'They must ban checking up on us,' Jorgenson had declared, when hearing of the call while he and Rita were taking breakfast together in the hotel's dining-room. 'Perhaps they ban up to something and wanted to be sure we wasn't watching them.'

Despite having made the explanation, the Professor had told the girl that he could not be able to accompany her that night because of a prior appointment. Although he had not made any mention of being otherwise engaged when they had parted company the previous night, she had asked no questions. His absence was not inconvenient, nor potentially dangerous for her as things turned out. Redmond had only gone to the Ambassador Restaurant with his cronies and, as usual, had come back to the hotel alone. He had taken a cab, which allowed her to do the same instead of walking after him and possibly being way-laid by the trio. Arriving at her room, she had found there was a lady's wristwatch she had admired in the hotel's gift shop attached to a blue silk ribbon around the bouquet brought there in her absence. Being aware of how much it had cost and perturbed by the note which accompanied it saying, 'For the one who I hold dearest in all the world', she had felt Jorgenson was carrying the deception too far. However, her attempt to call and protest had met with no response from his end of the telephone and she was informed by the receptionist that, as his key was still in its pigeon-hole behind the desk, he could not have returned to his room.

Deciding there was no point in waiting up, as she could deal with the matter in the morning, Rita had set about getting ready to go to bed. She had no liking for the reveal-ing clothing and amount of ostentatious jewellery called for by the character of a wealthy flapper, albeit one she hoped was now accepted as having a different motive from her real reason for taking such an interest in the author's activities. Nor was she any more enamoured of the exces-sive makeup she had on. Therefore it was with a feeling of relief that she discarded all the former and removed the latter before indulging in the relaxation of a long soaking in the bath.

Contemplating the disturbing way in which her associa-tion with the Professor was progressing, Rita donned and fastened the jacket of her pyjamas. However, the expensive present which had accompanied the bouquet was not the only reason why she wished Sergeant Alvin Dustine Fog would complete his current assignment and join her. There were other members of Company 'Z' whose arrival could have supplied an excuse for dispensing with Jorgenson's services, but she had a special reason for preferring him.[6]

6. *The 'special reason' for Rita Yarborough preferring the assistance of Sergeant Alvin Dustine—later known as 'Cap'—Fog over that of his equally competent fellow members of Company 'Z' developed to such an extent in later years that they were married.*

Thinking fondly of him, she walked into the main room.

The sight which met the girl's eyes drove everything else from her mind!

* * *　　　* * *

Rita Yarborough found she was no longer alone in her room. However, the unannounced visitor was not Professor Arne Jorgenson. In fact, the intruder was not even a man. Having gained admission by some means, a woman was standing by the dressing table reading the very romantic inscription on the card which had accompanied the expensive lady's wristwatch still fastened to the ribbon around the bouquet of flowers. Looking around as Rita entered, she had an expression of anger which was understandable in the circumstances. However, her appearance aroused the girl's curiosity as much as the reason for her presence.

Being a few years older and about an inch taller than Rita, the intruder had blonde hair done in a short straight bob. There was a suggestion of vitality, immense capability and utter fearlessness about her beautiful face. The bell bottomed red silk lounging pyjamas she wore were most complimentary to a figure which was willowly and shapely. Not only did the jacket indicate she was sufficiently well endowed to make the wearing of a 'flattening brassiere' a matter of considerable discomfort, but the very snug fit displayed beyond any doubt that she was wearing nothing underneath it. There was no sign of her having arrived in and removed a coat. Such was the close to transparent nature of her attire, she was hardly likely to have come through the streets dressed in that alone. Despite the implication being that she too was residing in the Capital Hotel, the girl could not remember ever having seen her.

While studying the woman, Rita found her response was surprising. Despite having no right to be there and clearly being angry, she showed none of the consternation a thief would have displayed at having been confronted by the legal occupant of the room. Instead of making a run for the door, she stepped towards the approaching girl.

77

Rising with speed and precision, the wide bottom of the trousers' leg riding back to show a calf with the muscular development of a well trained dancer, her right foot passed between Rita's reaching hands. It was covered with nothing more substantial than the thin rubber 'paddling pumps' popular for use at the beach, or around a swimming pool. Nevertheless, she proved to be aware of its limitations for what she was doing. Being caught under the chin by the ball of the foot, instead of the thinly protected toes, Rita might have counted herself fortunate. Although the unexpected attack sent her staggering until she sat involuntarily on the bed, it had arrived almost at the limit of its flight and was less effective than otherwise would have been the case.

Much to Rita's surprise, having delivered the attack, once more the woman did not behave as might be expected of a hotel thief caught in the act. Swinging around almost as a continuation of the kick, instead of making the most of her opportunity to leave, she darted to the dressing-table. There was a fluidity to her movements which reminded the girl of demonstrations given by Sergeant Alexandre 'Frenchie' Giradot, a member of Company 'Z' who claimed he was descended from a long line of Parisian apache[7] and whose talents included being a very skilful exponent of French *savate* fist and foot boxing. Watching her jerk at the bow of the ribbon around the bouquet and free the watch, as if being determined to take a piece of worthwhile loot with her when she fled, Rita wondered whether robbery was the real motive. She could be trying to create the impression that nothing else was the reason for the visit. The girl also decided that, if the latter alternative was the case, the delay offered her an opportunity to

7. *Used in this context, 'apache' does not mean a member of the Indian nation with a similar name. Pronounced 'a-pash' and not 'A-patchy', it is the sobriquet given by the French to a class of small time criminals who once infested Paris.*

prove the intruder was involved with Redmond and had actually come to search her room at his instigation.

'*This* is *mine*!' the blonde claimed, looking in a mocking fashion at Rita and gesturing with the watch. Her voice had slight traces of a Southron accent and she went on, 'So you stay right where you are, *fat butt*, or I'll give you some more of the same to make you wish you *had*!'

'You mean you'll *try*, you skinny *bitch*!' Rita spat back, placing her hands on the coverlet and thrusting herself erect.

Having lost none of the spirited nature which had brought her into contact with Sergeant Alvin Dustine Fog while she had been seeking to avenge the murder of her parents and gained her acceptance as a member of Company 'Z',[8] Rita would have felt a strong resentment even if the woman had done no more than come into her room without an invitation. Consequently, the way she had been treated and the less than flattering description she was accorded had done nothing to bring about a change of attitude. Even before the threat and insult were uttered, she had already decided to take whatever measures were necessary to learn why the unauthorized visit was being paid. What was more, her resolve was strengthened rather than decreased by realizing that she had heard the blonde's voice before. Although the declaration of ownership of the watch suggested her assumptions could be wrong with regards to the motive being connected with Redmond, it merely served to increase the puzzle. However, she was equally aware this was not the time to inquire why the other had called her room the night before and asked if Professor Arne Jorgenson was with her.

Concluding that Rita intended to resume hostilities, the woman placed the watch carefully at the far side of the dressing table. Then she scooped up the bouquet and turned to throw it at Rita. Advancing in its wake, she sent her left foot flashing upwards in a way which indicated the

8. *Told in*: RAPIDO CLINT.

previous kick had not been so effective by chance. However, the attack did not meet with the success of its predecessor. Coming to a stop before the flowers and their wicker basket container could reach her, Rita knocked them aside. Then, having avoided what she had guessed correctly was primarily intended as a diversion, she responded to the attack with one of the counters she had learned from Sergeant Alvin Fog.

Instead of trying to catch the swiftly approaching leg in her hands, Rita crossed and interposed her wrists, pointing downwards, so that it was halted by the bottom of the X shape they formed. Then she slipped the lower hand back until her fingers could close around the ankle and, with it secured, transferred the other to it. The twisting shove she gave propelled the blonde away from her. However, despite having been sent in a plunging rush towards a corner, the woman regained sufficient control over her movements to be able to extend her arms and have her hands make contact with the walls, preventing her head colliding with the unyielding surface. Twisting around swiftly, what she saw caused her to thrust herself from the confines of the corner. Once again, however, it was obvious that she was not seeking safty in flight.

Deciding that the way the blonde was behaving indicated a willingness to try to carry out the threat, Rita realized that the counter for the kick had been less effective than if the collision with the wall had taken place. However, despite the way she had been attacked on each occasion suggesting skill at *savate*, she was sufficiently confident in her own ability to consider she would be able to gain the upper hand and enforce a demand to have her curiosity satisfied. With that end in mind, she continued to move forward with her fists raised ready to resume the fray.

As they were moving towards one another, Rita keeping alert for another attempt to kick her, remembered just a moment too late that *savate* allowed the use of fists as well as feet. Before she could take precautions against such tactics, thrown with a skill and speed equal to that shown in the earlier attacks, the woman's right knuckles, caught her on the side of the chin in a far from gentle manner. Her own training in self defence had included using her fists and, although the blow hurt, she immediately retaliated by driving her clenched left hand downwards. Hit in the *solar plexus*, the blonde gasped and was unable to avoid the right uppercut which slammed beneath her jaw. However, despite staggering back, she proved she was far from incapacitated by driving her left fist into the girl's right breast. Pain bit into Rita and, before it passed off, she took a left cross to the cheek which jolted her head around. For all that, she hit back and, an instant after her blow landed, once again felt the impact of the blonde's bony right hand on her cheek.

Despite honours having been even up to that point, the woman showed no inclination to continue the exchange of punches on a give and take basis. Ducking beneath the next blow to come her way, she straightened and delivered two quick jabs to Rita's face. Circling like boxers, they used their fists with mixed results until the blonde was given an opportunity to repeat her evasive tactics just as successfully. However, giving her no chance to put them into effect a third time, Rita's right hand shot out to grasp the neckline of her pyjamas' jacket. Before the woman could react to the danger, a left cross to her jaw arrived with a force which caused the front of the garment to open and the slick material to be plucked from her assailant's grasp. Aided by her instinctive attempt to pull away, the punch sent the woman reeling until she sprawled on to her back. On alighting, she might have been grateful for the thick carpets which the Capital Hotel fitted in the best rooms. Helped by what were obviously well trained reflexes acting to reduce the impact of the fall, she had a comparatively soft surface upon which to descend.

Just how much the blonde benefited quickly became apparent to Rita. Rushing forward, her intention of diving on to the woman failed to reach fruition. Before she attained her objective, two hands shot out to grab and pull on the front of her blue cotton jacket. At the same time, she felt a pair of thinly covered feet being thrust against her stomach. Then the room seemed to rotate as she was propelled over her intended victim in a half somersault. However, she too was fortunate in her landing place. Coming down on the bed, she was saved from anything more serious happening by the depth of its mattress absorbing the force of her arrival. Although the velocity of the foot throw was sufficient to send her bouncing across until she dropped on to the floor at the other side, she was not so dazed or winded as would have occurred if she had landed even on the well carpeted floor. Aware that she was still in danger, she wasted no time in rolling over and thrusting herself upright with the aid of the bed. As she was doing so, she realized that she was not regaining her feet a moment too soon.

As if the response to the intended attack had not been proof enough, the blonde was already rising quickly enough to give warning that she was just as unaffected by the blow which knocked her down. Leaping on to the bed, instead of coming around it, she tried to return to the offensive with a kick. Ducking beneath the leg this time, Rita grabbed her by the other ankle and heaved. A yelp of alarm left the woman as she tumbled backwards on the mattress. Realizing what was intended as she felt the pulling to which the trapped limb was subjected, she flailed with her other leg and clutched the pillow in both hands. Neither stopped her being dragged over the coverlet until she was deposited on the floor. However, as her ankle was released and the girl bent with hands reaching for her, she put all the strength she could muster into swinging the pillow around. Struck in the face by it, Rita reeled a couple of steps and the woman rose before she could regain control over her movements.

Bending at the waist, the blonde darted forward. Thwarting the attempt to butt her in the body by stepping aside, Rita delivered a kick to the seat of the red trousers as the woman went by. Driven onwards, she disappeared through open door to the bathroom. Only briefly, however. Darting after her, the girl sank both hands into her hair and dragged her out again. Responding instinctively to the feminine mode of attack, the blonde plunged her fingers just as determinedly into the shortish rusty red locks. Staggering in a circle, jerking and tugging vigorously, they tumbled on to the bed. Crossing it, while changing from hair pulling to an equally primitive grappling which caused first one then the other to assume the upper position, they dropped to the floor and continued fighting with none of the skill previously shown.

After rolling over and over on the carpet for several seconds, the pair came to their feet. They broke apart, but only for an instant. Controlling her inclination to resume the hair pulling, Rita lunged forward with the intention of adopting more efficient methods to quell the woman. As they came together, she discovered the decision was mutual. The hold she took, meaning to throw the blonde over her hip, was countered in the fashion she had been taught by Alvin Fog. However, although it was she who was precipitated to the floor, she contrived to bring her assailant down with the counter she had learned for the attack.

The fighting continued in unabated fury, with elements of boxing, wrestling, *savate* and purely feminine hair pulling being employed indiscriminately. Regardless of the difference in their bodies' conformation, Rita discovered this did not give her any noticeable advantage over the blonde. Despite being slightly heavier, this was countered by the slender body of the woman possessing a wiry strength close to equalling her own and being capable of a rapidity of movement which tended to offset her few extra pounds. What was more, the girl found the blonde was able to match her skill when wrestling. Rita proved somewhat more adept in the use of fists, but this did not give her any appreciable advantage. It was nullified by the way in which the slender blonde seemed to be able to deliver kicks in every direction. Therefore, no matter what methods were being used, they were evenly matched in devising ways of inflicting punishment in return for that subjected by the other and, as neither showed any indication of wishing to quit, the struggle was not brief in duration.

In the course of being thrown, knocked, kicked, or pushed around the room, carooming off the walls and falling over the furniture in passing, each combatant had her pyjama jacket torn off and perspiration soon had the trousers clinging wetly to their legs. However, neither of them allowed the fact that her bosom was left without even a flimsy protection to deter her efforts. Both of them being totally engrossed in applying or escaping from a variety of throws, foot rolls, scissors to head or body, hammerlocks and other wrestling tricks, interspersed by punches, slaps and kicks launched with an equal impartiality, the loss of the garments went unnoticed.

Nevertheless, in one respect, the embattled pair might have counted themselves fortunate. If the girl had not removed her jewellery prior to taking the bath, the lumpy rings she had discarded would have been capable of inflicting disfiguring cuts. She was saved from a similar fate by the woman wearing only a flat gold wedding band. What was more, because of the strenuous and active life she led, Rita kept her fingernails trimmed short and, for some reason, the same applied to her opponent. Therefore, although each was treated in a way which would leave bruising, neither sustained any lasting injury despite the vigorous way they were mauling at one another.

After almost ten minutes of continuous brawling, having dropped from the bed on to their knees, the combatants interlocked their fingers and began an unthinking test of strength. Every muscle of their bodies, each shaped curvaceously in a different fashion, was brought into play until their mutual efforts caused them to come to their feet. For a few seconds, neither could achieve her desire to push the other backwards. With legs spread apart and feet digging into the carpet for added leverage, their arms rose from hip level to above their heads. Needing to replenish tormented lungs, they sucked in and expelled air in croaking gasps which set their pendulous bosoms rising and falling in what most have considered an attractive fashion.

Just as it seemed they had reached a condition of stalemate, Rita's extra weight proved the deciding factor by allowing her to bend the blonde's arms down and inwards. Then the woman's right foot slid back until its knee returned to the floor and her left leg slipped outwards. Alarmed by the development, she thrust her head forward and closed her mouth on the bare breast it reached. Before the teeth could break the skin, the girl yelped and retaliated. Snatching free her fingers, she brought up and drove her left knee into the blonde's bosom. However, although she went on to her back with both hands clutching at the stricken region, she was not rendered *hors de combat*. Stepping forward and lifting her right leg to stamp, the girl took both her opponent's feet in the stomach. The attack lacked the power which the slender limbs could have exerted earlier, but it was still hard enough to send her stumbling against the door.

For a few seconds, gasping in exhaustion, the combatants remained where they were. Then Rita saw the blonde get up and she forced her tormented body to do the same. They were both reeling in exhaustion, but moved towards one another without hesitation. Gasping for breath and swaying as they came to a stop, each braced herself to make what she sensed would be the last effort she was capable of producing. After a couple of seconds to call up their reserves of strength, they reached an identical solution over what action to take. Two right hands were knotted into fists and drawn back. Impelled by every remaining ounce of energy, they were swung around in twin arcs at the same instant. Delivered with the force of desperation, albeit having only a fraction of the power either could have attained when the fight started, the knuckles made simultaneous contact against the opposing jaws. Both heads were pushed rather than snapped back and around. Oblivious of the way in which the blonde went in the opposite direction to sprawl face down on the floor, Rita was sent staggering. She was saved from falling by stumbling shoulder first against the wall. Sliding helplessly to her knees and bracing herself on her hands, she fought to retain consciousness.

Although the struggle had been making a considerable noise from the beginning, nobody had come to investigate. The room upheld the reputation of the hotel for being sound-proof and would have prevented anybody passing by at such a late hour from hearing the commotion. Furthermore, while the thuds when one or both was dumped on the floor would have attracted attention in the bar below, it had been closed long before the fighting commenced.

Raising her head as she heard the room's door being opened, Rita saw a pair of legs in Levi's pants and flat heeled black boots come from the passage!

Despite the condition to which she was reduced by her exertions, alarm flooded through the girl as she remembered the way in which 'Leroy' and 'Tex' had been dressed!

* * *   * * *

'Cora-Ann, Cora-Ann!' said the man who stepped across the threshold, after glancing at the legitimate occupant of the room. Going to where the blonde was on her hands and knees, trying feebly to rise, he continued in a gently chiding tone, 'I told you Miss Yarborough didn't mean *anything* to me, excepting so far as our mutual interest in Broome and Redmond was concerned. But you will *insist* on doing things for yourself and look at what it's got you this time.'

Although Rita Yarborough had never seen the newcomer when he was clad in the fashion of a cowhand, nor even knew he owned such attire, she recognized him and lost the sense of alarm caused by his arrival!

Nevertheless, despite feeling on the point of collapsing, the girl was still sufficiently in possession of her faculties to realize something was wrong!

Then Rita realized what it was!

All traces of the Nordic timbre had gone and Professor Arne Jorgenson was speaking with the accent of a well educated Englishman!

Trying to work out the significance of the change of voice and finding it difficult to think in her exhausted condition, Rita watched the man gently turning the blonde until she was lying on her back. After examining her in the fashion of one possessing a knowledge of medical matters, despite the timbre of wry endearment with which he had addressed her, he rose and came back to Rita. Lifting her just as gently, he carried her across the room and laid her on the bed.

'Wh—Who—ar—are y—you?' Rita gasped, trying to sit up.

'Why I ban your friend Professor Jorgenson,' the man replied, reverting to the manner of speaking to which the girl had grown accustomed. Placing a hand lightly on her bare shoulder, he held her down without difficulty. 'Don't worry, I ban trained as a doctor. Lie still while I ban making sure you aren't hurt badly.' Having subjected her to as thorough a check as he had given the blonde, he went into the bathroom and returned after a few seconds carrying a tumbler filled with water. Easing her into a sitting position, he held it to her lips and said, 'Drink this.'

Much as Rita wanted to repeat her question, being sure she had not been supplied with the truth about the man's identity, she was suffering from such a severe thirst that she did as she was instructed. On her head being returned the pillow, she felt a lassitude coming over her. Trying to shake it off, as her suspicions had not been dispelled by what she was told, she watched him walk away. Instead of collecting more water from the bathroom, he crossed to pick up the blonde. Although she managed to force her shoulders upwards slightly and tried to speak, the effort proved to much. As he was carrying her now limp opponent from the room, blackness descended upon her.

With the return of her faculties, Rita was assailed by numerous throbbing and nagging pains. Remembering what had caused them, she forced herself to raise her head and look around. Becoming aware that daylight was coming through the window, across which the drapes had been drawn in her absence the previous night, she made the physical effort required to swing out her legs and sit on the edge of the bed. After the room stopped giving the impression of spinning violently, she took stock of her surroundings.

The first thing to make an impression upon the girl was that she was now wearing her bright yellow silk pyjamas instead of just the sweat-soddened blue cotton trousers to which she had been reduced during the fighting. What was more, a check showed she was much cleaner than she would have expected to be after having perspired so copiously and being in such extensive contact with the carpet while rolling on it. In fact, she decided her condition suggested she had been given a bath before the replacement nightwear was put on. She discovered next that, not only was the bouquet of flowers which had been crushed under their struggling bodies gone, but all other traces of the fracas had been removed. Feeling sure the blonde would not have been capable of tidying up, or giving her the bath and change of attire, she realized there was only one other possible candidate. Feeling a blush come to her cheeks at the appreciation of what had been entailed, she wondered why the man had taken it upon himself to do treat her with such consideration.

Wanting to divert her thoughts from the embarassing subject and recollecting the cause of the fight, Rita rose and walked unsteadily to the dressing-table. Seeing no sign of the wristwatch on it, or the floor, her first inclination was to send for the house detective and report it was missing. However, a moment's thought warned her that such a course was undesirable under the circumstances.

Wondering whether to contact Major Benson Tragg, or put a call through to the Professor's room, demanding an explanation she felt so thirsty that she decided to slake it before doing either. Going to the bathroom, she drank two tumblers of cold water, hardly stopping to draw breath.

Feeling somewhat better, Rita studied her reflection in the mirror. There was a bruise on the left side of her jaw and another blackish-purple blotch below her right eye. She did not need to remove her pyjamas to conclude that several other parts of her body were likely to be marked in a similar fashion and a sense of annoyance flooded through her. While she felt sure that she could conceal the facial injuries beneath the amount of makeup used for her portrayal of the wealthy flapper, it would be impossible to do so when she was following Philip Redmond in her guise of the intellectual student. Furthermore, despite being able to put up with the aching caused by the bruises until they faded away, hiding those which would be exposed by her more revealing flapper attire would be difficult.

'Cora-Ann, whoever you might be,' the girl said wryly, the memory of "Professor Jorgenson's" comment having remained in spite of the condition she had been in when he arrived. 'I hope you feel as *bad*—no, even *worse* than I do!'

Having delivered the sentiment, Rita decided to make the postponed telephone calls. Concluding it would be advisable to inform Major Tragg of her suspicions regarding the man before talking with him, she limped into the main room. Opening the drawer of the bedside table upon which the telephone was standing, she took out the wristwatch she wore as an adjunct to her second *alter ego*. What she saw caused her to assume she had failed to rewind the mechanism and it had stopped. A cluck of annoyance left her. She had two numbers at which the Major could be reached. Needing to know the time so she could decide where to call, she was on the point of going to find out when she remembered the marks on her face and realized they would attract unwanted attention from who-ever she questioned in the passage. Returning to the bath-room, she applied enough powder to make them less noticeable. With this done, donning the robe hanging behind the door and wrapping it around her so she was concealed from neck to ankles, she set about acquiring the necessary information.

Picking up the key which was lying not far from where she had collapsed at the end of the fight, the girl guessed it had fallen there on being pushed out to make way for whatever means the blonde had employed to gain admit-tance. On unlocking and opening the door, the copy of the *Austin Gazette* she had delivered each morning to help keep a check upon the daily activities of Philip Redmond fell against her foot. However, as she bent instinctively to pick it up—an action which provoked a painful protest from her sore body—her attention was diverted to the sign reading, '*Please Do Not Disturb*!' hanging on the knob. Knowing she had not put it there, she glanced in each direction along the passage. The only person in sight was the maid with the excitable temperament.

'Will it be all right for me to come in and make up your bed now, please, ma'am?' the woman inquired, hurrying forward. 'I'm going off in a quarter of an hour and the housekeeper always expects chores like that to be done before I leave.'

'Come in,' Rita assented, before the implication of what she had heard struck home. 'You're going *off*. What time is it, for heavens sake?'

'Four fifteen, ma'am,' the maid replied and a knowing look came to her face. 'That must have been *some* party you and the Professor had last night, for you to have slept so late. Was it because he was going away?'

'Going away?' the girl repeated, being aware that her apparently intimate relationship with ''Jorgenson'' had become common knowledge amongst the staff of the hotel. 'When is he going?'

'He's left already,' the woman answered, in the tone of

one who had acquired an interesting piece of gossip. 'In fact, his room's already been taken by a French gent. Didn't *you* know he was going?'

'He said something about it last night,' Rita lied, picking up the newspaper and moving aside to let the maid enter the room. 'But, after all that happened and having only just recov—*woken up*—it slipped my mind. What time did he go?'

'Just before noon,' the woman supplied, clearly having drawn the conclusion required of her from the way the reply was made. 'I expect he didn't knock and tell you goodbye because he saw the sign.'

'He always was considerate,' the girl claimed, hoping the pain caused by every movement did not show on her face. Tossing the paper unopened on to the dressing-table, she continued, 'I think I'll take a shower to clear my head and dress while you're tidying the room. Then you can finish up after I've gone downstairs for a meal.'

'Yes, ma'am,' the maid agreed, albeit with reluctance, having hoped to acquire further titbits of information to spread amongst her workmates.

Collecting a long sleeved frock with a high heart shaped neckline and a deep cloche hat with a turned-down brim from the wardrobe, Rita was grateful that such attire was fashionable for daytime wear amongst the kind of flapper she was pretending to be. Adding undergarments, stockings and shoes to the ensemble, she retired to the bathroom. Feeling a little better after having had the shower, she applied the makeup needed to conceal the marks which her clothing did not cover. Then, having dressed and donned the jewellery which was still where she had placed it the previous night, she went on with the course of action she had outlined. Ignoring the woman's obvious desire to learn more about her reaction to the 'Professor's' departure, she was stepping into the package when she heard the door of the next room opening. Turning her head so quickly that the movement sent a stab of pain which made her wince, she studied its new occupant as he came towards her. She felt there was something vaguely familiar about him, but could not decide what it might be.

Because her father had frequently done business with Frenchmen, even if she had not received the information from the maid, Rita would have guessed the nationality of the man who had replaced 'Jorgenson' as her neighbour. Bare headed and white haired, he was a tall, with a ramrod straight carriage giving the impression he was marching rather than merely walking along the passage. Being sallow of complexion, his skin having a texture implying he was of late middle age, and a grey moustache waxed to sharp points in the Gallic fashion to which she had become accustomed, his handsome aquiline features were set in lines suggestive of a disciplined control. Such was his soldierly bearing, he made the excellently tailored grey suit he had on seem more like a military uniform than civilian attire. There was a red rosette in the lapel of his coat which she identified as the insignia of an *officer* and it came almost as a surprise to see he was wearing ordinary, albeit highly polished, black footwear and not a pair of Hessian leg cavalry boots.

'Good afternoon, *mam'selle*,' the man greeted as he came up, making a quick inclination of his head.

'Good afternoon, sir,' Rita replied, realizing she might have made her interest too apparent and starting to walk in the same direction.

'Pardon me for what may appear a liberty,' the man requested. Slowing down, he kept pace with the girl and they went the stairs leading to the reception lobby side by side. Although his English was excellent, it had a pronounced Gallic timbre. 'I notice you are limping a little. Perhaps you have met with an accident while playing tennis, or riding?'

'Neither, I'm afraid,' Rita replied with a smile, not being averse to continuing the conversation in the hope of discovering whether they had met somewhere. 'I bumped into the corner of the dressing-table in my room this morning.'

'I trust you aren't hurt too badly?'

'No, although I'm annoyed at having been so clumsy.'

'Accidents can happen to the best of us,' the man claimed sympathetically. 'And, if I may say so, I am sure you are one of the best of us.'

'Why thank you for the compliment, kind sir,' Rita replied. 'I don't believe I've seen you around the hotel before?'

'I only arrived a short while ago,' the man explained. 'And, as I know *nobody* in Austin, if you have no other plans, perhaps you would do me the honour of dining as my guest this evening.'

'I may be going out with my—*uncle*,' the girl answered, feeling puzzled. Despite the reputation for taking a very active interest in the opposite sex credited to members of his nation, those from the *Ancien Regime*—to which her neighbour apparently belonged—and which she had met had never been so forward in their behaviour at such a short acquaintance. Deciding he could be an exception and she might have given him a wrong impression by continuing the conversation, she pointed across the lobby. 'Here he is now. Hello, *Uncle* Benson!'

'Howdy, Rita-gal,' Major Tragg responded. Coming to a stop, he darted a quick look at the Frenchman before going on, 'I was expecting you to call me earlier, so I came 'round to see if you're all right.'

In his late forties, the commanding officer of Company 'Z' had a deeply bronzed rugged face and brown hair turning grey at the temples. His six foot tall frame was lean and had the wiry build of one who was engaged in strenuous outdoors' occupation. There was nothing about his appearance and attire, except for a slight bulge at the left side of his jacket caused by the short barrelled revolver holstered on his waist belt, to suggest he was a peace officer from a family which had long been involved in the enforcement of law and order in Texas.[9] Rather he gave

9. *As is recorded elsewhere in this volume, one of the Tragg family is still actively engaged on the enforcement of law and order in Texas. Some information about two earlier members who served the Lone Star State as peace officers is given in*: SET A-FOOT *and* BEGUINAGE IS DEAD.

the impression of being a prosperous rancher who still put in as hard a day's work as any of his cowhands.

'I've been too *busy* to call,' Rita stated. 'By the way, Professor Jorgenson has left and this gentleman is my new neighbour.'

'Howdy, sir,' the Major said, making his manner redolent of jealous suspicion.

'Good afternoon, sir,' the Frenchman replied, a slight smile twisting briefly at his lips. 'I trust you will forgive me for taking the liberty of opening a conversation with your—*niece* when we met in the passage upstairs. Allow me to present myself. I am the Marquis de Crevitte-Soligny.'

'Pleased to meet you, sir,' Major Tragg acknowledged, shaking the hand he was offered. However, instead of supplying his name, he turned his attention pointedly to the girl. 'I've got us a table for *two* in the dining-room.'

'Excuse me, please,' the Marquis requested, with the air of one who wanted to establish that he could take a hint. 'I must ask at the desk if the rest of my baggage, which was put on the wrong train in Houston, has caught up with me.'

'What happened?' the Major inquired, after he had escorted Rita to a table which was sufficiently far away from the few other occupants for them to talk without being over heard. 'Did Jorgenson give you the shiner?'

'I didn't know it showed,' the girl claimed. Then having told of what had happened the previous night without describing in any detail or mentioning the name of her opponent, she concluded, 'I bet dear Cora-Ann has already left, too. And I ho—!'

'*Who?*' Major Tragg demanded and for the first time in their acquaintance Rita saw his face register genuine surprise.

'I wasn't at my best and brightest at the time,' Rita admitted wryly. Although she had intended to say that she hoped the wristwatch which seemed to have caused the fight would not work, she decided it was not the time for levity. 'But I'm almost sure that's what he called her when he came in.'

'What did she look like?'

'About my age, a little taller, slender, with close bobbed straight blonde hair—!'

'Beautiful?'

'Very,' Rita confirmed. 'What is it, Major?'

'It seems you've been in even more exalted company than we realized,' Major Tragg answered sombrely. 'Thing being, what is *he* doing here?'

'Who?' the girl asked, knowing only something of considerable importance could have elicited such a response from the normally imperturbable commanding officer of Company 'Z'.

'Henry Arthur Milton,' the Major replied. 'He's better known to peace officers all over the world as the Ringer!'

* * *　　* * *

'Excuse me, ma'am!' the excitable maid said, as Rita Yarborough opened the door of her room and was bending to pick up the copy of the *Austin Gazette* from the floor of the otherwise unoccupied passage. 'Can you help me, please?'

'What's wrong?' the girl inquired, straightening with the care still required to avoid arousing twinges of pain from her bruised body beneath the yellow silk pyjamas and dressing-gown she had on.

'I've been banging on Mr. Redmond's door as hard as I can,' the woman explained. 'But I can't wake him up!'

'Well it is only just eight o'clock,' Rita pointed out. 'Perhaps he's decided to lie in late.'

'He *hasn't*!' the maid denied, her expressive face showing alarm. 'He said he wanted calling at eight without fail, so he can be ready to catch the eastbound train.'

Although her excellent physical condition had helped her throw off the worst effects of the fight, Rita had not been required to exert herself the previous afternoon and evening!

95

Before satisfying the girl's curiosity further in the dining-room, Major Benson Tragg had gone to the reception desk. He returned to explain how he had described the blonde to the clerk and discovered she had been a resident at the hotel. She had arrived the same day as 'Professor Arne Jorgenson', signing the register as 'Mrs. C.A. Barford, Seattle' and had left shortly after he checked out. Then Rita had been told what was known about the true identity of her former escort.[10] Scanty though the information had been, she was most impressed by what she had heard.

Although he had not received any awards for gallantry, reputedly because he had declined those he was offered, Captain Henry Arthur Milton had had a distinguished career as a fighter pilot with the Royal Flying Corps during the 'Great War'. Retiring when peace came, he had for some unknown reason taken it upon himself to conduct a particularly effective crusade against those who evaded the consequences of serious crimes, and he did not hesitate to inflict the ultimate penalty if he considered death was warranted. However, despite the authorities throughout the world knowing that much about him, none could give a description of exactly what he looked like. Only one 'group' picture of his Squadron in which he appeared had been located. Not only had he been on the rear row, but he had contrived to prevent his features from being recognizable. No other photographs of him which might have supplied the information were known to exist. Since then, because of his ability to alter his appearance by means of a superlative ability at disguise—'ring the

10. On taking the precaution of contacting the Norwegian Embassy in Washington, D.C., by telephone, Major Benson Tragg was informed that Professor Arne Jorgenson was a well known arctic explorer and matched the description of the man acting as escort to Rita Yarborough. He was travelling in the United States, but because of his aversion to publicity his itinerary was not known.

changes', in the argot of the British underworld—he had been given the sobriquet, 'the Ringer'.[11]

There was, the commanding officer of Company 'Z' had stated, one thing more than any other about the Ringer which was certain. By all accounts, he was completely devoted to his wife, Cora-Ann, who was reputed to be a willing and active accomplice in his activities. Therefore, despite his behaviour and the very romantic note attached to the wristwatch he had had delivered to her room, it was unlikely that he had formed his attachment with Rita because of her undoubted feminine physical attractions. Nor had he merely been in Austin for a vacation and, having accepted her story of being a hopeful newspaper reporter, he had obviously been impelled by nothing more than a quixotic wish to help her. According to the comment he made when coming into her room, he too had an interest in Philip Redmond and John Broome. However, no matter what this had been, the fight appeared to have caused the Miltons to take their departure from the Capital Hotel. Although the Major had said he would try to find out if they had also gone from the city, she had not been told whether there was an answer as yet.

Apologising for not having kept the author and his secretary under observation that day, Rita had said she would do so in the evening. However, the need had not arisen. While she and Major Tragg were parting company in the reception hall, Redmond had come in alone from whatever had occupied him during the afternoon. They had heard him ask whether Broome had returned and, on receiving an answer in the negative, he had gone to his room with a worried look on his unprepossessing face.

Returning to her quarters, even though she had been assured by the Major that only a trained observer could detect the black eye, the girl had concluded it would be

11. *Some of the known details of Captain Henry Arthur Milton's career after his retirement from the Royal Flying Corps are recorded in*: THE RINGER *and* AGAIN THE RINGER, *by Edgar Wallace.*

97

advisable to keep on the less revealing attire no matter where Redmond elected to spend the evening. However, the decision had proved immaterial. Having kept her door just sufficiently ajar to allow her to see the entrance to the author's accommodation, when he emerged, she had been ready to follow him. Coming out to continue her observations, her concern over seeing the Marquis de Chevitte-Soligny step into the passage had proved unwarranted. Despite having followed them into the hotel's dining-room, he had not pressed his attentions upon her.

Watching from the nearest table she had been able to get, Rita had decided Redmond was even more perturbed than when she had seen him last. What was more, he had shown even greater evidence of alarm when he had read the note which accompanied a small package brought to him by a bellhop. Leaving his food unfinished, although he had not made the kind of complaints about its quality or the service which usually accompanied his meals no matter where he was taking them, he had hurried to the reception desk. Having had a brief conversation with the clerk, he had gone upstairs darting several glances behind him as if he expected to be followed.

Keeping an eye on the reception hall in case Redmond came downstairs to go out, Rita had finished her meal without this happening. She had been on the point of returning to her room when she had seen a couple of his regular companions come in. Crossing to the reception desk, she was in time to hear the clerk informing them that the author had said he would not be joining them as he was feeling ill and he did not want to be disturbed. After they had left, she had contacted the clerk, using the pay-phone in the coffeeshop to give the impression of speaking from outside the hotel, and learned that Broome was still absent. Telephoning Major Tragg from her room and reporting what had happened, she had stated her intention of maintaining the surveillance for the rest of the night. However, having done so until two in the morning without either the secretary putting in an appearance or Redmond coming out, exhaustion had caused her to retire to her bed. The habit she had developed of rising early had caused her to wake just after seven and she had decided to collect the newspaper before doing anything else.

* * *   * * *

Hearing what the maid had to say, Rita Yarborough wondered whether yielding to the impulse at two o'clock had allowed her quarry to leave unobserved!

'Oh ma'am!' the woman went on. 'If I don't wake him and he misses his train, he'll report me *again*—!'

'But it isn't *your* fault if you can't wake him,' the girl asserted.

'That's not what the housekeeper'll say,' the maid claimed, growing more distressed. 'You don't know what he's *like*. He's reported me for something or other *every* day he's been here and the last time, the housekeeper warned me that I'd be fired if it happened again.'

'I'm sure she'll be understanding when you explain,' Rita suggested, without admitting she did know what the author was like in the context of the statement. From the beginning of the surveillance, he had displayed arrogance towards everybody he considered a social inferior and seemed to delight in making complaints about them on the slighest pretext. 'In fact—!'

'Is anything *wrong*?' inquired a masculine voice with a Gallic accent, before the girl could offer to confirm the reason for the maid's failure to waken the author.

Glancing around, Rita saw her new neighbour coming from his room. It was apparent from his attire that he had not long since left his bed. Although wearing his trousers and well polished black boots, the long and voluminous black dressing-gown he had on failed to conceal the fact that he had not yet donned more than his undershirt.

'It's the gent in there, sir,' the maid replied and, having explained the reason, went on, 'I can't wake him up.'

'Then, under the circumstances, you would be justified in using your—pass-key—I believe it is called,' de

Crevitte-Soligny suggested. 'Don't you agree, *mam'selle*?'

'Yes,' Rita seconded, wanting to find out whether the author had slipped away in the night.

'His's still in the lock inside his room,' the maid reported as she was trying to use her pass-key. 'There, I've pushed it out.' However, on turning her pass-key and trying the door, the look of consternation returned and she yelped, 'He's put the bolt on as well!'

'*Mon dieu*!' the Frenchman barked. 'The last time I saw something like *this* happen, the man in the room had committed *suicide*!'

The supposition Rita drew that such a comment was most ill-advised in the present company was immediately proved correct!

'*Suicide*!' the maid screeched, jerking her thin body erect and gesticulating wildly. 'D—Do you *think* th—that's what he's *done*?'

'Of course not,' de Crevitte-Soligny replied, yet somehow his voice lacked conviction. 'But let *me* take a look!' Easing the far from comforted woman away from the door, he removed the pass-key and, bending to peer through the keyhole he ejaculated, '*Mon dieu*!'

'Wha—Wh—What is *it*?' the maid inquired, clearly suspecting the worst.

Instead of replying, the Frenchman straightened up. Pushing the woman aside with less gentleness as she tried to approach the door, which also compelled Rita to move away, he stepped back the full width of the passage. Using the wall he had reached as an aid to thrusting himself forward, he advanced to charge the door with his shoulder. The way in which he did so and the result of his efforts reminded Rita of how she had seen Sergeant Ranse Smith of Company 'Z'—an exceptionally handsome blond giant with the muscular development of a Hercules—gain admittance in a similar fashion. Such was the force he employed, the door burst inwards to the accompaniment of a screech as the screws which had held the bolt and lock in place were driven violently from the surrounding woodwork.

'*Sacre bleu*!' de Crevitte-Soligny gasped, halting on the threshold and expanding his arms so the voluminous dressing-gown spread like a cape on either side until it blocked the doorway. '*Horrible*!'

Having moved forward more quickly than Rita was able, until she was behind the Frenchman, the maid let out a screech which seemed to give credence to his brief summation of the situation!

'What is *it*?' the girl asked, trying to see past the woman and over the man's dressing-gown.

'Keep *out* both of you!' de Crevitte-Soligny commanded and his voice had a timbre of chilling warning which increased the consternation being displayed by the woman. He continued without lowering his arms, 'It is not for *you* to see!'

'No, ma'am!' the maid howled, twisting and throwing herself into Rita's arms. 'It *isn't*!'

Wanting to satisfy herself on the point, as she felt sure Major Tragg would expect her to do so, the girl tried to get free. Instantly, the already distraught maid began to struggle and shriek in a hysterical fashion. Although he glanced over his shoulder, de Crevitte-Soligny went into the room instead of offering to help Rita. Much to her annoyance, she was too engrossed in restraining the woman to be able to follow him and, either by accident or design, he kicked the door closed.

For a few seconds, the girl was too fully occupied to even think of going after the Frenchman. Then, pushing the woman away from her, she employed a means she had been told was most suitable for such behaviour. The slap she delivered with her left hand did more than bring the hysterics to an abrupt end. Giving a gasp, the maid crumpled to the floor. Startled by the response to her treatment, Rita knelt down. She was examining the maid when she heard the door open and, as had happened when 'Professor Arne Jorgenson' had arrived on the night of the fight, a pair of boots came into her range of vision. Starting to raise her eyes, she jerked them down again and satisfied herself that the thing which had come to her notice was correct.

'I—Is he—?' the girl asked, looking up and hoping that no hint of the implications she had drawn from what she had seen showed on her face.

'He is,' the Marquis confirmed.

'Was it—*suicide*?' Rita inquired, standing up.

'*Perhaps*,' de Crevitte-Soligny replied, his manner expressing doubt. 'Would you go to your room and call the police, please. Tell them it would be advisable to send whoever specializes in *murder*!'

'Of cour—!' the girl began. 'But how could it have been murder when the door was locked and bolted on the *inside*?'

'That, I would imagine, my dear *mam'selle*, is what the police officers are going to find *puzzling*,' the Gallic looking man said sombrely. 'Particularly as I noticed the window is also fastened.'

* * *   * * *

'*M'sieur le Marquis*,' Rita Yarborough said, holding the door of her room open with her right hand and grasping her vanity bag in the left. Since the preliminary stages of the investigation into Philip Redmond's death had ended, using the means she had employed when keeping Redmond under observation, she had watched for the Frenchman to come into the passage so she could make the suggestion. 'Will you come in, please?'

By the time the girl had called for the police and reported the latest developments to Major Benson Tragg, several people occupying rooms on the first floor were gathered in front of the dead author's door. It had been closed and the hotel's house detective was there to prevent anybody entering until the authorities arrived. Having recovered from her faint, the maid was explaining volubly the horror she claimed to have seen when the Marquis had gained admission. He, on the other hand, was declining to comment with a chilling politeness which defied further questioning.

102

Despite Company 'Z' having been involved in Redmond's affairs for several days, on seeing who arrived, and remembering what she had been told when receiving her assignment, Rita had agreed with her superior's summation that neither he nor a member of her sex—especially one who had no official standing—would be welcomed as participants in the investigation by the senior member of the officers of the Austin Police Department. Big and bulky, Captain Myles Riordan of the Homicide Bureau was known to be ambitious, with aspirations more towards political advancement than merely getting promotion in his profession. Always determined to gain whatever kudos might personally accrue from the successful outcome of an investigation, he was noted for his objections to any other law enforcement agency becoming involved in his cases. In fact, according to the Major, he had on a couple of occasions refused assistance from conventional Texas Rangers which could have helped him make an arrest and procure a conviction against a person with political connections whom he had considered it would have been an unsound career move to antagonize.

Despite not having supplied an official reason for being present, the girl had been able to learn some of the circumstances surrounding the author's death. Always willing to let people he considered important see him carrying out his duties and clearly regarding the occupants of the first floor at the Capital Hotel as coming into that category, Riordan had left the door of the room wide open and had made no attempt to keep the body concealed. Contriving to look between the other members of the investigation team around the bed, she had wondered why the Marquis de Crevitte-Soligny expressed such horror when gaining admission. While she knew Frenchman were supposed to have very excitable natures, he had not struck her as being possessed of that trait. Nor could she imagine why the maid had responded as if having seen something horrific. Except for the hilt of the knife which must have killed Redmond rising through the blankets, there was nothing—

not even the slightest trace of blood—to indicate the author was doing other than sleeping peacefully on his back.

Questioning de Crevitte-Soligny, Riordan had displayed a respect which indicated he was considered sufficiently influential to warrant such treatment. He had stated that he had only arrived at the hotel the previous day and was unacquainted with the dead man, then he described the reason for the door being forced and the discovery made on entering. Rita's explanation of how she had come to be involved was received with a similar civility, which nevertheless left the impression that the Captain considered she had nothing useful to add. Deciding against mentioning a theory she had formed, she had moved aside and allowed the interrogation of the maid to take place. Continuing to express her horror, yet speaking with a relish which implied she was not averse to finding herself at the centre of attraction, the woman had told about the attempts she had made to waken Redmond and verified the Frenchman's story. Having heard what they had to say, Riordan had instructed them—politely when addressing de Crevitte-Soligny and the girl, but less so where the maid was concerned—to remain on the premises in case there was anything further he wanted from them.

Riordan had next allowed himself to be seen examining the broken bolt on the door. Then he had carried out an equally ostentatious check which established that Redmond had made use of the facility which allowed the occupant to lock the window. However, he had made no mention of whatever conclusions he had drawn from the evidence suggesting there was no way in which the man who used the knife could have gained admission and left. Nor had he been any more forthcoming when the doctor had claimed the killing had taken place within the past hour. Instead, speaking loudly enough for his audience in the passage to hear, he had commented upon there being ashes from some burned paper and cardboard scattered upon the floor. Claiming these, some cigarettes and the contents of the ashtray on the bedside table were certain to be informative when submitted to tests in the police laboratory, he had announced his belief that the matter would speedily be cleared up and the murderer brought to justice. Then, telling his men to report anything they discovered, he had taken his departure exuding the air of one who believed he had done everything that was necessary and could leave the rest of the investigation in the hands of less competent officers.

With their superior gone, the detectives who remained had closed the door and conducted the rest of the examination in the privacy which was generally employed by peace officers when on such a case. Expecting to be questioned further, Rita had gone to her room and changed into her street clothes, then returned to join the other spectators. However, what she had envisaged did not occur. The detectives had left about fifteen minutes later, taking the body and giving orders for the room to be kept locked until instructions to the contrary were issued, but without having asked her, the Marquis or the maid any more questions and she had concluded that she would learn nothing about whatever progress, if any, had been made in the investigation.

Although the girl had informed Major Tragg of what had taken place, she had refrained from mentioning the speculations aroused by what she had seen and heard. Instead, despite realizing she could be taking a very grave risk, which might even prove fatal if she was wrong in one summation, she had elected to put them to the test herself. Although she did not believe it would prove necessary, she had taken a precaution before making ready to do so.

* * *   * * *

'Come into your *room, mam'selle*?' the Marquis de Crevitte-Soligny replied, his tone and manner at its most Gallic. 'Would that be *proper*?' He paused for a moment. Then, as there was no response, he went on, 'After all, you know what they say about us Frenchmen.'

'I know what they say about *Frenchmen*,' Rita

Yarborough admitted. 'But, in *your* case, I'm sure I'll be as safe as if you were *Norwegian*—or even an Englishman known for "ringing the changes".'

'What a quaint expression,' the man said, without so much as a muscle in his face giving a hint at whether he knew what it meant in any context. 'Of course I will come in, *mam'selle*. My white hair is sufficient of a chaperone, I think, to cover the proprieties.'

'It is,' Rita confirmed. Having moved back and allowed the man to pass her, she closed the door. Locking and placing her back against it, she slipped her right hand into the vanity bag. Although delivered politely, her next words were more in the nature of a command than a request. 'Please take a seat, *Captain Milton*.'

'So you *did* notice the stain on my boot,' 'de Crevitte-Soligny' said, his voice becoming that of a well educated Englishman, as he sat on the chair at the dressing-table.

'Yes.'

'I suppose I shouldn't have kept on wearing them. But, as I told you the night we met, they're so comfortable they're my favourites. Did you suspect anything before?'

'Not while you were being "de Crevitte-Soligny",' Rita replied. 'That's a *magnificent* disguise.'

'And my "Professor Arne Jorgenson" not ban so good?' Captain Henry Arthur Milton inquired, reverting to the Nordic accent.

'It was just as good,' Rita assessed. 'Mind you, I think I like you better without those bushy eyebrows, the promi-nent false teeth, the scar and whatever you used to bulge out your cheeks.' Watching the smile which came to the man's face, she continued, 'And, looking back, I think you made yourself *sound* just a *little* too much like a stage Norwegian. You didn't go so far as saying, "Yumping Yiminy" as the "Swede" comedians do, but you tended to overdo the "ban".'

'I'll keep it in mind,' the Ringer declared in his natural voice. 'And now, Miss Yarborough, what have you in mind for me?'

106

'Why did you kill Redmond?' the girl asked, instead of replying to the question.

'*Me*?'

'*You*!'

'But the maid saw—!' Milton began, yet there was a timbre in his voice more redolent of admiration than being disturbed or angry over the accusation.

'Nothing except the back of your dressing-gown,' Rita interrupted, keeping her right forefinger resting lightly on the trigger of the Remington Double Derringer pistol she had concealed in the vanity bag. 'She's so excitable and impressionable, you convinced her that she had seen him lying killed in a horrible fashion, when he was actually still alive.'

'*You* were there too,' the Ringer pointed out.

'And must have caused you a problem, as you had hoped to have nobody but her in the passage,' the girl guessed. 'But, fortunately for you, her hysterics kept me occupied while you went in and killed him. Why did you do it, Captain Milton? It certainly *wasn't* a spur of the moment impulse. Unless I miss my guess, you've been watching him and preparing to do it for days.'

'I felt the world would be a better place without him,' the Ringer replied. 'You may have guessed he is more interested in male than female—companionship?'

'I suspected it.'

'I don't approve of that kind of thing. Nor did it end there. He also had a taste for *children* of *both* sexes.'

'And that was why you decided to kill him?' Rita suggested, sensing the Englishman felt a similar revulsion to her own at such sexual deviations.

'No, but I must admit it gave me an added inducement to consider he deserved the shades,' the Ringer replied. 'Although he was already well established as an author of books deriding everything most people hold dear, he also worked as a civil servant with a well paid sinecure which was a reserved occupation and kept him from military service during the Great War. He stayed at it for a couple of years after the war. We wondered why, until one of our agen—a friend of mine engaged on something else recently discovered that he supplied information to the Bolsheviks which cost the lives of a number of our sailors, including two of my cousins, during the campaign in the Baltic after the War ended. Unfortunately, my friend was unable to bring the documentary proof he'd acquired from Russia with him and that meant there was no legal way in which the traitorous devil could be brought to justice for his betrayal, any more than for his sexual perversions as he had always kept them carefully covered up. I hoped to settle accounts with him in England, but he had come over here before I was able to reach him. You, of course, had a different motive for keeping him under observation and it *isn't* because you're trying to become a newspaper reporter.'

'It *isn't*,' the girl conceded. 'But how did you know?'

'I'm afraid I'd been eavesdropping on your telephone conversations with Major Tragg, using a tumbler placed against the wall. You know the trick?'

'I know it.'

'The last time we met, George Manfred told me that, if the Governor of Texas acted on some advice he had been given while he was over here with Gonzales and Poiccart, the Major was the most likely candidate to lead the organization which was to be formed.[12] You are helping him against the alliance which the Brothers of the Red International have formed with some Mexican revolutionaries?'

'Yes. The Major thought Redmond might be involved in it.'

'And the Major was right,' the Ringer confirmed. 'Although he was leaving all the dirty work and risks to Broome.'

'Then I was wasting my time—!' Rita said bitterly.

'Not at all,' Milton denied. 'I saw you coming out of Redmond's room dressed as a maid and, although you didn't notice him, so did Broome. It's my suspicion that

12. *See*: APPENDIX THREE.

he was lurking in the alley meaning to kill you after his two helpers left you badly beaten. Anyway, with you doing such a good job of following Redmond, he wasn't able to act as the go-between for the Brothers and the revolutionaries.'

'But why did you come with me in the evenings?' the girl asked, feeling somewhat better at what she had just been told.

'Partly for your protection and partly because I suspect they'd become a little suspicious of "Professor Jorgenson",' the Ringer explained. 'You were safe enough during the daytime, which let me do some snooping to supplement Cora-Ann's efforts.'

'She was helping you?'

'She often does. Incidentally, you were right about us being watched the night Redmond took the Victoria ride. We were, by her. She was following the leader of the Mexicans who was meaning to meet him on the way round, but was prevented by us being behind.'

'And she became jealous when she saw the way we were acting?'

'Good heavens, *no*! I'd told her about you and she knew why we were behaving like that.'

'Then it wasn't she who called to ask if you were with me that night.'

'It *was* she,' the Ringer corrected. 'She'd learned something important and wanted to tell me. Unfortunately, for once, the ringing of the telephone didn't wake me up and she thought I might have had to stay with you—in the nicest way, of course. So she came back to the hotel and, telling the switchboard operator she was a private detective after evidence of infidelity for your husband, bribed him to put her through to your room and, if you checked, to say she'd called "the Professor" just before speaking to you. By the way, about that wristwatch. By the kind of coincidence you wouldn't believe if you read it in one of that chap Edgar Wallace's books, Cora-Ann had been admiring it too. Unfortunately, when I bought it as a birthday present for her, I didn't notice until too late that Broome was in the shop and watching me. So I had it sent to your room, along with the bouquet, feeling sure you'd return it in the morning. The trouble is, as you've probably guessed, Cora-Ann's just a little touch *impetuous*. As it was her birthday that morning, she decided to collect it herself. I guessed what she might be doing when I found she wasn't in her room, but I wasn't back in time to stop her. She asked me to tell you how sorry she is about the way things turned out.'

'I should *hope* she is too,' Rita claimed, keeping the Remington concealed in the vanity bag with her right hand and feeling gingerly at her black eye with her left forefinger. However, there was no animosity in her tone. 'Because I know I am.'

'It may make you feel a little better to know she had *two* of them to hide,' Milton suggested with a smile. 'And she said to tell you that she hopes there's no hard feelings.'

'There aren't,' the girl asserted, also smiling. 'It was as good a workout as I've ever had, but tell her that if she wants a rematch, not to call me, I'll call her.[13] But where did you go to get back from?'

'We'd heard that the Brothers had sent a supply of arms to the revolutionaries and they were awaiting collection at a ranch house a few miles from town!' the Ringer explained. 'So we—!'

' "*We*",' Rita interrupted. 'But your wife couldn't have been with you.'

'I was using the editorial "we",' the Ringer replied, after a brief pause in which the girl suspected he was thinking

---

13. *A month later, Rita Yarborough received a registered packet mailed in New Orleans. In it were a small pair of golden boxing gloves—which she still wears on a charm bracelet—and a note, without an address to allow her to reply, saying,* 'A little tribute to the best sparring partner I ever had and I agree with what you told Arthur about a rematch. All best wishes from Arthur and myself, Cora-Ann Milton'

up an explanation.[14] 'So *I* followed Broome and found out that our information was correct.'

'I'll call the Major—!'

'There isn't any rush for that. As I said, we—*I*— followed Broome there and you'd be surprised how much damage a hand grenade thrown amongst boxes of ammunition can do. The whole consignment was destroyed, along with everybody who had gone into the barn to fight the fire we'd started. That's why Redmond was looking so worried yesterday. Broome hadn't come back.'

'So Broome is dead,' Rita guessed.

'Yes,' the Ringer confirmed. 'And, in my opinion, the world is a better place for that. I don't suppose it would have been any consolation for him if he had known, but I'd marked him for the shades along with Redmond and for the same reasons.'

'Did you intend to kill Redmond the way you did it this morning?'

'Yes.'

'You couldn't have guessed he'd be sleeping so deeply the maid wouldn't be able to wake him up.'

'I didn't *guess*, I made sure he wouldn't. You remember that packet and note he received while he was having dinner last night?'

'Yes.'

'I arranged for it to be given to him. The note told him Broome was dead and the consignment destroyed. It was signed "Fuentes", the leader of the Mexican revolu-

14. *We suspect that, far from being a private individual motivated by a desire to ensure malefactors did not evade the consequences of their misdeeds, Captain Henry Arthur Milton was a member of the British Secret Service and had the special grading which Ian Fleming refers to in the* James Bond *biographies as a 'Double O' number, authorizing him to kill if this was required in the line of duty. Unfortunately, as yet, we have not been able to confirm our supposition. Neither can Alvin Dustine 'Cap' Fog supply us with more detailed information about the activities of Captain and Mrs. Milton during their stay in Austin.*

tionaries,[15] I knew he would want to get away from Austin as quickly as possible, but there wasn't another east-bound train until this morning. If he'd tried to leave by some other means—Well, we—*I* had a contingency plan for that.'

'But how could you be certain he wouldn't wake up when the maid came?'

'You've seen the way he behaved when he was cele-brating with his friend around town,' the Ringer answered. 'Didn't you think he was unusually gay and light-hearted considering how miserable and sober he acted at other times?'

'I did,' Rita conceded. 'In fact, I was sure he was smoking muggle, or even on something worse in the way of drugs.'

' "Muggle"?'

'*Marijuana.*'

'Ah yes!' Milton said, nodding in understanding. 'We call it *bhang, hashish*, or Indian hemp. Anyway, the packet had what he took to be a few such cigarettes, "with the compliments of Fuentes". They actually contained a narcotic which sent him into a sufficiently deep sleep to make certain he wouldn't wake up when the maid came in the morning. I was just as confident that she would behave as she did and I knew I could convince her she had seen much more than she had. Once I got into the room, it was simple enough to put the knife into his heart. The medical training I mentioned to you when I put you on the bed after the fight helped me locate it without needing to remove the covers. I hadn't counted on you being there as well, or that you'd notice I was still wearing my favourite boots, but the maid fainting diverted you at the vital time and I decided that you'd missed seeing the stain.'

---

15. *This was not the first time members of the Fuentes family had been leaders of Mexican revolutionaries. See:* NO FINGER ON THE TRIGGER.

'I suppose the fight must have made carrying out your plan more difficult?'

'Not really, except that poor Cora-Ann had to use quite a bit of makeup to hide the battle damage. Even if you hadn't let me know you'd heard me speaking normally and realized I wasn't "Professor Jorgenson", we intended to leave yesterday. You see, I was sure Captain Riordan would take charge of the investigation with such a famous victim involved and, from what I'd learned about him, I decided he would be less likely to question something he was told by the Marquis de Crevitte-Solingy, who sounded vastly more important and potentially influential than an obscure Norwegian explorer. My guess that he would bring those of his men who he felt sure wouldn't be bright enough to steal the limelight from him by solving the case was just as correct. Then, he did what I anticipated he would do when he realised he had come up against a very difficult mystery. He left them to deal with it and face the consequences of having to report a failure.'

'But it won't be left without a lot more investigation,' the girl warned. 'The State Attorney General will insist on *that* and whoever is put in charge will be inquiring a lot more closely into your story. Particularly as, with the door and window being locked on the inside, it will take a lot of explaining as to how anybody else could have got in and killed him, then get out again.'

'I know,' Milton admitted, standing up slowly and reaching in a casual seeming fashion into the right side pocket of his jacket. 'And, when those questions arise, there'll be another mystery. The Marquis de Crevitte-Soligny will have disappeared without a trace, except for the one small suitcase and a few items of clothing which hadn't "got lost by the railway". In fact, I was going to do the disappearing when you stopped me. The question now is, will I be able to do it *now*?' I don't doubt you know how to use that gun you're holding in your vanity bag, perhaps even as well as I can the one I am now holding in my right hand.'

'You won't need it,' Rita claimed, bringing her empty hand from the bag. 'I'm sure Captain Riordan wouldn't welcome having his case solved by a mere *woman*. It was he who caused a proposal to have female officers in the Austin Police Department to be cancelled. And he might consider it could jeopardize his political aspirations to arrest somebody of the Marquis de Crevitte-Soligny's importance.'

'Major Tragg might not see it that way,' the Ringer warned.

'I'm sure he will, when I tell him the circumstances,' Rita answered. 'You see, you were right. The Governor did act upon Mr. Manfred's advice and the Com—*group* Major Tragg set up does have more latitude than other law enforcement agencies in dealing with situations such as these.' Thinking of how she had recently been involved in an operation by Company "Z" which led to a vicious murderer receiving the appropriate penalty even though he had contrived to be acquitted when brought to trial,[16] she also accepted that two men had met a fate they deserved and agreed with the Ringer that the world would be a better place without either. Unlocking the door and drawing it open, she went on, 'Goodbye, Captain Milton. Give my regards to Cora-Ann when you join her.'

16. *Told in*: THE JUSTICE OF COMPANY 'Z'.

PART THREE

DAWN DRUMMOND-CLAYTON
In
ACCIDENT—OR MURDER?

A sharp crack broke the silence of the woodland!

Although the shelter offered by the foliage of the trees around the clearing should have made it a good place in which to relax, the solitary bull elephant in the centre was already restless and irritable. Therefore, hearing the sound caused it to start searching for the cause immediately. Yet, at first sight, there did not seem to be any reason for its reaction.

Measuring a few inches over eleven foot at the highest point of its back, its grey skin being etched by creases and folds beyond the norm, the bull was carrying almost seventy-five pounds of ivory in each now yellowed and discoloured tusk. However, even though it was clearly past its prime, it had nothing to fear from any animal it was likely to encounter in the woodland. Despite the indications of its advanced age and there being a wound encrusted by dried blood on its right shoulder, it was still sufficient of a match in size and bulk to ensure a full grown rhinoceros would be willing to accept its presence with no more than a state of mutual wary neutrality. Nor, regardless of the injury, was it yet so declined in physical condition that a pride of lions, or mob of hyenas, might consider it sufficiently weakened to be a candidate for being attacked and eaten.

Nevertheless, like any creature which was by nature a dweller in a herd, the instincts of the old bull were to exercise a continual caution when it was alone. This was especially the case when it was compelled by circumstances

115

to move into an area very different from that in which it had spent all its life. Therefore, since having been driven by a younger and more virile male from the group over which it had, until recently, exercised domination, loneliness had turned it morose and inclined to behave with greater aggression than when it had been in the company of its own kind. Furthermore, recent events had been such as to increase this trait of latent savagery.

Driven from what had been its 'home' territory for over forty years, the bull had travelled many miles across open savannah offering none of the shade or shelter and nowhere nearly as much of the nourishment provided by the hilly bush country which it had roamed since birth. Then, having been kept moving by the pangs of extreme hunger it was experiencing, it had discovered a source of easily attainable and succulent food. Unfortunately, this had been in the cultivated land of the Gasali villages which lay along the borders of that section of the great Ambagasali Wild Life Reserve. Such a change of feeding habits had quickly brought it into conflict with the owners of the *shambas* it had selected to help supply the four to five hundred pounds of mixed vegetation it required daily as sustenance for its still vast bulk.

During its first confrontations with the human beings, when resisting the attempts which were made to drive it from amongst the crops, the bull had had no need to do more than squeal savagely and behave in a threatening fashion. This was sufficient to chase away the women against whom it had been in contention. However, the defenders of the crops it had selected that morning had been men. Dashing at them with a similar demonstration, which would have ended harmlessly if unresisted, it had received a spear in the right shoulder. Lacking more effective weapons and seeing they had aroused its temper, the men had hurriedly retired to the safety of the sturdy wooden stockade around their village. Foiled in its attempts to reach them and having vented its fury by destroying the *shamba* in which the incident occurred, the

116

bull had followed the habits it had adopted since arriving by chance in the area and discovering the crops offered such a nutritious feeding ground.

Returning to a patch of woodland it had discovered rising like an island from the surrounding open plains, the elephant was able to avoid the unwanted attentions of the tick birds which had plagued it as it was traversing the savannah by attacking with their well adapted bills the already raw and painful edges of the wound. Once in the shade of the trees and undergrowth, it had spent its time browsing upon the foliage and resting until ready to make another foray during the cool hours of darkness.

However, although the bull had snapped off the wooden shaft of the spear with its trunk—that most effective all-purpose tool, which served for gathering water and food, capable of selecting a single small leaf, or ripping a thick branch from a tree, occasional 'fly-swat', shower-bath, dust spray and weapon—the steel head still remained embedded in its flesh. The bleeding had now stopped, but the pain still nagged at it and increased its spirit of aggression to such an extent that it had charged and scattered a previously tolerated herd of impala when they were unwise enough to enter the small clearing where it was sheltering.

Still in a similarly aggravated mood, on hearing the crack of dry wood breaking so close by, the elephant stopped feeding and became alert. Out spread its great sail-like ears, flapping and questing to pinpoint the exact source of the sound. Then it raised its head until its tusks were parallel to the ground. Possessing reasonable eyesight, it scanned its surroundings so as to ascertain whether the noise heralded any kind of danger. After a few seconds of searching, aided by the gentle breeze carrying a scent to the exceptionally keen nostrils situated behind the triangular shaped prehensile 'lip' at the tip of the trunk, its efforts met with success. The scent wafted to its nostrils was that of the kind of creature responsible for its injury and, although differing in some way from the body odours of the people it had previously encountered, this served as a reminder of how it had sustained the wound which was now causing a continuous nagging pain.

The disturbance had been caused by a magnificent female representative of the species *Homo Sapiens'* Caucasian sub-division. Although it might have struck some people that she was inadequately clad for traversing such terrain on foot, her obvious racial origins notwithstanding, somehow the appearance she presented seemed to be as much a part of the patch of East African woodland as the elephant.

In her early twenties, the girl was about five foot eight inches tall and bareheaded. Being cut short and curly, her tawny hair set off almost classically beautiful features whose lines denoted breeding, strength of will and intelligence beyond the norm. Bronzed from head to toe by the sun, clad only in a far from excessive bikini made of leopardskin and simple heeless leather sandals, she wore no jewellery and was not armed in any way. Regardless of the latter omission, she exuded an aura of close to primeval wildness, and of being completely at home in her present surroundings. The skimpy nature of her attire indicated that, while she possesed the kind of figure many a 'sex symbol' movie actress sought to attain with the use of artificial aids, she needed none to create her richly curvaceous contours. Adding to the suggestion of primitivism, but without causing any loss of femininity from her appearance, clearly powerful muscles—limned by a sheen of perspiration until they were so well defined they would have been welcomed by many a competitor in a female 'body building' competition—played under the smooth skin of her arms, legs, shoulders and stomach.

Whatever her reason for being in the woodland might be, the girl had succeeded in approaching through the undergrowth until reaching the edge of the clearing without disturbing its solitary occupant. Now, after having stepped upon and broken a fallen branch, she appeared to be showing a poor appreciation of the situation. Instead of withdrawing behind one of the large trees between which she was passing, either being of sufficient breadth to have offered complete concealment, she stepped forward until in plain view of the elephant. Instantly, attracted by her movements, its head turned until it was studying her with only one eye. Anybody cognisant with the habits of *Loxodonta Africana* would have been aware that, while such behaviour was always a very dangerous sign, it was not invariably followed by a charge. Rather it was in the nature of a preliminary examination of the situation, wherein a decision would be made whether to attack or retreat.

Regardless of her appearance conveying the impression of belonging in such an environment, it seemed the girl was unaware of the meaning of what she saw. If she had frozen into immobility the moment she had found herself under observation, she might have been left unmolested. However, having committed the error of disturbing the suffering elephant and allowing herself to be located, she further compounded the gravity of the situation by letting out a yell which sounded like that of an alarmed Gasali woman, then began to wave her arms in the way they had when trying to frighten the bull from a *shamba*.

Under the circumstances, such behaviour could produce only one response!

Curling its trunk upwards and still keeping the tusks pointing straight at its objective, showing what anyone with knowledge of its species would have recognized as being signs of deliberate intention rather than mere bluff, the elephant gave a savage trumpeting squeal and dashed forward!

Immediately the huge animal started to move, despite having behaved in such an ill-advised manner after having disturbed it, the girl swung around and took her departure in a way which suggested she had at last become aware of the precarious situation she had created. What was more, she proved she was capable of selecting the means most suitable for trying to extricate herself from the very

119

dangerous predicament. Certainly there was nothing about her movements to imply she was fleeing in blind panic. Rather she was running as swiftly as her potently muscled legs could carry her in the direction from which she had come.

Because of the nature of her surroundings, the girl could not take her departure in a straight line. Nevertheless, such was her agility and superb bodily control, she was able to maintain a very rapid pace while swerving and weaving between trees or through openings in the undergrowth. What was more, her retreat was not impeded by having on the style of clothing and footwear which the majority of members of her gender and race would have considered suitable for use in such terrain. Inadequate as her skimpy costume might appear, it proved advantageous under the circumstances. There were a couple of places where, if she had been attired in a more conventional fashion, the gaps in the bushes were so narrow that the material of the garments might have become snagged and delayed her flight. As it was, the foliage tended to brush over instead of finding a purchase upon her glistening bare skin.

However, regardless of the speed with which the girl was carrying out her flight, making good her escape was far from a sinecure!

The behaviour of the intruder had driven the bull into a state of fury which was increased rather than diminished as a consequence of the extra pain its movements were producing. Therefore, it was goaded to keep up the chase by its intended victim remaining in sight. Although subjected to a similar need to swerve when passing between the bigger trees, which slowed its progress to some degree, it suffered from no such disadvantage elsewhere. Its massive bulk was able to crash through the narrow gaps as if the undergrowth did not exist. Just before reaching the edge of the woodland, although its eagerly extended trunk had failed to make contact, its swiftly moving body smashed down a sapling and she felt the wind of the upper

120

foliage against her back as it descended to her immediate rear.

Having had a very narrow escape, a few more steps took the girl from amongst the trees!

Not thirty seconds later, the still thoroughly enraged elephant burst into view!

Ahead was comparatively open ground rolling away as far as the eye could see!

Once again, the girl appeared to be committing an error of judgement. If she had remained in the woodland, she might have been able to find somewhere to hide from her pursuer and cause it to give up the chase. Having emerged on to the savannah, the only possible place of concealment was a couple of bushes some seventy-five yards away and, even if she could arrive there, they would be totally inadequate as protection against the furious bull!

The girl was still running with a style which would not have disgraced a well trained sprinter at an athletics' meeting, but she was at a disadvantage. While the elephant probably would have attained a top speed in a charge of around twenty-five miles per hour in its prime, age and its wound had slowed it down to a certain degree. Not sufficient, however, for her to be able to outdistance it. The terrain was level, with nothing to prevent her from moving in a straight line, but it was covered by short and spiky grass. Therefore, despite her obvious ability, she could not hope to attain the kind of pace which was possible when wearing spiked running shoes and on a smooth cinder track.

With each raking stride covering more ground than the swiftly moving legs of the girl were capable of achieving, the elephant was continuing to close the gap as they passed across the open ground. Its ears were flapping wildly, the trunk curled upwards and it repeatedly emitted screams indicative of its growing rage.

Suddenly, with the bushes still about thirty yards away—despite having negotiated the woodland without mishap—something caused the girl to lose her balance!

Whatever the reason, pitching forward, the tawny haired beauty went sprawling to the ground!

* * *   * * *

'It should've been *me* who went to fetch him out,' *Mbili Mbogo* complained, speaking English as he was aware that the woman kneeling at his side behind a couple of small bushes knew only a few basic words of Swahili—the *linqua franca* of East Africa—learned since her arrival in Ambagasali less than a week ago, and none at all of his native language. 'But she *never* would listen to *reason*. White men have *some* good ideas, but they're not so smart in others. We Wa-Kamba always keep our women in their place and beat them with sticks if they forget what their place is.'

'I really *must* remember to keep you and my husband *apart*,' Beryl Tragg replied, her accent English and "upper class". Without taking her gaze from the clump of trees some seventy-five yards away, into which the person about whom her companion had spoken had disappeared a short while ago, she went on, 'I have enough trouble keeping him in line already, without letting you give him ideas like *that*.'

Five foot seven in height and thirty years of age, the second speaker was willowly without being either skinny or flat chested. Cut short for convenience, as she had always led a most active life, her ash-blonde hair needed no artificial additives to retain its natural colour. Long hours spent in the open air around Rockabye County, Texas—where she had lived since her marriage to Sheriff Jack Tragg—had failed to harshen the texture of her golden bronze skin to any noticeable extent. Devoid of make-up and glowing with health, her maturely beautiful face exuded self confidence and the possession of an inborn faculty for instinctive leadership. She had on a wide brimmed, lightweight off white Western style hat, held in place by a fancily plaited leather *barbiquejo* chinstrap. A scarlet silk bandana was tightly rolled and knotted about her throat, trailing its ends over a loose fitting khaki bush jacket with eight spare cartridges, for the manificent Weathery .378 Magnum bolt action rifle she was holding, in loops on its breast pockets. Matching lightweight trousers, tucked into ankle high brown hunting boots, completed her ensemble.

Small, grey haired, with a wrinkled cheerful face indicative of one well past the prime of life, but still sprightly and sturdily built, *Mbili Mbogo* was a Wa-Kamba from the Machakos district of Kenya.[1] Amongst the white officers and n.c.o's of the King's African Rifles, and others who had the privilege to serve with them, they were a race who shared with the Samburu of the Northern Frontier District the distinction of being regarded as East Africa's equivalent of the Asian sub-continent's Ghurkas. He had, in fact, retired with the rank of company sergeant major after twenty-one years 'with the colours'. As was befitting one with such a background, he was as smartly turned out as was always the case unless working undercover on anti-poaching duties. He wore a brimless red felt *tarbush* hat, embellished by the brightly polished buffalo head cap badge of the Ambagasali Wildlife Service, a neatly pressed khaki bush jacket, shorts and a pair of elephant hide sandals. There was a bandoleer of ammunition suspended across his torso. He held a Holland & Holland .500 calibre double barrelled rifle and a second was leaning against the bush behind which he was concealed, within easy reaching distance of his right hand. A small knapsack, a rolled up bundle of what was obviously khaki clothing, a pair of brown hunting boots and a wide brown belt with a long bladed knife sheathed at its left side were near his feet.

In the course of her life, the blonde could lay claim to numerous achievements. Since settling in Texas, she had become known as the most successful breeder of horses for working cattle since Colin Farquharson ran the C On F

1. 'Mbili Mbogo', *Swahili for, 'Two Buffalo'*.

ranch from the middle to the turn of the Nineteenth Century.[2] Four hunting trophies she had taken had won places in *Rowland Ward's Records of Big Game*. She had also attained championship status at rifle, pistol and clay pigeon shooting. Yet, despite all she had achieved elsewhere, she felt considerable pleasure at having the elderly Wa-Kamba address her with such obvious dry levity. She considered it implied that, regardless of his remark about the status of women amongst his people, he believed she was capable of carrying out her part in what lay ahead. Of course, her train of thought continued, he could also be trying to ease the tension which she decided she must be showing. Competent as she knew herself to be, she had never had so much dependent upon her skill as at this particular moment. The task was not what she had expected would be her lot when she and her husband had accepted an invitation from Dawn Drummond-Clayton and James Allenvale 'Bunduki' Gunn to take a hunting trip in Ambagasli.[3]

Being a most progressive ruler, as was only to be expected of one who was a product of Eton public school and the Royal Military Academy at Sandhurst before succeeding to the throne, Prince *Simba Nyeuse*[4] was well aware of just how valuable, as a money earning tourist attraction, were the vast variety and numbers of his country's animals. He also accepted some kind of culling was essential to avoid over-grazing in what was, of necessity, a comparatively restricted domain. Therefore, on receiving a warning from Bunduki—his Chief Game Warden—he

2. *Some details about the career of Colin Farquharson are recorded in*: .44 CALIBRE MAN *and* A HORSE CALLED MOGOLLON.

3. *Details of the family background and special qualifications of Dawn Drummond-Clayton, also her connection with James Allenvale 'Bunduki' Gunn are given in*: APPENDIX ONE.

4. *'Simba Nyeuse', 'Black Lion'. How the name was meant to be used by Russian backed agitators in an attempt to cause the death of the Prince is recorded in*: Part Two, 'Death To *Simba Nyeuse*', J.T.'S LADIES.

had decided to adopt the system of prevention they considered most suitable in every way for keeping the various creatures at a level which the terrain of the enormous Ambagasali Wildlife Reserve could support. Instead of paying professional hunters to do the work, or leaving it to the Game Scouts, he had elected to allow the surplus to be either taken by a small group of Government appointed animal trappers—for sale to suitable zoological gardens—or removed as trophies by wealthy sportsmen and women willing to contribute a high price for the privilege. However, such big game hunters were not only to be most carefully selected, they would also be strictly supervised to ensure the stringent rules for their conduct were obeyed.

The system was, many considered, a most sensible solution to a very serious problem facing every African nation which maintained sanctuaries for wild animals. Culling by hunting offered the advantage that only the biggest and best trophies were removed, those just passing their prime and starting on what was invariably a rapid downwards path to being eaten while still alive by hyenas and other scavengers. What was more, instead of costing money, the revenue their disposal brought in was put to good use in preserving the stock which remained.

Although the Traggs were not the first hunters to receive an invitation since the scheme was implemented, they had arrived at a fortuitous time. Having reached numbers where their feeding was threatening the existence of the rhinoceros, the elephant herds needed culling before they duplicated the catastrophe caused by their kind in the great Tsavo National Park of Kenya. What was more, an old bull was being troublesome and potentially dangerous to human lives in an area of the Reserve where its kind only very rarely put in an appearance. It had to be removed, before it did further damage or carried out an attack resulting in the death or injury of some villager. In addition to being a cause of ill feelings amongst the people concerned, such an incident would be used as a means of strenghtening their case by those local politicians who sought easily attained popularity and votes by constantly demanding the Wildlife Reserve be thrown open for agriculture. Therefore, as the time available to them was comparatively limited and there were other trophies they could hunt, Bunduki had suggested he took Jack Tragg to help with the culling, while Beryl went after the *shamba* raider accompanied by Dawn and the head Game Scout, *Mbili Mbogo*.

Having arranged to be notified by the next village to be raided, on word being received that morning, the trio had travelled there from their luxurious base camp in Dawn's Land Rover. Before starting the hunt, knowing villagers sometimes faked evidence in the interest of getting a supply of free meat—as this was part of the customary recompense when an animal had to be dealt with for similar offences—they had checked the damage to make sure it was inflicted by the elephant. Satisfied they would be after the actual culprit, but aware that the wound it had received gave a greater urgency to the situation, they had set out to follow it. As Beryl had realized, from what she had been told about the leathery-featured old Wa-Kamba, she had witnessed Dawn accorded a rare honour by being allowed to carry out the actual tracking. Knowing he would have behaved in exactly the same fashion had he condescended to permit even Bunduki—who, being the adopted son of and trained by *Bwana M'Kubwa Sana*, was considered to be *very* competent at such matters[5]—to carry out a task of that nature, she was amused to notice how he kept a careful watch upon what Dawn was doing all the time they were moving.

Knowing something of tracking, the blonde had been impressed at the skill possessed by the girl. Although she herself could only rarely detect a trace of the bull's passing, Dawn had shown no hesitation. Only once was there

5. 'Bwana Mkubwa Sana', *Swahili sobriquet for Lord Greystoke— who was also known as 'Tarzan of the Apes'—meaning 'Very Big Lord', literally, 'Lord Big Very'*.

any plainly visible evidence. Having paused for a drink at a waterhole, the old male had left clear imprints in the mud. Examining them, Dawn had indicated to Beryl one of the ways in which African elephants differed from those of Asia. There were only three visible toes at the front, but four on the hind feet. Pointing out how evenly the steps had been taken, the girl had said the bull was not yet showing any sign of its movements being impaired by the spear wound it had received. However, a short distance further on, she had announced that the signs established that it had charged at a lion which had crossed its path without there being any suggestion of provocation, and she had stated this implied its behaviour was rendered violent by the pain from the injury.

After covering another six miles across what Dawn had described lovingly as the M.M.B.A.A.—meaning, she had explained, the Miles And Miles Of Bloody Awful Africa which referred to the great game-haunted savannahs which covered much of the eastern and southern sides of that continent—the hunters had come into sight of their quarry. The girl and *Mbili Mbogo* had each studied it through field glasses to ascertain it was the bull they sought before pronouncing what amounted to a death sentence. However, carrying out the execution was proving to be more difficult because of what had happened.

As the blonde was aware, hunting elephant was not a matter of long range shooting. Instead, to ensure a clean kill, it was carried out at ranges of not much over fifty yards and generally even closer. Powerful though the Weatherby rifle she carried undoubtedly was, and although it was custom built for the greatest possible accuracy under all conditions, this still held true where the world's largest land-dwelling animal was concerned. The bull was still far beyond an acceptable distance when they had received their first sight of it and there was little cover which would permit them to move closer. What was more, before they could attempt to advance into an acceptable firing range, it had entered a patch of woodland and disappeared from view.

Without needing to be told, Beryl had realized the situation would require very careful handling if she was to carry out the remainder of the hunt in the only manner she was willing to contemplate. She had been in wholehearted agreement with the very strict rules, created by the Wildife Service, to ensure the best possible sport without inflicting unnecessary pain to the quarry, which were explained when she and her husband were invited to hunt in Ambagasali. Therefore, she had been willing to let her much more experienced companions lay out the plan of campaign.

Pointing out there was little chance of all three of them being able to approach through the woodland without being detected by their quarry, the girl had warned of the consequences if the attempt ended in failure. Should the elephant be alarmed into flight, there would not be time before darkness descended for them to hope to catch up with it on foot, and it would be given an opportunity to raid another *shamba* that night, perhaps with fatal results to one or more of the villagers. While agreeing that such a state of affairs must be avoided if possible, the blonde had been startled and perturbed by the solution proposed by Dawn.

'You *must* have a back-up gun with you under the rules, which means you can't go in alone after him,' the girl had reminded when the blonde began to protest. 'So, although I've never met anybody who looks *less* like Mohammed, I'm going to see whether I can bring the mountain to you!'

Advancing until reaching the nearest suitable place of concealment, having refused to allow *M'bili Mbogo* to carry out the dangerous task, Dawn had made ready to put her plan into effect. What was more, it had become apparent to Beryl that some such contigency had been contemplated by her companions. Leaning her heavy calibre Holland & Holland double barrelled rifle against a bush, the girl had taken off her hunting boots, socks and outer clothing. Their removal had established she was wearing a leopardskin bikini instead of more conventional under garments, and she had donned a pair of leather sandals taken from the small pack carried by the Wa-Kamba. With the change of attire completed, leaving the other two kneeling behind the bushes holding their rifles ready for use, she had made her way into the woodland.

'She's found it!' Beryl said, her voice becoming almost breathless, as the scream of the enraged elephant rang out from amongst the trees and brought the brief exchange of comments to an end. Listening to the crashing of breaking foliage, she went on, 'And it's after her!'

'Be ready to shoot straight!' *Mbili Mbogo* replied, standing up and gesturing with his rifle. 'Because, *good* as she is, it will be needed. Neither Bunduki nor even *Bwana Mkubwa Sana* himself could outrun an elephant, especially once they're clear of the trees.'

'You'll be ready to back me up?' Beryl stated rather than asked and, also straightening up, she moved the leather sling of the Weatherby rifle until it was beneath her bent left elbow, then ensured she could line the barrel without it being obstructed by the bushes.

'If you *need* it,' the Game Scout promised, handling his big Jeffrey's elephant gun with the casual assurance of one well versed in its use. 'But you *won't*.'

All she had to do, the blonde told herself, was prove worthy of the confidence which *Mbili Mbogo* was putting in her!

* * *   * * *

The moment Dawn Drummond-Clayton appeared, with *Mbili Mbogo's* Holland & Holland duplicating the action, Beryl Tragg began to line the Weatherby through the narrow gap between the tops of the bushes. Although she had fired it many times before, never had she felt a deeper sense of urgency than at this moment. On the other occasions, she had known only her own life would be put at risk should she fail to bring down the dangerous animal at which she was aiming. This time, failure could cost the life of a girl whom she had come to like and respect. Forcing herself to put such thoughts from her mind, she concentrated upon the task.

Squinting her right eye along the barrel of the rifle, gaining extra support from the leverage applied against her left elbow by the sling, Beryl appreciated the wisdom of having taken Dawn's advice in leaving behind the telescopic sight with which it was mostly equipped. At such close quarters, useful as it had been on other occasions, the precision-made visual aid would have proven more of a liability than an asset. In fact, the range was so short, she had not even raised the 'leaf' backsight with its adjustable graduations to produce increased elevation for firing at various distances. Instead, she was employing the V-shaped notch which was set at right angles on the lower end of the backsight. Keeping her breathing steady and so gentle that it did not affect the alignment to any noticeable degree, remembering what she had been told about dealing with such a situation, she selected the target best suited to her needs.

Unfortunately, the bull had its trunk curled in a way which covered the exact point of aim. What was more, Dawn was posing a problem for Beryl. Wanting to bring the elephant into the best possible position for an instant kill, she was running straight towards the centre of the bushes.

Then, just before Beryl yielded to an impulse to shout for the girl to swerve aside, she plunged forward as if having tripped over something!

'My god!' the blonde gasped. 'She's gone *down*!'

However, such was the strength of Beryl's nerves that she did not allow the drastically changed situation to cause her to freeze into immobility!

Instead, even as the thought struck home, the blonde decided the mishap could prove beneficial. While Dawn's fall was putting her in even greater peril than at any other moment during the pursuit, it also paved the way for her salvation. As she fell, the bull's trunk was lowered until extending between the still close to horizontal tusks. The movement exposed the target area, the point in the centre of the head just below an imaginary line drawn beneath the eyes. Immediately, Beryl's brain rapped out a message and her well trained reflexes responded to it.

Taking a split-second to ensure her aim had not wavered, then being satisfied upon this vitally important point, the blonde tightened her right forefinger until the firing cycle was commenced. The crash of the shot was far from quiet and the thrust of the recoil anything but gentle, despite the rubber shoulder pad affixed to the rear of the butt, but she was conscious of neither. Nor anything else, for that matter, during the brief interim—which seemed vastly longer to her—between the powder charge being detonated and the bullet arriving at its intended destination.

Travelling as it was directed, through a rifled barrel manufactured to ensure as true a flight as was possible, the round nosed, three hundred grain 'full jacketed' .378 calibre bullet had its steel coating further covered by copper-and-zinc alloy gilding metal. This was to produce the greatest possible penetration from the three thousand feet per second muzzle velocity it attained. Dealing with such large quarry as the bull elephant, particularly when restricted to making a frontal shot, this was essential.

The species *Loxodonta Africana* had one of the most oddly shaped skulls of any living animal. Running to the level of the eyes, the tusks left a space not much more than three inches high by five inches wide through which the brain could be reached. Just about eye level, a circular orifice went back from the base of the trunk to the section of cellular bone which covered the brain. A miss of even an inch on either side meant striking a tusk or more solid bone capable of deflecting even the heaviest bullet. Lower down produced a similar unsatisfactory contact with the heavier bone coming out over the upper molars and nasal passages.

However, on this occasion, the contact was made at the ideal spot. A small puff of dust erupted as the bullet met the central point at which it was aimed. Ploughing onwards, it tore through the brain. Halted in its tracks, for all of its swiftly moving close to six tons weight, and killed almost instantenously, the bull's enormous body seemed to crumple. Its legs buckled and it toppled sideways to the ground—not more than two feet from its intended victim.

'Good shot, *memsahib*!' *Mbili Mbogo* praised, relaxing from the position of readiness he had adopted in case Beryl could not cope with the situation.

'I agree,' the girl seconded, coming to her feet and reaching behind quickly to fasten the clips of the bikini's bra, which had separated in the midst of her vigorous evasion. She had deliberately provoked the elephant into chasing her, leading it from the shelter of the woodland and towards where her companions were waiting in concealment. On realizing that she was in the line of fire, despite having been all too aware of the risks involved, she had made a rolling dive to leave the way clear for Beryl to have an unimpeded point of aim. Although her confidence in the blonde had proved justified, without the Wa-Kamba needing to open fire in his capacity of "back up gun", she continued with mock severity, 'But I thought you'd *never* shoot!'

'I wanted to make sure of him,' Beryl replied, lowering the Weatherby and, as had happened on other occasions when she had faced a dangerous charging animal, becoming aware of the throbbing its recoil had inflicted upon her right shoulder. Then, looking with sympathy at the sprawled out body of the elephant, she continued with a touch of sadness. 'I'm pleased to have the tusks, but I *wish* there had been some *other* way to deal with him.'

'There *wasn't*,' Dawn asserted definitely, despite sharing the emotion. 'And, as long as we keep open places like the Wildlife Reserve for animals to live in with human beings as neighbours, it's something which will have to keep on being done, regardless of what any "animals-

must-come-first'' conservation freak might try to make
people believe to the contrary.'

* * *   * * *

'Is that Bunduki and Jack coming?' Beryl Tragg asked,
pointing to a cloud of red dust rising from beneath the
wheels of a fast moving Land Rover approaching along a
track across the plains.

'No,' Dawn Drummond-Clayton replied, shading her
eyes with her left hand.

'Visitors then?' the sylph-like blonde woman suggested.

'You *could* call them that,' the tawny haired girl
admitted.

As the hunters had been checking to ensure the elephant
was dead, a Land Rover and a three-ton Bedford truck
carrying a number of Africans who had been attracted by
the sound of the shot had appeared over a distant rim.
Before they had arrived and the latter vehicle had
disgorged its delighted passengers, the girl had resumed
the clothing she had removed to allow the necessary freedom of movement required by her role as decoy. Making
no mention of her part in the proceedings, she had given
the blonde all the credit for the disposal of the *shamba*
raider, and the Gasali villagers had been profuse in their
expressions of gratitude. Waiting only until the elderly
Wa-Kamba Chief Game Scout had taken a *panga* bush-
knife from the smaller vehicle and removed the tusks,
which subsequently proved to weigh seventy-two and
seventy-four pounds, they had boarded it. Then, leaving
the Bedford to assist in transporting what was required of
the carcass back to the village, and knowing the remainder
would be devoured by various scavengers, they had set off
on their twenty miles' return journey.

The trio had reached their base camp some three miles
inside the Ambagasali Wildlife Reserve by the middle of
the afternoon. Nestling in the crook of a low hill's arm, by
a stream which still held plenty of water from the last rainy
season, it offered a vista of the surrounding plains with

their vast quantities of wildlife and was a very pleasant location. Supplied by the Government controlled *safari* company,[6] it was adhering to the traditions established when professional big game hunting provided a considerable addition to the economy elsewhere throughout East Africa. Therefore, its standards of luxury went far beyond those of the days when hunting parties travelled on foot, with whatever was required by way of supplies being carried in packages upon the heads of porters. Four major pieces of transportable accommodation were available. Beryl and her husband occupied a big double-fly tent, outside which the tusks were now propped up on display, with the single-fly versions for Dawn and Bunduki flanking it. At the other side of the campfire, the large open fronted dining tent also acted as a store for boxes of food to supplement whatever meat might be brought in as a result of the hunting. Nearby stood the small cook tent, from which seemingly inadequate base a surprising variety of dishes were produced by the very competent staff. Of their own choice, the dozen African members of the party had set up shelter-half tents a short distance away.

Having taken hot baths in the portable water-proof containers of the ablutions' tent, Beryl and Dawn had elected to celebrate the successful hunt by donning attire other than that worn during the day. Although it still wanted about an hour to sundown and the men had not returned, they were wearing cool halter necked and sleeveless evening dresses which were most complimentary to their respective feminine physical attributes. As was shown through the slits extending up the outer seams and from beneath the long hems, their legs were bare and they had on heeless Grecian type sandals with cross-straps running upwards to knee level.

'Do you know them?' Beryl inquired, noticing the

6. *Although the Swahili word* 'safari' *has become synonymous with a hunting expedition in East Africa, it actually means a journey of any kind.*

comment had been made in a tone which was less than enthusiastic.

'I've never been formally introduced, thank heavens,' Dawn answered, possessing better eyesight than her companion and being able to make out details which the other could not detect. 'But I've seen them and heard about them. They're from the Ambagasali Research Project over at *Tembo Niguu*.'

'You sound as if you don't like them,' the blonde estimated. Having read the travel brochure for the area, she knew "*Tembo Niguu*"—meaning "Elephant's Foot"— was the name of a hunting lodge presented as a base camp for the Project by Prince *Simba Nyeuse* and she was aware of how it had received its name despite being a considerable distance from the region occupied by the animals in question. It was built at that location by the Prince's father in honour of this being the place where he had killed a rogue bull elephant behaving much as had the one she shot that afternoon, and which had subsequently proved to carry the largest tusks ever to be taken in Ambagasali. The front feet had been removed and hollowed out, then equipped with supporting straps inside, to be used for an annual ritual. To ensure the continuation of the good luck with which he had been favoured by acquiring such a trophy, they were left on the porch of the lodge and each year, on the anniversary of the event, he walked around the building wearing them. Instead of commenting upon the matter, despite feeling sure the question she posed did not apply, she continued, 'Or is it conservationists in general you don't like?'

'I've nothing against *some* conservationists,' Dawn claimed. 'They're dedicated people and do really useful work.'

'But that bunch don't come into that category?'

'I don't know anything about how they do their work on the Project,' the girl admitted. 'But, from what I've seen of them, they're the kind who think conservationists must go around looking like they *never* wash and've been

135

rolling in the red *murram* dust and wear clothing, even when they're in town for the evening that any self respecting African would be ashamed to be seen in.'

'I bet they wear rings on every finger and other jewellery which makes them look even more cheap and shoddy,' Beryl guessed, having seen the kind of persons described by the girl in the United States and on visits to Kenya.

'They do.'

'But there's *more* than just that making you dislike them?'

'There is,' Dawn confirmed. '*Sandru Katamunboni suspects* they could be more interested in political agitation than conservation.'

'I'd have thought he would have taken *action* in that case,' Beryl commented. She knew the man in question was a Sandhurst trained colonel of the Ambagasali Army who was the very efficient head of the Bureau of Internal Affairs and was responsible to Prince *Simba Nyeuse* for the maintainence of law and order throughout the country. 'After all, he isn't hampered by having to "respect the rights" of thieves and rabble-rousers in the same way that knee-jerk, bleeding heart "liberals" try to compel Jack and every other peace officer throughout the States and the United Kingdom to do.'

'Ordering them to leave without *definite* proof would be impolitic, Sandru told me,' Dawn explained. 'You've heard how strongly *Simba Nyeuse* feels about keeping narcotics out of Ambagasali?'

'I have,' the blonde agreed, in a tone which implied approval of the Prince's attitude. 'Sandru told Jack and me when he came to meet us at the hotel the night we arrived how the anti-narcotics laws proscribe very severe punishment for sale and possession of even the so-called "soft drugs".'

'They *do*,' the girl confirmed. 'Well, this bunch's predecessors started to grow *marijuana* in what was supposed to be a maize *shamba* at *Tembo Niguu*. Sandru heard about it, but they managed to burn off all they'd planted

136

before his men could collect samples for evidence. So he issued an order for them all to be deported, using the excuse that their negligence nearly caused a bush fire which could have endangered the lodge, the Reserve and the adjacent villages.'

'I heard something about the expulsions in the States, but there was no mention of it being for raising pot.'

'That part never got out. When they got back to England, they claimed they were expelled because they'd spoken out against *Simba Nyeuse's* so called repressive Right Wing regime and there was considerable adverse comment raised in the media by 'liberal' conservation circles.'

'Why didn't the Prince have the truth of the matter announced?'

'As I said, there was no *proof* of what they'd been up to and, having heard how blatantly one-sided the coverage of the incident was by the media in the U.K., he didn't want an international slanging match which could have had an adverse effect upon Ambagasali's good relationship with England and the U.S.A. So he wouldn't let Sandru give the real reason. After all, Professor Henry Wilbraham runs the Project. Not only was he unaware of what they'd been doing, or he'd have stopped it, but he's achieved world-wide renown for the excellence of his conservation work. Although he's been unlucky in the helpers who've joined him since he came down here, including this bunch unless I miss my guess, he's been very helpful in his suggestions for maintaining the Reserve. What's more, he's stated publicly that he's in agreement with the way in which the decision to allow culling by hunting is being regulated and put into effect.'

'They do look as if they've been rolled in the dirt, and I've seen better dressed scarecrows,' the blonde remarked, studying the occupants of the vehicle as it came to a stop a short distance away and brought to an end the conversation. 'But being scruffy's part of their image, I suppose. They wouldn't want anybody to mistake them for us

137

horrible tourists, who're only here for *pleasure* while they were doing such *serious* and *vitally important* work.'

Climbing out of the vehicle, there was much about the appearance of the three men and two women, all being in their early twenties, to justify the comments made by Dawn Drummond-Clayton and Beryl Tragg. Even with the excessive rate at which they had been approaching, blatantly ignoring that the speed limit for the Reserve was thirty miles per hour, it seemed highly unlikely they could have acquired such a coating of the red dust raised from the *murram* soil of the track during the eight or so miles' journey from *Tembo Niguu*. It covered every one of them from head to foot and practically rendered the respective colour of their hair indistinguishable.

Having the almost obligatory long hair and beards, the men were all clad in sleeveless shirts, knotted instead of being fastened by buttons. Below very short shorts, their legs were bare and ended in open toed sandals. However, as Katamunboni had pointed them out and named each for her benefit shortly after their arrival in the country, Dawn was able to identify them by the differences in their heights and builds.

Tallest and bulkiest, with a surly and arrogant expression, was Christopher Holmes. Slender to the point of being bony and having gaunt features little improved by their straggly hirsute adornment, Peter Carter was next in height. Thickset and shortest of the three, David Short was equally unprepossessing in appearance.

In keeping with their male companions, Frances Morrell and Sharen Laurence wore what amounted to the uniform of their kind. About five seven, with reasonably good figures, the former had her brunette hair in an unkempt semi-Afro style and the latter's locks—naturally red beneath the dust—were cropped raggedly and boyishly short around her skull. The tank-top of indeterminate colour each wore established all too obviously that nothing else covered their torsoes. Contriving to have been raggedly trimmed until even briefer than those

138

of the men, their cut-down patched blue jeans more than justified the term 'shorts' and they were both barefoot. Although the only jewellery worn by Dawn and Beryl was the latter's wedding ring, the conservationist duo had several pendants around their necks and a number of thin bracelets on each wrist. As was the case with the men, who also sported a variety of pendants, all four sets of grubby fingers bore the kind of rings which Beryl had commented upon with justifiable disdain.

* * *   * * *

'Look *there*!' Peter Carter said, pointing in an accusatory fashion at the pair of tusks. Sprinkling his words with profanities, a habit all of the group indulged in as an ego trip intended to bring their conversation down to the level of the "little people", he continued, 'They've been working off their blood-lust by slaughtering an elephant in the reserve!'

'What can you expect from their useless, money-grabbing, parasitic kind?' David Short inquired. 'I say they need teaching a *lesson*!'

'That's why we're here,' Christopher Holmes asserted.

Which was true enough!

Ever since the decision was announced to allow limited and carefully controlled fee paying hunters to perform the necessary culling on the Ambagasali Wildlife Reserve, although Professor Wilbraham had declared concurrence, the quintet had been amongst those most loud in condemnation. As was the case with so many of their kind, their objections to the so called bloodsports were based mainly upon opposition to the politics of, and envy towards, the wealth of the people who participated, rather than for any genuine concern over the animals. In fact, ever since their arrival in the country, they had given support to those local 'liberal' politicians who sought to win votes by suggesting the Reserve be reduced in size and the land given over to agriculture, even though this would result in the death of many of the wild creatures displaced from it.

139

That morning, because Professor Wilbraham was absent, the five had not been carrying out any of the duties for which they received munificent grants from a prominent conservation organization. Instead, getting 'high' on a recently arrived supply of *marijuana*—which they and their kind always insisted was harmless and even beneficial—they had started discussing the hunting taking place in the vicinity of their headquarters. Remembering a sequence in a movie supposedly set in East Africa and which carried a 'message' dear to her heart, Sharen Laurence had said they should do something along the same lines. In it, a group professing 'liberal' persuasions had visited a similarly luxurious camp and, terrifying the occupants without difficulty, proceeded to inflict summary corporal punishment upon the wealthy sportswoman who was the white hunter's client.

Despite the rest having agreed the suggestion had merit, being the kind they were, nothing would have come of it if they had not been aware that Bunduki and Sheriff Jack Tragg were absent. Satisfied there would be no opposition from the 'poor, down-trodden blacks' who would be present, nor the two women who were left behind, they had decided to visit the camp and teach what Laurence had described as the 'blood-lusting American neo-fascists and their upper class bootlickers' a lesson. Doing so, they had told one another, would bring the attention of the world to the way in which animals were being slaughtered indiscriminately for the perverted pleasure of the idle rich.

When Carter had pointed out they might be arrested and even thrown into jail for what they were planning to do, he had been reminded by Laurence of the benefits which had accrued to a prominent British conservationist who had been incarcerated for a short period after joining a demonstration against the making of a dam in Tasmania. Having taken the measures they were contemplating in the sacred name of conservation, she had asserted, they too could hope for numerous well paid television and radio interviews on their return to England. With that prospect in mind, they had boarded one of the Project's Land Rovers and set out on their mission of retribution. Having halted on a distant rim and used binnoculars to ensure the two men had not returned, being disinclined to take any risks, they had finished the journey when satisfied it was safe to do so.

'Do you mind telling me what brings you here?' Dawn requested, sounding meek and not a little afraid, as she watched the three men approaching in a rough half circle, followed at a short distance by the no more clean nor tidy girls.

'Your kind believe in inflicting corporal and capital punishment on the poor victims of your materialistic society who fall foul of what *you* call law and order,' replied Laurence. She also punctuated her words with profanities, for the same reason they were used by the rest of the group. 'So we're going to let you find out how it *feels* to be on the receiving end.'

'In other words,' Frances Morrell went on. 'We're going to put you across that table and give you the thrashing you deserve.'

'Oh dear!' Dawn gasped, seeing Carter was close behind Beryl and sensing that Holmes was just as close to her rear. 'Did you hear *that*, Mrs. Tragg?'

'I *did*, Miss Drummond-Clayton,' the blonde confirmed, also giving the impression of being close to terrified. 'And I'm so *afraid*, I'll just have to do—*This*!'

Saying the last word, Beryl took a pace to the rear. Doing so carried her within reaching distance of the arms which had been raised to grab her. However, before Carter was able to do so, she pivoted and rammed back her right elbow. Taken in the *solar plexus*, with a force powered by muscles to which long years of hard work around horses had given considerable strength, all the breath was driven from his lungs in the strangled croak he involuntarily emitted. Driven away from his intended victim, he folded at the waist clutching the point of impact with both hands. Nor were his sufferings at an end. Turning

141

and grabbing him by the shoulders, Beryl hurled up her right knee. It caught him on the descending forehead, for which he might have felt grateful as contact elsewhere could have broken his already unlovely nose. The blow forced him to reverse directions until he went sprawling supine.

While the blonde was dealing with her skinny would-be assailant, fortune seemed to be favouring Holmes. Moving more swiftly than Carter, he succeeded in encircling Dawn's biceps with his arms and pulled her towards him. However, at that point, he too learned that the frightened posture was only simulated to induce the sense of over confidence it had created. Proving just as competent as the blonde at protecting herself, the girl jerked her neck sharply when concluding she was at the optimum distance. The back of her skull struck and crushed her assailant's nose even as he was opening his mouth to give an exclamation of profane satisfaction. Pain caused him to release his 'captive' and, blinded by the tears which burst involuntarily from his eyes, he stumbled in a half circle away from her with blood gushing out of his nostrils. He was speeded in his departure by a push to his rump from Dawn's left foot which propelled him onwards.

On the point of falling as a result of the powerful shove he had received, the largest of the trio was brought to a halt while still erect by arriving at the table where the small and almost globular cook was preparing the evening meal. By then, he had regained something of his blurred vision. Assailed by the pain from his crushed and gory nose, he saw the means of avenging himself. However, as his right hand reached for the razor sharp butcher's knife which had come to his gaze, it was knocked away by the African. Snarling in rage and forgetting all the condescending pretended affection he expressed where all blacks were concerned, he drew back his fist. The blow he intended to deliver was not struck. Showing surprising speed for one of such bulk in comparison with height, the cook grabbed up a heavy skillet in both hands. Its side was jabbed into

142

Holmes' stomach hard enough to cause him to retreat and double over. Then the base came around to arrive with a resounding clang on top of his head and he subsided limply face down.

Having dealt with the first two proposed captors, who had been expecting that the intended victims would prove as easy to deal with as was always the case in the kind of movies they favoured when conservationists were in contention against hunters, Dawn and Beryl turned upon the last male member of the group. Although he had started to lunge at them, seeing what happened to his companions, Short realized things were not going as easily as he too had anticipated. He tried to halt and adopt a defensive rather than offensive attitude, but was too late to achieve his purpose. Having swung to confront him, so perfectly did they co-ordinate their attack, the girl and the blonde might have rehearsed their actions for some considerable time. Catching hold of him by a wrist each, they spread his arms apart. Rising from the slits along the seams of the evening gowns, which allowed practically unrestricted freedom of movement, two shapely and potently muscled legs delivered kicks from different directions in rapid succession.

Knowing the open toes of the sandal precluded a direct attack, Dawn ensured it was the hard leather of the left sole which made very effective contact with the unprotected stomach of the third male conservationist. An instant later, passing just as forcefully between his inadvertently open thighs, the top of Beryl's right foot arrived at an even more vulnerable point of the masculine anatomy. The recipient of the double assault let out a strangled yelp of pain and dropped first to his knees, then face forward to lie writhing in agony on the ground.

Despite being feminists of the most pronounced kind, Laurence and Morrell had allowed the men to precede them. During the journey from the Project's headquarters, they had had time to consider the more than possible benefits they hoped to acquire on returning to England. Knowing that the authorities in Ambagasali regarded the tourists with considerable favour, as supplying a sizeable proportion of the country's finances, they realized a complaint from their victims was likely to see them all arrested and put in jail. Without the protection they could count upon from the media and left wing Members of Parliament, even if the stay was not long in duration, such an incarceration would be far less pleasant than would be the case in the British Isles. Therefore, having discussed the matter in whispers, they had decided to let the men do the dirty work so that they could plead ignorance of what was intended when the police arrived to deal with the complaint laid by their victims.

Nevertheless, seeing their companions were failing so badly, the women conservationists felt it incumbent upon themselves to take a more active part than was intended. Having found the television series *Kung Fu* acceptable to their tastes, despite their middle class-middle management backgrounds having taught them action-escapism-adventure Westerns were beneath their intellectual superiority, they had taken instruction in the fighting art it potrayed. Like many others who did so, they considered their knowledge rendered them as invincible as the hero of the series when in contention against white 'baddies' who invariably spoke with what were supposed to be the accent of the Southern States. Confident they had nothing to fear, particularly as they had witnessed enough to have an awareness of the danger which the men had lacked, they let out the traditional yells and went into the postures of readiness they had been taught.

At which point, the brunette and the red head discovered there was a vast difference between attempting to employ *kung fu* in earnest, instead of during practice sessions where everybody else had performed in a pre-arranged routine!

Exchanging glances, Dawn and Beryl dealt with the latest development as efficaciously as they had coped with the three men!

Instead of responding by adopting a similar position of

144

readiness, which the red head instinctively anticipated, the tawny haired girl stepped forward and swung a fast and well done right cross. The rising knuckles caught Laurence under the jaw, snapping her head around and stretching her neck. Knocked out on her feet, her raised hands flopped limply to her sides and she twirled away to alight flaccidly on the ground.

Nor, although she was able to launch a kick, did Morrell fare any better against the slender blonde. Her rising ankle was caught in two surprisingly strong hands before the foot could make contact. Then the trapped leg was given a powerful swinging heave. Spun around with no control over her motions, as she completed the circle, she met a similar blow to that which Dawn had delivered. Rendered unconscious, she landed supine across the equally inoperative body of the red head.

'Here endeth the first lesson,' Dawn remarked, shaking her throbbing right hand and looking around. She saw none of the men would be able to continue hostilities and gave her attention to the camp staff who were gathered with various kinds of extemporised weapons in their hands. Speaking Swahili, she continued, 'Get them on their feet and into their *gharri* so they can go back where they came from.'

'Is that all you're going to do?' Beryl inquired, working the fingers of the fist she had used to deliver the knockout blow.

'I don't want the kind of anti-bloodsports publicity the British left wing gutter press and all four channels of the television over there would give them if we had them arrested and brought to trial,' the girl replied. 'But I intend to go and have a word with Professor Wilbraham in the morning. When he hears what they tried to do, I'm sure he'll be able to *persuade* them that their services will be more use in some other country.'

'I hope so,' the blonde claimed. 'They might not get off so *lightly* if they try this kind of game against some other hunting party.'

* * *

'Hello!' Dawn Drummond-Clayton said, as the Land Rover in which she and her two companions from the elephant hunt were riding came to a halt on a rim overlooking the headquarters of the Ambagasali Research Project. 'It seems we aren't the only visitors for Professor Wilbraham!'

As she was paying what she wanted to be known to the five unsavoury looking conservationists as an official visit, the girl was wearing the clothing which she had discarded the previous day before going to lure the *shamba* raider to its death. As visual evidence of this, on each rolled up sleeve of her khaki bush shirt was a large cloth shield inscribed, 'AMBAGASALI WILDLIFE SERVICE, Assistant Chief Warden'; a status she had been granted by Prince *Simba Nyeuse* in addition to her regular duties as an instructress of physical education at the University of Ambaga. The legs of her khaki trousers were tucked into the calf high tops of hunting boots and, around her waist, the broad brown leather belt still carried the sheathed Randall Model One 'All Purpose Fighting' knife with a sambur horn 'finger-grip' hilt. Although she did not believe she would need it as a means of defence against the quintet, a Winchester .375 Magnum bolt action rifle—one of the battery she and Bunduki had brought with them—reposed with *Mbili Mbogo's* elephant gun on the back seats.

'It does,' Beryl Tragg agreed, also looking at the vehicle painted in the dark blue and white livery of the Ambagasali Police Department which was parked in front of what she guessed to be the main building. She too was dressed as she had been during the hunt for the wounded bull elephant, but had tactfully left her Weatherby rifle at the *safari* camp. 'I wonder if *they're* making an official call?'

'What do you think, *Mbili Mbogo*?' Dawn asked. 'Did any of our people send word of what happened yesterday to the police?'

'*Hapana*!' the Chief Game Scout replied from his place

behind the steering wheel, saying the Swahili word for "no" with certainty. He reverted to English as he went on, 'Since I caught a couple of them using the camp radio to send messages to their girl-friends in Ambaga, I've kept it locked up.'

'You've got no *romance* in your soul,' the girl accused with a smile, no mention of the incident having been made to her or Bunduki until that moment.

'I've got plenty of romance in my soul, even though I'm too old for it to do me any good,' *Mbili Mbogo* asserted, his seamed face showing no emotion although there was a twinkle in his eyes. 'But it's the Game Department who has to pay for the batteries, not the *safari* company, and I don't see why *we* should have to make it good when their people run them out.'

'Spoken like a true Civil Servant, *mzee*,[7] although that's a *terrible* thing to accuse *anybody* of being,' Dawn sniffed, but Beryl noticed there was no animosity in her tone. Rather she spoke in the bantering fashion of one addressing an old, respected and well-liked friend. 'Let's go down and see what's brought the police out here.'

'It'd better be something *important*,' the Wa-Kamba said in a coldly authoritative voice which the blonde concluded was far from being as officially disapproving as the words implied. 'Not just to scrounge a cup of tea or a *Tembo, baridi sana* or two.'

'I *know*!' the girl declared, eyeing the Chief Game Scout in a manner which Beryl realized she often adopted when conducting an equally acrimonious seeming conversation with her elderly, competent and respected *Chicano* head stablehand on the ranch in Rockabye County. 'If there's any scrounging of cups of tea to be done, or more particularly *Tembo* whether it's *baridi sana* or not,[8] you

7. 'Mzee': *Swahili word meaning an old and respected man.*
8. 'Tembo, baridi sana': *because the trademark of Tusker beer is an elephant, it has been given the sobriquet,* Tembo, *the Swahili name for that animal in those areas of East Africa where it is brewed.* 'Baridi sana' *means 'very cold', literally, 'cold very'.*

consider that it's you and your motley crew of Scouts should be doing it.'

'This *is* the *Wildlife* Reserve, not farming land,' *Mbili Mbogo* pointed out with mock severity, starting the vehicle moving once more. 'So anything like that should come to the Game Scouts, not the police.'

While her companions were talking, Beryl was studying their destination. The main building of *Tembo Niguu* was a large and substantial structure made with mud walls and a thick thatched roof after the native fashion. Nevertheless it showed signs of possessing modern conveniences which included the aerial for a two-way radio. There was a lean-to at one end under which was parked a Land Rover, but neither the second nor the larger truck belonging to the Ambagasali Research Project were in evidence. Nor was there any sign of life from the four smaller buildings which housed the African staff. The camp had been set up close to the wooded banks of a small river and already grass was starting to grow over the area burned out by Professor Henry Wilbraham's previous assistants to destroy evidence of their illegal crop of *marijuana*.

Approaching the buildings, Dawn noticed only three of the group who had visited her camp yesterday afternoon emerged, accompanied by a sergeant and two constables whose smart bearing and clean, well pressed, khaki uniforms were a marked contrast to their slovenly appearance. Wondering where Sharen Laurence and Christopher Holmes might be, as they did not follow the others, she was just as puzzled by the absence of Professor Wilbraham, although she could see from the number of the license plate that it was the Range Rover he used for his work in the otherwise empty lean-to. Nor did any of the dozen Africans who were employed in various capacities put in an appearance. Knowing three of them always liked to be involved in anything that happened, this also surprised her.

'What do *you* want here?' Frances Morrell demanded sullenly from the porch, moving until in front of her male companions and scowling at the new arrivals as *Mbili Mbogo* brought their vehicle to a halt behind the police Land Rover. 'This's private property and—!'

'*Tembo Niguu* isn't *private* property.' Dawn interrupted, dismounting and putting her hands on her hips in a way which displayed the official insignia on her sleeves. 'It was donated to the Game Department by Prince *Simba Nyeuse* when he established the Ambagasali Wildlife Reserve and has been loaned to *Professor Wilbraham* by the *Game Department* as headquarters for his Project.' Gesturing at the inscription on the right sleeve's cloth shield with her left hand, she continued, 'So, as an *Assistant Chief Warden*, I'm *entitled* to come here any time I wish.'

'That's true,' the sergeant declared in good English and without hestitation, as the conservationists expectantly looked his way. Ignoring the obvious disappointment caused by the confirmation, he walked towards the newcomers and went on, using the sobriquet by which the girl was known throughout Ambagasali, 'I'm pleased you've come, Miss D-C. They tell me that Professor Wilbraham is dead.'

'*Dead*?' Dawn repeated, remembering a rumour she had heard about a medical problem which was threatening to cause the man in question to retire from the Project he had developed. 'Was it a heart attack?'

'No,' the sergeant denied. 'They say he has been killed by an elephant.'

'*What*?' Dawn gasped, swinging her gaze from where the conservationists had remained on the verandah, and having her attention diverted before she could decide what was missing on it. On the point of saying that the area had never been what was termed as "elephant country" being only very rarely visited by solitary members of the species driven from their normal terrain, she concluded it might be advisable to learn more before making the declaration. 'When did it happen, Sergeant Matsuni?'

'This morning,' the *N.C.O.* replied. Like the constables,

149

he was just over medium height, stocky and had the dusty black skin pigmentation which differentiated the Bantu Gasali people from the Nilotic Ambagas with whom they shared the country.[9] 'Mr. Carter called on the radio and asked for *us* to come. I told him *Tembo Niguu* is inside the Wildlife Reserve, but he insisted that it was a *police* matter and not for the Game Department to handle. He didn't say anything about the elephant until after I got here.'

'I didn't,' the young man in question confirmed, glaring defiantly at Dawn and advancing with his companions. There was a suggestion of something furtive mingled with truculence in his attitude and neither he nor the others were showing any noticeable grief for the death of their superior. 'We decided, under the circumstances, it would be advisable for the *police* to handle the investigation.'

'What circumstances?' Dawn queried.

'We all know an elephant never attacks without being given a very good reason,' Carter claimed. 'So this one must have had that reason.'

'It could have been *wounded*,' Morrel supported, her manner indicating she was suggesting something significant.

'In a fight with another elephant,' Dawn inquired, 'or by an accident?'

'*Neither*!' Morrell claimed. Waving a hand to her male companions as if wishing to make it plain she was expressing a unanimous opinion, she went on and gave an even greater emphasis to the last word than she had to her denial. 'We *all* believe it could have been *shot*!'

'By poachers?' Dawn suggested, although she felt sure this was not what had been implied.

---

9. *'Bantu': pertaining to one of the many Negroid nations such as the Zulu, Matabele, Bechuana, Xhosa, Damara, Swahili, Kikuyu, Wakamba, etc., of Southern and Central Africa.*

9a. *'Nilotic': possessing the physical characteristics of people native to the Nile Basin. The Masai are probably the best known examples of this ethnic group, but it also includes the Samburu of Kenya's Northern Frontier District.*

'Or *hunters*!' Morrell replied, looking pointedly to where Beryl had remained in the Land Rover, and the mutter of concurrence from the male conservationists confirmed the tawny haired girl's supposition.

'Where did it happen?' *Mbili Mbogo* injected, having correctly interpreted the glance Dawn directed his way that meant he should take over the questioning.

'By the ford across the river,' Carter supplied.

'Let's go and take a look,' the Chief Game Scout suggested to the sergeant. 'If there's a wounded elephant on the rampage, I want to get after it as soon as I can.'

'I can understand that,' Matsuni answered. 'Show us the body, Mr. Carter.'

'May I come too, please, sergeant?' Dawn requested.

'Certainly, Miss D-C,' Matsuni confirmed, again without hesitation. However, his ready response was not solely due to accepting she had an official right to participate in her capacity as Assistant Game Warden. Nor did it come from knowing she was a friend of Colonel Sandru Katamunhoni and Prince *Simba Nyeuse*. He was aware of her relationship with *Bwana Mkubwa Sana* and how this had given her a considerable knowledge of animals which could prove beneficial in the forthcoming investigation. 'Let's get started.'

Led by Carter, the whole party went along a narrow track through the woodland. They stopped at the sergeant's command when the ford across the river came into view. Already a few vultures had gathered on the upper branches of the trees, but none had dropped to the ground. Lying on the muddy bank near the edge of the water, the body of the Professor was supine and covered by a blanket which had kept the winged scavengers from descending to begin feeding.

'We decided we'd leave him there until you'd seen him, sergeant,' Carter claimed, then he pointed. 'Look at all the elephant tracks!'

'I can see them,' Matsuni answered. 'Everybody stay where you are, except Miss D-C and *Mbili Mbogo*!'

151

'But we found the body and sent for you,' Morrell protested, after exchanging glances with her companions and beating both to speaking.

'That was what you're supposed to do, even though this is on the Wildlife Reserve,' the sergeant answered, before the red head could continue. While he was willing to accept co-operation from Dawn and *Mbili Mbogo*, nothing he had seen of the three conservationists since their first meeting had led him to believe they could render assistance. 'Now it's a matter for the police and the Game Department, so stay where you are and let us get on with it.'

Despite her instincts warning her there was something more than met the eye about the affair, being aware that the conservationists would be more inclined to accept whatever conclusions were drawn by the sergeant and the Wa-Kamba than any she might reach, Dawn allowed them to precede her. Glancing over her shoulder as Matsuni was approaching the body, she noticed the grubby trio were standing a short distance away from Beryl and the two policemen. There was an increasing of the furtive air which they were showing and she concluded this was because they did not care for having herself and *Mbili Mbogo* so closely involved in the affair. Although they had obeyed the order to remain, having muttered briefly amongst themselves, they were now obviously listening so as to hear whatever passed between the two Africans and herself. Her thoughts on the subject were brought to an end by what she saw.

Making a wry face, Dawn looked down as the sergeant pulled aside the blanket. Exposed to view, the tall and lean Professor's usually cheerful features were twisted into an expression of agony. He was clad in khaki trousers, socks, shoes and a tartan shirt, the front of which was thickly smeared with mud. However, when it was unbuttoned and drawn open by Matsuni, the position of the injury indicated that the thin chest had been stove in from the side, rather than crushed underfoot. What was more, the deep indentation looked as if it had been inflicted by the fairly blunt tip of a square stake of some kind rather than the roundish and padded sole of an elephant's foot. In her opinion, neither a tusk nor even one of the toenails could have caused it.

Having seen a couple of poachers who had been killed by elephants, Dawn felt certain such was not the cause on this occasion. A glance at *Mbili Mbogo* assured her that he had reached the same conclusion. Seeing him nod towards the numerous tracks in the mud, she gazed at them. They had the unmistakable shape caused by the feet of an elephant, but a moment's study brought a frown to her face and she looked closer. Another quick glance at the elderly Chief Game Scout informed her that he too had reached the conclusion at which she had arrived.

'Well, *sergeant*,' Carter called. 'What do *you* make of it?'

'Going by the tracks, it certainly looks as if he was killed by an elephant,' Matsuni admitted. Having drawn an accurate conclusion from the way in which Dawn had remained in the background, despite having the official status to take charge of the affair on behalf of the Game Department if she was so inclined, he went on instead of objecting when the conservationists moved closer, 'What do you say, *Mbili Mbogo*?'

'It looks that way,' the Chief Game Scout conceded. 'But it must have been a *very* strange elephant that did it.'

'How do you mean?' the sergeant inquired.

'There're only *three* toes on *all* of the footprints,' the elderly Wa-Kamba explained, pointing to the clear imprints which had been left in the mud. 'Which means they can only have been made by the *front* feet, because those at the back of *every* elephant I've seen—and that runs into *thousands* here and back home in Kenya—have always had *four* toes.' Knowing Matsuni was a member of a pastoral race which had never gone in for hunting and only killed wild animals when it became necessary to protect their *shambas*, he paused to let what he was saying be

153

absorbed. Satisfied his summation was being accepted by the sergeant and noticing the consternation being shown by the trio, he continued, 'And there's something else.'

'What is it?' Matsuni asked, having darted a glance to and received a nod of confirmation from Dawn.

'Those imprints are *very* clear,' the Wa-Kamba obliged. 'But they aren't deep enough to be made by an elephant, particularly if it was walking on its front legs as this one must have been.'

'I don't follow you,' Matsuni admitted, frowning in genuine puzzlement.

'What *Mbili Mbogo* means is that the Professor was killed by a human being,' Dawn explained, having kept the conservationists under observation while the Africans were talking. Noticing the suggestion of growing alarm playing upon each grubby face, she had decided an intervention by herself might provoke some involuntary response which would shed light on the puzzling aspects of the situation. 'But to make it seem this wasn't the case, the killer brought the body here and, putting a pair of elephant's hollowed out front feet over his own, made tracks which he thought would lead us astray.'

'How *very* convenient for this killer of *yours*,' Morrell sneered, stepping closer although she looked as uneasy as her companions. 'He just happened to have brought a pair of hollowed out elephant's feet with him. Or did he find them lying around in the woods here?'

'Not "in the woods here", as you put it,' Dawn corrected, realizing what she had missed seeing while speaking to the unkempt looking brunette on her arrival. She also concluded the men were not reacting as she would have expected. Instead of advancing to give greater emphasis to what their companion was saying, they remained where they had halted the second time, moving closer together as if seeking mutual support. 'But there's a pair on the porch of the lodge.'

'Wilb—!' Morrell snapped, then made an amendment to what she had concluded just too late was the wrong kind

154

of reference to the dead man under the circumstances. '*The Professor* said such things were an affront to a conservation project and threw them away just after we got here!'

'He *didn't*,' Dawn denied with conviction. 'In fact, he *couldn't* have thrown them away, even *if* he had felt as you claim about them. They were taken from a very big rogue bull Prince *Simba Nyeuse* shot near here as a boy. That's how the Lodge got its name. They are regarded as being symbols of good luck and one of the conditions under which it was loaned to the Professor was that he left them on the porch.'

'Are you accusing one of *us* of killing him?' Morrell challenged, but there was less of the earlier truculence in her voice and, like her companions, she was now looking even more distinctly ill at ease.

'I haven't accused *anybody*, as far as I can remember,' Dawn corrected. 'But neither have I seen anybody except you three in the area.'

'There are a dozen Africans on the staff of the Project,' the brunette pointed out sullenly, moving back until standing by the men as if seeking their support.

'No *African* would try such an easily detected trick,' Dawn countered, noticing no mention was made of the absent pair of conservationists and hoping that none of the trio knew that the pastoral background of the local Gasalis made them less knowledgeable than *Mbili Mbogo* where the habits of wild animals and tracking were concerned. 'Anyway, I haven't seen any of them about this morning.'

'That's because none of them are here,' Matsuni supplied, before any of the grubby conservationists could speak. 'They've all been attending a wedding over at Wakoli village since yesterday afternoon and, going by what I saw before I left this morning, *none* of them were in any condition to have come back to do something like this.'

'Which means,' Dawn said, looking at the trio in a

pointed fashion which she felt sure would elicit an informative response from them. 'Unless there's been a *stranger* in the area—and *none* have been reported by our Game Scouts, who keep a *very* careful watch for such things—the choice of suspects appears to be limited to just you *three*.'

'Just us *three*?' David Short repeated, speaking for the first time and his tone was as filled with perturbation as the glance he directed at his companions.

'Aren't there two more of you?' the sergeant asked, eyeing the trio in a speculative fashion which did nothing to reduce their obviously growing consternation. 'Where are they?'

'Th—They went to Ambaga for some supplies this morning,' Morrell answered, glancing at the man on either side of her.

'They were taking a *very* funny route to get *there*,' Dawn stated. 'We saw them as we were coming here. They were driving on the *safari* bus track which leads to the *eastern* side of the Reserve and I remember saying to *Mbili Mbogo* that, if they kept going at the *speed* they were travelling, they might cross the border with Ballinganda without realizing.'

'*Cross the border*?' Carter growled and his tone was redolent of suspicion. 'But they said they were going to—!'

'What if they've—!' Short began at the same moment.

'Seeing Wil—*the Professor* like that's made me feel ill!' Morrell declared loudly, her face twitching with an emotion which was other than grief for her dead superior. While speaking, she glared from one to the other man and brought their comments to a halt. 'I—I've got to go back to the house!'

'And me!' Short seconded, but his pretence at distress over what had happened to Professor Wilbraham was just as lacking in conviction.

As the grubby looking brunette and the no cleaner thick-set man swung around to walk away, Carter gave an angry hiss and followed them.

'I say, Dawn,' Beryl commented, watching the conservationists hurrying in the direction from which they had come. 'As far as I can recall, we didn't see *anybody* on the way here.'

'I know that and you know that, but *they* don't know it,' the tawny haired girl answered, having supplied false information instinctively in the hope that she might satisfy the conclusions she had reached. Seeing Matsuni was also looking after the departing trio and concluding he meant to order them to stop, she went on, 'If you don't mind a *suggestion*, sergeant, I'd let them go and follow in a couple of minutes. You might learn something which will help clear up what's happened.'

* * *   * * *

'There's a bunch!' Sharen Laurence said, halting the Land Rover she was driving and pointing beyond a stream which had just come into view to where the rolling savannah changed into a different type of terrain.

'So what?' Christopher Holmes replied, also looking to where a small herd of elephants were walking down a slope thickly dotted with 'wait-a-bit' thorn bushes and flat topped acacia trees. 'It's taken *you* a long time to find them and *you* haven't been going at any speed.' Before his companion could launch her intended protest over having been given the blame for the delay, he gestured to two bulky knapsacks lying in the back of the vehicle with a sporting rifle which had belonged to Professor Wilbraham and went on, 'With what we've got in *them*, the sooner we're over the border and into Balinganda, the better I'll feel.'

Although Dawn Drummond-Clayton had only been pulling a bluff in the hope of discovering the real facts behind the death of Professor Wilbraham, she had inadvertently spoken the truth regarding the intentions of the pair.

There was a very good reason for the way in which Laurence and Holmes were behaving!

By aligning himself with the West when Ambagasali

157

was granted independence by the United Kingdom, Prince *Simba Nyeuse* had made himself very unpopular with the Communist bloc. Under his firm yet scrupulously fair rule, he had created a prosperity and economic stability almost equalling that of Kenya. Furthermore, he had instituted a system for protecting the rights and liberty of all his people regardless of the tribe to which they belonged, which was far in excess of those countries throughout Africa embracing Marxist policies. Although attempts to overthrow him and replace his government with a regime more amenable to the ideals of Russia had failed, there were those within and outside his country who still sought to bring this about. The presence of the quintet of 'conservationists' at *Tembo Niguu* was to play a part in a scheme directed towards achieving the desired result.

Finding the activities of an 'anti-bloodsports' group to which they belonged was becoming the subject of too close an investigation by the police for their liking, as a result of a campaign of sending letter bombs to people connected with various field sports, Laurence and her four companions had been delighted to be offered an opportunity to leave England. Nor, despite their strong left wing point of view, had they objected when informed they would be going to Ambagasali as replacements for the party deported by Colonel Sandru Katamundoni. They knew they were being sent to a pleasant location and would have a far better standard of living than would have been forthcoming if their destination had been a country ruled by a one-party Marxist regime. What was more, having acquired university degrees which—on paper at least—qualified them for the duties involved, they were to take up well paid occupations and felt sure these would not entail doing too much work.

The five had been less enamoured when informed that they would be expected to resume the cultivation of *marijuana*, to be employed in Ambagasali as a prelude to diverting the users on to more potent narcotics. This in turn, it was hoped, would help create the social unrest their kind sought to bring about everywhere in the Free World as a means of attaining the complete control of the governments they found unattainable by obtaining a majority of votes in democratic elections.

However, the people who had made the selection knew far too much about the quintet's illegal activities for them to be able to refuse. As an added inducement, they were told they would be given sufficient of the narcotic to supply their own needs until the first crop was available for use. They were also warned against repeating the mistake of their predecessors, who had attempted to cultivate a supply in the immediate vicinity of the Project's headquarters for the purposes of personal profit. Instead, they were instructed to pass on the seeds with which they would be issued to be planted in other parts of the country on *shambas* owned by local 'liberal' sympathisers who were just as eager to benefit from the crop.

While they were waiting for the means to set about the task they had been sent to carry out, conditions at *Tembo Niguu* had come up to the expectations of Laurence and her companions. As anticipated, they had found their duties were far from arduous and these were carried out with just enough competence to avoid provoking complaints from Professor Wilbraham. Nor did they entirely transgress in another way. Reports about some of the company they kept on visits to the capital city, Ambaga, had reached Colonel Katamundoni. However, as they had followed the orders they were given in the United Kingdom to refrain from becoming involved in any activities which would have served as a reason for them to be deported, Colonel Katamundoni, being told of the conversations they had engaged in, had realised it did no more than supply him with a clear indication of their political persuasions. He suspected they had brought *marijuana* with them, but they had kept it to themselves and he had decided not to take any action against them unless they started to share it with members of the local population.

159

Having all the selfish and self-centred qualities of their kind, despite suggestions from their acquaintances, they had refused to part with any of it. Nor, possessing natures prone to being distrustful of everybody, had they mentioned their main purpose for being in the country to anyone.

Prior to the arrival of the five at *Tembo Niguu*, the people who had procured their appointments made arrangements with supporters in the otherwise unaware international conservation organization for the processed *marijuana* and a large quantity of *Canabis Sativa* seeds to be sent concealed in supplies for Professor Wilbraham. Fortune had seemed to be favouring them when the consignment arrived. Its coming coincided with their superior being absent on business at the capital city, Ambaga. As a precaution against accidental discovery before the supply could be put in a secure hiding place, and taking advantage of his absence, they had insisted that all the African assistants for the Project—none of whom, they suspected, would be sympathetic to their plans—accepted an invitation to attend the wedding festivities of a well-to-do friend at a nearby Gasali village.

The quintet had only themselves to blame for the scheme failing to continue proceeding in such a satisfactory fashion. Instead of waiting until after they had hidden the containers filled with the seeds they had started smoking some of the processed *marijuana* as the supply they had contrived to bring into the country with them had run out a few days earlier. The boost given to their delusion of self importance along with a spurious courage as they became 'high' on the narcotic had led to them carrying out the disastrous visit to the hunting *safari* camp. When they had come back to their headquarters, as a result of their defeat at the hands of their intended victims, none had been in any condition to think of concealing the rest of the illicit addition to the legitimate supplies. The situation had not been improved by the unexpected return of the Professor just before sundown.

Going to the storeroom shortly after breakfast that morning, Wilbraham had found the processed *marijuana* and containers holding the seeds to produce further crops. Meeting Laurence and Holmes as he was coming out, he had stated his intention of using the radio to report the matter to the authorities. The pair had been driven to a state of near panic by the thought of the consequences. Each had realised these could go far beyond the loss of the narcotic upon which they were so dependent. If arrested for being in possession of such a large quantity, they would find themselves facing trial by a legal system much less easy going than the one to which they were accustomed in the United Kingdom. Recovering her wits quicker than Holmes, the red head had given an order which both acted upon. Grabbing the Professor by the front of his shirt, they had delivered a violent shove and propelled him in a spinning twirl through the door of the room he had just left. On following to ensure his silence, they had found that he was already dying as a result of the left side of his chest having been caved in by colliding with the corner of an unopened crate.

Appreciating that they had made the predicament they were in even more serious, the pair had given thought as to how they might escape facing the consequences. As was generally the case when some decision had to be made, possessing a forceful character and connections in left wing circles which gave her a moral ascendancy over the other four, it had been Laurence who thought up a solution. While she went to collect her own and his knapsacks, to take away the consignment of *marijuana* and seeds instead of their clothing, Holmes had carried out her instructions. Gathering the other three conservationists, he had told them that he had found the Professor lying dead in the storeroom apparently as the result of a fall against a crate. He had also pointed out how the 'mishap' might be turned to the advantage of their anti-hunting campaign. They would use the two feet of the elephant on the porch of the building to create the impression that he had been killed by such a creature.

161

If any of the three had suspected the truth about how Wilbraham met his end, sharing Holmes' belief that it could be ill-advised, even dangerous, if Laurence was antagonized, they had kept the thought to themselves. After the body had been taken to the edge of the river, the 'evidence' was created and the pair of feet thrown into the water. When he had informed the rest of the red-head's scheme to the civil authorities at Wakoli—refraining from mentioning how the Professor was supposed to have died, so the Game Department would not be involved in the early stages. Laurence and he would then create a diversion by taking the rifle which was kept on the premises for self defence purposes, and wound a few elephants.

There would be no difficulty in convincing the local police officers that one of the injured animals was responsible for Wilbraham's death, Holmes had asserted. Furthermore, they would be just as easily induced by the trio to put the blame elsewhere. Once the news got out, he had declared to strengthen his suppositions, it would be seized upon by the very local anti-bloodsports lobby in the media of the United Kingdom and other countries of the Free World as an argument against allowing a continuation of the culling by hunters who paid for the privilege. There had been no arguments over the proposals. Instead, all three had been in agreement with his summation that the policemen who came in response to their summons would be willing to accept without question their explanation of what had happened and would be guided along the required lines on how to deal with the situation.

It had not occurred to any of the trio to look in the Land Rover which Laurence had driven from the lean-to. If they had, they might have been made suspicious by the sight of the knapsacks on the floor. What was more, if an examination had been made, it would have disclosed that all the illicit consignment—with the exception of the quantity of the processed leaves they had concealed amongst their respective belongings—was missing from the storeroom. As neither check was undertaken, the pair had been allowed to leave without question. However, they had had no intention of returning. Instead, they meant to cross the border with the neighbouring country of Balinganda. Having done so, should things not go as envisaged and the truth be discovered, they felt sure the Marxist government of that country would refuse any application by the Ambagasali authorities for their extradition. Nevertheless, the painful treatment they had suffered at the hands of Dawn Drummond-Clayton and Beryl Tragg was still fresh in their memories and further inflamed by the *marijuana* they were smoking. Therefore, they had decided it would be a measure of revenge to carry out the other part of the scheme before leaving the Wildlife Reserve and offer their deserted companions an opportunity to lay the blame for the animals suffering from gunshot wounds upon the offending pair's hunting party.

Instead of sticking to the trail along which—unbeknown to them—the tawny haired girl had said they were seen, the pair had taken a more circuitous route in search of their intended quarry. However, as the red head had never driven across country, they had been unable to travel as quickly as they would have preferred. What was more, if either had given the matter any thought, they might have foreseen there was a major point against their story being accepted. In spite of its name, *Tembo Niguu* was not even near 'elephant country'. Because they had overlooked this point, they had covered a considerable distance without having located any of the great animals. Instead of having drawn any conclusions from this, but keeping in mind the possibility that the police might not be convinced by the 'explanation' they had induced their companions to supply, they had been discussing whether to give up the quest when they had reached the fringe of the hilly bush country and the herd had come into view.

'We can do it and then go over,' Laurence stated. 'It won't take that much longer.'

'I can't hit them from here,' Holmes pointed out sullenly.

'They're coming down that slope towards the stream, so

I'll go behind the clump of bushes on this side,' the red head replied, her tone taking on a note which her companion knew meant she was determined to have her way. 'You'll be able to hit some of them from that close.'

Looking surly, but concluding he would be wasting time by arguing, Holmes reached over then picked up the rifle. Despite professing an abhorence for all forms of military training and physical violence, he had been taught handling weapons while attending a gathering of left wing activists during his time at university and he felt sure he could carry out his part in the affair. Glancing at the camera with the telephoto lens which was on the seat between them, he worked the bolt to feed the uppermost round into the chamber. By that time, the red head was driving the Land Rover down the slope towards the bushes she had indicated. Although the elephants looked their way, being accustomed to vehicles, none showed any alarm or inclination to turn back. Instead, although the Land Rover was in plain view beyond the clump of bushes, they arrived at the stream and spread along the opposite bank not fifty yards from where it was halted.

'Get out and use the bonnet for a rest!' Laurence commanded rather than suggested, as the burly young man started to thrust the barrel of the rifle through the window. 'That way, I can take the photos we need of the animals with their wounds bleeding.'

Accepting that the red head had made a valid point, Holmes did as he was instructed. Not only would obtaining additional support for the rifle increase his chances of success, but they would be able to use the camera they had brought to take photographs of the injuries he intended to inflict as 'proof' of the allegations to be made against hunters. Resting his elbows upon the bonnet, he cradled the butt against his shoulder and lined the sights at the nearest animal. He gave no thought to the fact that, like all the others which were fully grown, it was a cow with such small tusks it would be unlikely to attract the attention of sport hunters seeking trophies.

'Go on!' Laurence commanded from inside the vehicle, remaining seated behind the steering-wheel and focusing the camera. 'Start shooting!'

Aware that having the vehicle ready for immediate departure was a sound precaution, in case the elephants should attack when he started shooting, Holmes did not ask for the engine to be switched off. He was convinced that, particularly with the range being so short, he could make the required hits in spite of the slight vibration caused by the idling motor. Satisfied upon that point and with his aim, he started to tighten his right forefinger upon the trigger.

* * *   * * *

'Damn it!' Dawn Drummond-Clayton ejaculated, bringing the Land Rover she was driving to a stop. 'They've managed to find some elephants!'

'I thought you said there wouldn't be any this near the plains?' Beryl Tragg queried from her place between the tawny haired girl and *Mbili Mbogo*.

'They must have been driven down this way by shortage of food in the bush country,' the elderly Chief Game Scout replied, also looking at the massive grey shapes descending the slope towards where the vehicle which he had been tracking was halted at the nearer side of a stream. Having learned enough to suggest a weapon might be needed, he was holding Dawn's bolt action .375 Magnum sporting rifle—with which he had elected to arm himself instead of his shorter ranged double barrelled elephant gun—between his knees. 'I've been saying for months that we should've thinned the herds out before they had to start looking for new feeding grounds.'

The suggestion made by the tawny haired girl to Sergeant Matsuni had proved worthwhile!

Following the trio of conservationists back to the hunting lodge, Dawn and her companions had waited until they discovered enough to make them suspect they had been tricked and deserted by the other two. Entering the

165

building without letting their presence be known to its irate occupants, once again acting upon the advice which the tawny haired girl had given in his tribal language—which none of the conservationists could understand—the sergeant had demanded they accompanied him while he inspected the storeroom. Still allowing himself to be prompted by the same means, he had stated the belief with Dawn's suggestion that the injury resulting in the death of Professor Wilbraham was not accidental.

Already angered by the loss of the consignment, the trio had not taken into account that its removal by their companions prevented it from being found and incriminating them in its possession. Instead, they had behaved as Dawn had hoped when she remarked that the other two were absent and must be considred innocent on that account. As each possessed a full measure of the distrustful nature and blatant self-interest of their kind, all three had sensed danger to themselves. Realizing that the ploy suggested by Christopher Holmes had failed to produce the desired results, leaving them 'holding the bag', they had respectively and with equal speed acquired a determination to gain whatever leniency might accrue from supplying the truth about the situation. In fact, all three were so eager to gain personal exculpation, Matsuni had had difficulty in keeping the men quiet while allowing Morrell to provide the explanation.

According to the brunette, with the two men supporting her story, Holmes and Sharen Laurence had asserted they had found the Professor dead as the result of a fall against a crate and had decided to use his body as a means of arousing sympathy for the anti-bloodsports campaign by making it appear he was killed by an elephant which hunters had wounded. Making no mention of the *marijuana*, but furious at its loss and the pair's desertion, she had declared they had already carried out the production of the false evidence unaided and had asked for the police to be informed while they went to make sure there would be elephants suffering from gunshot wounds in the area.

Dawn had not been surprised to discover the blame for the death of Professor Wilbraham was placed upon the absent pair. This was the course she had anticipated would be taken once the trio realized the plan had failed, regardless of whether true or not. However, she was very disturbed by learning of the proposed attempt to use the killing as a means of creating anti-hunting propaganda. An examination of the Professor's quarters had established that his rifle and some ammunition was missing and she did not doubt the pair would attempt to carry out the purpose now revealed. Asking Matsuni to deal with the situation at *Tembo Niguu*, after having given him further advice regarding the line of action he should take, she had left with Beryl Tragg and *Mbili Mbogo* to prevent the vicious scheme being brought to fruition.[10]

Knowing the Wa-Kamba was better at tracking than herself, Dawn had done the driving and left the selection of the direction they took to him. Once the point at which Laurence and Holmes had turned on to the savannah was discovered, he had had no difficulty in following them. Equipped for the special needs of the Game Department, the vehicle had a canvas roof over the front seat and, with this rolled back, *Mbili Mbogo* was able to stand up when necessary and see over the windshield instead of needing to dismount. Such was his skill, the pursuers were able to

10. *Following advice she had received from Beryl Tragg, Dawn Drummond-Clayton had suggested that Sergeant Matsuni searched the trio's rooms. On doing so, he found the marijuana each had taken for personal use from the consignment. However, circumstances were to prevent them from being charged as accomplices in the killing or in the proposed planting of the seeds. Instead, faced with the possibility of standing trial for possession of the processed narcotic—taking a course proposed by Colonel Sandru Katamundoni, in the interests of retaining good relations with England, when he interviewed them at his headquarters in Ambaga—they were only too willing to declare publicly that they were leaving Ambagasali for 'reasons of ill health'. In that way, their expulsion was carried out with none of the distorted publicity employed by the media in the United Kingdom over the ejection of their predecessors.*

travel much quicker than their quarry. Furthermore, as the terrain they were traversing had never been 'elephant country', they had hoped to catch up with the pair before such territory was reached. Unfortunately, because of the increase in the number of the enormous animals following the abolition of hunting, it had become apparent that a herd had been compelled to seek new domains in search of food and was now in danger.

'Shout and scare them!' Beryl suggested, watching Holmes descend and rest the rifle on the bonnet of the Land Rover. 'Or blow the horn!'

'That won't work!' Dawn answered, knowing the elephants were used to both sounds and, especially at that distance, were unlikely to be bothered by hearing either. It was also possible that the couple they were following might decide her party was too far away to intervene more effectively and Holmes would wound at least one of the herd before taking flight. 'But *this* might!'

Coming to her feet and standing on the set, the tawny haired beauty cupped her hands around her mouth. Throwing back her head, she gave the call of the 'Great Apes' which she and Bunduki had learned from *Bwana Mkubwa Sana*.

'*Aaah—Eeee—Aaah—Eeee—Aaagh*!'

Intended for signalling and claiming dominance over an extensive piece of territory in thickly wooded terrain, the sound which left Dawn had acoustic qualities far in excess of those a normal human voice was capable of producing. It lacked the full resonance which Bunduki and their teacher could accomplish by virtue of their larger lungs, but it still possessed excellent carrying qualities and was sufficiently awesome in timbre to be most impressive. Rolling across the intervening distance, the effect was not as efficacious as had frequently been suggested when the sound was duplicated for use in 'Tarzan' movies. Nevertheless, the result it achieved served her purpose.

Hearing the call, although it did not induce them to take flight or come towards its source, as had invariably happened in the movies, the elephants began to respond by milling restlessly around. On the other hand, the eerie and unexpected sound produced a more desirable effect upon the two conservationists. Startled, Holmes jerked his head around as his finger completed tightening on the trigger. Doing so caused the barrel to lose its alignment and the bullet which left the muzzle tore harmlessly above the animals across the stream. Allowing the camera to slip from her grasp, Laurence twisted on the front seat until she was able to locate the cause of the disturbance.

'It's those bitches from the hunting camp!' the red head screeched, turning forward to grasp the steering-wheel and gearstick. With her left foot starting to depress the clutch, she went on just as vehemently, 'Kill the driver!'

Snarling with rage which—despite the stimulating effects of the *marijuana* he had been smoking—was nine tenths fear, Holmes set about doing as he was told. Working the bolt to eject the empty cartridge case and replace it with a loaded round, failing to notice what his companion was doing, he swung the rifle in the required direction. He was aligning his sights towards where the tawny haired girl was resuming her seat when he heard the engine of the Land Rover being revved up. Believing this implied no more than that Laurence was making ready to quit the area as soon as he had fired and climbed back into the cab, he squeezed at the trigger. The crack of discharging powder was accompanied by a rasping as the red head slammed the vehicle into gear and, as she had had no need to use the hand brake on halting, set it into motion. Even as a realization that he was being deserted assailed the burly man, he was too late to do anything to prevent it. More by luck than skill, his bullet came close to achieving its purpose. However, this proved more of a disaster than a benefit for him.

Seeing the windshield impaled by the lead from the burly white man's rifle, which fortunately passed between his companions, *Mbili Mbogo* responded with the speed and effectiveness he had acquired and never lost in the

Kings African Rifles. Thrusting himself erect and deftly swinging the Winchester he was holding into a firing position, he took sight and touched off a shot. In doing so, he justified the selection of armament he had made. Powerful as the elephant gun undoutedly was, it did not offer the kind of accuracy required to attain a hit at the range over which he was shooting. Leaving the rifle and flying as it was directed, offering a tribute to the skill with which it was dispatched, the heavy bullet struck Holmes in the centre of his chest. Pitched backwards by the impact, with the rifle he had stolen leaving his hands, he measured his length on the ground as his companion drove away.

'Sit down!' Dawn snapped. '*She* isn't going to get away!'

Waiting only until the Wa-Kamba had resumed his seat, the tawny haired girl set their vehicle into motion. Across the stream, the elephants swung around and loped away. Paying no attention to their departure, she concentrated upon getting up speed to counter that of the red head she was pursuing. However, on arriving where Holmes was sprawled writhing on the ground, she brought the Land Rover to a halt.

'Look after him until I get back, Beryl, *Mbili Mbogo*!' Dawn commanded. 'She's *mine*!'

Nodding in grim approval, instead of exchanging the Winchester for his elephant gun, the Wa-Kamba worked its bolt to recharge the chamber. Then, even before Dawn had brought the Land Rover to a halt, he slipped out of the front door with the rifle held ready for use if it should be needed. However, the blonde did not follow him. The way in which the girl had spoken reminded her of a similar response she had heard from one of her husband's deputy sheriffs in Rockabye County on being told where the man who had shot his partner could be located. If the girl caught the red head while in such a frame of mind, anger over the death of Professor Wilbraham might cause her to behave in a fashion which she would later regret. It was unlikely that the fleeing conservationist was armed in any

170

way, but Dawn might not give this any thought if resistance was offered. In addition to the heavy calibre Holland and Holland elephant gun on the rear seat, she was wearing the Randall Model One 'All Purpose Fighting' knife which her father—acknowledged as one of the world's foremost authorities on the subject—had taught her to wield as a most effective weapon. Even if she did not take the firearm from the vehicle should the chase prove successful, she might draw the knife and strike to kill instinctively if faced in a hostile manner by the woman she had no doubt was partly responsible for the death of the kindly head of the Ambagasali Research Project.

'I'm coming with you!' Beryl stated. Seeing Dawn look around, she went on in a tone of grim finality. 'I *am* and arguing will only let her get further away.'

Accepting the inevitable and appreciating the validity of the second statement, the girl started the Land Rover moving!

Although Laurence had not driven at any speed while looking for elephants, a fear of capture caused her to abandon her previous caution. A second consideration for the leisurely pace had been frequent reminders from Holmes to avoid bursting open the containers holding the seeds for future crops of *marijuana*, with which they had hoped to ensure co-operation from the Marxist authorities in Balinganda. Glancing over her shoulder and seeing she was being pursued drove all such considerations from her mind. The African who had shot her companion was no longer in the other vehicle, but she remembered how the two women had dealt with her party during the disastrous visit to their camp. Even if they did not have any weapons, they were certain to be able to overpower her should they be granted an opportunity to do so. After she was taken prisoner, aware of what her own reaction would be under similar circumstances, she felt certain the trio whom she and Holmes had abandonned at *Tembo Niguu* would seek to lay the full responsibility for the death of the Professor so as to try to save themselves.

With such considerations in mind, the red head kept her foot down on the accelerator and accepted the jolts caused by the rapid progress of the Land Rover as it sped across the savannah. These decreased in violence as she reached an area of more level and open ground. What was more, despite a glance to the rear informing her that her pursuers were gradually closing the gap, she saw the reddish-brown earth of a *safari* bus track ahead. Reaching it, she turned in the direction which she felt sure would lead to the border with Balinganda.

'Now we've *got* her!' Dawn declared with satisfaction, watching what the red head was doing.

'She's still going towards the border,' Beryl replied, having studied maps of the Reserve and possessing an excellent sense of direction acquired by traversing the large area of range in Texas which comprised her ranch. 'And she might get across it before we catch up with her.'

'Not on *this* track,' the girl denied, swinging the Game Department's Land Rover so it was following the other vehicle along the red *murram* surface. 'It turns at Crocodile Point and goes back to the Tangana River *Safari* Camp.'

'Crocodile Point?' Beryl queried.

'It's an almost sheer slope above the river on this side,' Dawn explained, trying to coax more speed from the swiftly moving Land Rover. 'The Game Department allow the *Safari* Camp's staff to throw in carcasses of animals too old for human consumption so as to keep crocodiles in the vicinity to make sure the tourists get photographs. That's it, where the white marker posts are.'

Seeing several stones painted white flanking where the track she was following turned right, Laurence gave a hiss of satisfaction as she drew an erroneous conclusion. In addition to having been too lazy to acquire more than fragmentary information respecting the anatomy and ways of elephants, she was just as poorly informed about the local geography. Nevertheless, she believed salvation was at hand. According to what little she remembered about the latter subject, due to the absence of clearly defined physical features such as a river, the dividing line between Ambagasali and Balinganda was designated in such a fashion. Therefore, she decided that she had almost reached it and her escape was secured. Glancing in the rearview mirror, she was satisfied there was no way the pursuers could catch up with her before she crossed. Knowing that the Marxist government across the border took the gravest exception to any intrusion upon its territory, she felt sure the tawny haired girl would not chance causing a diplomatic incident by following her.

Nor did the red head draw any conclusions from being unable to discern what was immediately beyond the markers. More of the rolling and fairly open savannah spread ahead where she could see, which she took as an indication that it could be reached by descending a slope as yet not in view. As she was approaching, satisfied all was well, she paid no attention to a signpost towards which she was heading and gave no thought to the fact that the track curved past it. However, drawing closer, she instinctively read what was printed on its white surface in somewhat faded—but still legible—red letters.

'CROCODILE POINT
BEWARE
DO NOT GO BEYOND
THE MARKER POSTS'

Even as her *marijuana*-slowed mind began to appreciate the message, it was too late for Laurence to act upon its warning. Belatedly appreciating that the land immediately beyond the edge of the rim fell at a much steeper angle than she had envisaged, she tried to avert the disaster. Applying the foot and hand brakes, she wrenched at the steering-wheel in a desperate attempt to turn aside as the nose of the Land Rover was passing between two of the markers. Travelling at around seventy miles per hour, there was no time for either measure to take effect before the vehicle tipped forward and commenced its plunge down the close to perpendicular slope. Striking a rock and flipping over, with a crash which drowned out her screams, its top smashed on to the unyielding surface. Having her torso crushed against the steering-wheel, she was killed as the rolling motion continued. In addition to bursting open the knapacks and dislodging the contents, two containers of the *Canabis Sativa* seeds being thrown out of the back to burst open on the ground, another impact ruptured the fuel feed pipe. The contents of the petrol tank ignited and turned the vehicle, along with the remainder of its cargo of potential misery and suffering, into a blazing mass which plunged into the deep pool formed in the river at that point.

Bringing the Game Department's Land Rover to a rubber-squealing stop just short of the marker posts, Dawn thrust herself from its cab. Looking down, she was just in time to see several large crocodiles which had been basking upon the bank at the other side plunging into the water. Descending just as quickly, Beryl darted around the bonnet to catch her by the arm as she began to move forward.

'Where do you think you're going?' the blonde demanded, as the tawny haired beauty tried to shake off her grasp.

'Down there!' Dawn replied, gesturing with her free hand to where a cloud of steam was rising from the churned up surface of the river. 'She must be trapped—!'

'She'd be dead before she reached the water!' Beryl assessed, without relinquishing her hold and feeling sure the red headed conservationist would not have shown any such concern if their positions had been reversed. 'And, even if she isn't, you'd be killed by the crocodiles if you went into the water after her. They've become accustomed to living on the food which is thrown into the river from the Point here and that's how they'll regard *everything* edible, dead or alive, they find down there. Strong and capable as he is Bunduki couldn't survive down there with just a knife for protection, nor even Lord Greystoke for that matter, and I'm not good enough with the elephant gun to be able to keep them off you.'

'You're right, I suppose,' Dawn conceded, stopping her attempts to get free and do something her own instincts had already warned would be futile and might end in her own death. Waiting until the surface of the pool settled down, without any sign of Laurence emerging from the wrecked vehicle, she went on, 'All we can do now is collect *Mbili Mbogo* and the chap he shot, then let Sergeant Matsuni know what's happened.'

Boarding the Land Rover, the tawny haired girl drew what consolation she could from knowing the killers of Professor Wilbraham had met no worse fate than had been warranted by their actions. What she did not know, until the *Canabis Sativa* seeds were found on the slope and the surviving trio of conservationists sought exculpation for their part in the attempt to create anti-hunting propaganda by telling the full story—blaming their dead colleagues for the arrival of the consignment and the purpose to which it was to be put—was that Ambagasali had again escaped a plot to inflict upon its population the curse of addiction to narcotics.

175

PART FOUR

WOMAN DEPUTY ALICE FAYDE
In
NO MAN ABOUT THE HOUSE

'Howdy there, Miss Fayde!' greeted the greyish-haired and thickset patrolman, his leathery brown face having a welcoming smile as he bent towards the open window of the Fort Mustang. On seeing it approaching, he had stepped into the centre of the street and given a wave which caused it to be brought to a halt. In addition to bearing the medal ribbons awarded for military campaigns and denoting departmental citations, the shirt of his dark blue uniform had badges indicating several years' service in the Gusher City Police Department on its sleeves. While his manner was redolent of politeness and respect, this was not caused by his being aware that—as a deputy of the Rockabye County Sheriff's Office—the woman he was addressing had the equivalent rank to a lieutenant in the Patrol Bureau. Rather it was an attitude arising from knowing her to be a very competent peace officer, who had earned her rank by the effective manner in which she carried out her duties. 'You've surely moved *pronto* on this one.'

'*This one*?' Woman Deputy Alice Fayde queried, throwing a quick look to where four black and white radio patrol cars of the G.C.P.D. were standing at the right side of the street. Then, looking at the man who had caused her to stop and who was opening the door with an air of expecting her to alight, she picked up the bulky brown Pete Ludwig shoulder bag—which was specially designed for use by female peace officers—from beside her on the front passenger seat and continued, 'I don't like the way you said *that*. What "*this one*" are you talking about?'

Leaving the vehicle Alice, by any standards, presented a picture pleasing to the masculine gaze. While she could not be termed ravishingly beautiful, her red hair—having grown again to a suitable length, after circumstances had caused it to be cropped short, for a return to the 'flip' style she preferred[1]—framed a face which was very good looking and suggested considerable strength of will. Despite being of a casual nature, the attire she had on did little to conceal the fact that her five foot seven inches tall figure was graced with well formed 'vital statistics' of 'thirty-seven, twenty-five, thirty-five'. What was more, the nature of her clothing gave an indication that her curvaceous contours were firmly fleshed and she kept herself in excellent physical condition.

The time was just after nine o'clock on Sunday morning and, making the most of not being engaged upon a case, Alice was taking the weekend off duty. However, under the regulations laid down by the Rockabye County Department of Public Safety—which controlled and administered the local law enforcement agencies—she was required to have a handgun with her even when not on watch. Therefore, before leaving her apartment, she had placed her Colt Commander .45 calibre automatic pistol in the removable holster supplied with the shoulder bag—which was also equipped with receptacles for handcuffs and other items she might require in the line of duty—she used unless she was working undercover.

Normally, being on much closer terms than merely as members of an investigation team in the Sheriff's Office, the red head and her partner, Deputy Sheriff Bradford 'Brad' Counter, would have spent their leisure time together.[2] However, as he was very keen on improving his

---

1. *Why Woman Deputy Alice Fayde had her hair cut is told in*: RUN FOR THE BORDER.
2. *How Alice Fayde and Brad Counter developed a much closer relationship than just working together as an investigation team is described in*: THE 1/4 SECOND DRAW.

skill with all kinds of police firearms, he had gone to El Paso to represent the Rockabye County Sheriff's Office in a combat pistol shooting competition. Appreciating how the possession of competence was of vital importance to a peace officer, she shared his interest and had acquired the rating of 'Expert' on the exacting firearms' training course—intended to instil a thorough knowledge of how to handle various types of combat situations, rather than concentrating upon formal target shooting—at which the Department of Public Safety required all local peace officers to qualify each month. Although her ability was of such a high standard that she too had been invited to compete at El Paso, wanting to catch up on some housework, she had elected to remain at home.

However, instead of making a start at her chores immediately after she had had her breakfast, Alice had donned a blue towelling headband, a loose fitting grey sweater, the dark blue trousers from a track suit, white ankle socks and white rubber soled jogging shoes. Dressed in this fashion, she was driving to a gymnasium and 'keep fit' centre her cousin, Hazel Holiday, owned in the Evans Hill District. It was her intention to have a more thorough physical training workout than was often possible due to the irregular hours required by her duties. Seeing four 'black and whites' by the side of the street, two facing in each direction, had suggested to her that they had met so the crews could have a conversation. Being aware that Lombard Crescent was a very law abiding neighbourhood, she had decided such a concentration of official vehicles implied there might be some serious trouble. Her supposition had been given strength by the oldest of the patrolmen having stepped into the centre of the street and, as she had misconstrued the wave he had given as a salutation, signalling for her to stop.

'You mean you haven't come from the Sheriff's Office?' the patrolman inquired, finding nothing unusual about the way the red head was dressed as he was aware that the deputies—who performed the functions of a

Homicide squad in Gusher City[3]—generally wore civilian clothing of one kind or another when on duty.

'No,' Alice denied. 'I'm off watch.'

'When I saw it was your Mustang coming, I couldn't figure out how you'd got here so soon after I'd called in,' the patrolman admitted. 'And I was wondering where Brad Counter was.'

'Showing *better* sense than it seems I am, Mr. O'Malley,' Alice said wryly, reading the name tag above the left breast pocket of the "harness bull's" dark blue shirt. They had never worked together, but she remembered often having seen him riding a black and white or patrolling on foot when passing through Evans Hill and she felt sure his memory was just as good. Therefore, she was not in the least surprised by him having recognized her private vehicle and knowing the identity of her regular partner. Realizing that—despite being technically off duty—she would be required to take charge if the matter was of extreme urgency, instead of waiting for the arrival of whichever team of deputies was sent by the Day Watch Commander at the Sheriff's Office, a brisker tone came into her voice and she continued, 'What's doing?'

'It could be something we'd rather do without,' the patrolman replied and jerked his thumb towards an unoccupied private vehicle a short distance away. 'My partner and I were cruising along here and found that heap, but the fellers who'd been in it've gone and not too long ago.'

'They must be real *heavy* for you to have called so much back-up,' the red head suggested with a pointed look at the four r.p.'s. 'And for a team from the Sheriff's Office.'

'Heavy enough, by all accounts,' O'Malley admitted and his tone became bitter. 'They pulled a multiple homicide at Sergeant Dan's Diner over on the county line. Were

3. *Information regarding the way in which the Rockabye County Sheriff's Office in the county seat, Gusher City, operated is described in* APPENDIX TWO.

four of them involved, according to the fry-cook, who they didn't know was around.'

'Was Dan there?' Alice asked, knowing the man in question was a retired soldier who had won the Congressional Medal of Honour in Korea and was well liked throughout the county.

'Yeah!' the patrolman confirmed grimly. 'From what I heard, the bastards who downed him were saying out loud what murderous sons-of-bitches our boys in 'Nam are and spicing it with real foul language. You know how he felt about 'Nam, seeing his boy was killed out there. And he never took to cussing in his place, 'specially when there were women and kids about.

'And there were women and children about?' the red head inquired, but the words were more of a statement.

'A woman and her three young 'uns,' O'Malley answered. 'Well, Dan told the yoyos to clean up their talk or get out. One of 'em yelled, 'Go to hell, you murdering redneck son-of-a-bitch!' and hauled a Uzi out of the knapsack he'd got with him. He started shooting and the others joined him at it. They didn't stop until they'd blown Dan, the woman and her kids away and shot the hell out of his picture wearing the Big One and a N.R.A. poster that were on the wall. Then they emptied the cash register and took this heap because their own had all but worn through two tyres. Must have hid out somewhere until this morning, then came back through town. Only it ran out of gas here not too long back and they've lit a shuck on foot.'

'Well now, just look who's here,' Alice said quietly, gesturing at a well dressed young man leaving a car which had just come to a halt a short distance to her rear. 'They may be even heavier than you expected, Mr. O'Malley.'

'You know him?' the patrolman inquired, also looking around.

'It's Andrew Wilson and he's only recently been assigned to the F.B.I.'s field office in town,' the red head replied. Although she too was angered by the report of what had happened at Sergeant Dan's Diner, her voice held a friendly timbre as she walked towards the new arrival. 'Hey there, Andy. I'd've thought you'd be *trying* to beat Brad at the combat shooting match in El Paso.'

'I decided I'd stay out and give somebody else a chance of winning,' the F.B.I. Special Agent answered, shaking hands. Then his voice took on a more serious tone. 'Looks like you could've got yourselves a problem here.'

'There's some might say that,' O'Malley drawled, but he too showed none of the animosity which practically every local law enforcement officer in the majority of the current television "cop" shows was potrayed as feeling towards members of the Federal Bureau Of Investigation. 'Four suspects in a multiple shooting dumped their wheels when they ran out of gas and, according to what we've heard, they *could* be hid up in a house down the street a ways.'

'Then I hope to God it isn't an *occupied* house,' Wilson said with quiet vehemence, before the patrolman could continue.

'It's *occupied*,' O'Malley stated grimly and gestured to where a youngster with a bicycle loaded with newspapers was talking to two of the patrolmen. 'The boy there said he saw a couple of men looking through the window while he was tossing the papers on to the porch of Number *Eighteen-Twenty*!'

'*Eighteen-Twenty*!' Alice repeated, with a similar emphasis.

'What makes *that* house different from the rest along here?' Wilson inquired, realizing the local officers had a knowledge of the area which he lacked.

'The Stenhart Sisters live there,' the red head replied, having grown up a few streets away from Lombard Crescent and being acquainted with the occupants of Eighteen-Twenty.

'Would that be the same Stenhart Sisters who keep showing up on old movies?' the F.B.I. Special Agent inquired.

'That's them,' O'Malley confirmed, before Alice could

speak. 'Only the movies aren't all that *old*. Fact being, I used to have the hots for Miss Amelia when I was in the Service.'

'Sorry,' Wilson apologised with a grin, noticing some of the medal ribbons on the patrolman's shirt were given for participation in campaigns during World War II.

'They were quite well known in their day and settled here when they retired,' Alice explained. 'They aren't really sisters, but everybody calls them by their stage name. And, unless things have changed since I was a kid selling girl scout cookies with Cousin Hazel around here, their's is the only house on Lombard which doesn't have at least one man in it.'

'It still *might* not have any men in it,' O'Malley claimed. 'I went along there and knocked. Miz Emmy-Mae answered and I told her what the kid reckoned he'd seen. When I asked her if they'd got any visitors or workmen in, she said they hadn't.'

'But you think she might not be telling the truth?' Alice guessed.

'I dunno and that's a fact,' the patrolman answered. 'Hell, I know Miz Emmy-Mae always looks and acts like the kind of dumb and fluttery Southern gal she used to play when they were doing their act, but I can't see her lying to us. Trouble is, the boy still says he's certain he saw two fellers' faces and there's no way the bunch who left that heap could have got by all our cars on foot without us seeing them, and their chances aren't much better if they've stolen another set of wheels. Soon as I called, Cen-Con put out an A.P.B. to check everybody found walking in the neighbourhood who fitted their descriptions, even if alone, and to start eye-balling every heap with four fellers in it that goes by to make sure it isn't them.'[4]

'Is the boy *sure* it was *men* he saw?' Wilson asked.

---

4. *'Cen-Con': Central Control, the permanently manned radio station operated by the Gusher City Police Department's Bureau of Communications and capable of transmitting to all parts of Rockabye County.*

4a. *'A.P.B': an 'all points bulletin'.*

'Allowed one had a moustache,' O'Malley replied. 'Which's how come he noticed 'em.'

'Would he be reliable?' the Special Agent inquired.

'I'd say so,' the patrolman estimated. 'I've known him since he was in diapers and I don't see him making up something like that just to give us the runaround.'

'Then they could have got into the house and forced Miz Emmy-Mae to lie by holding guns on her sisters,' the red head assessed. She sensed that Wilson, like herself, was willing to accept the summation regarding the boy and did not doubt both men had reached an identical solution. 'The way she always acts, they'd think she wasn't smart enough to try to tip you off, but her sisters might have been.'

'That's the way it hit me,' O'Malley conceded. 'And, in which case, could be *we've* got us a hostage situation on our hands!'

'That's how it looks to me,' Alice agreed, having noticed the emphasis placed on the word "*we've*" by the leathery featured patrolman. With a sensation much as if she had been touched by an ice cold hand, she realized that he accepted her appointment as a woman deputy from the Sheriff's Office in the city made her the senior local peace officer present. Therefore, as nobody else from her department had arrived—regardless of a member of a law enforcement agency with country-wide jurisdiction being on the scene and in spite of her being off watch—she must take at least the preliminary steps for dealing with the situation. 'What do we know about the fellers from the car?'

'Not much beyond their descriptions and what went down at the Diner,' the patrolman replied. 'According to the report Buck Shields sent in from Euclid,[5] they took off west over the county line after they'd looted the cash

5. *Deputy Sheriff Buck Shields, First Deputy in charge of the Sheriff's Sub-Office at Euclid. Some details of his career can be found in*: THE 1/4 SECOND DRAW *and* POINT OF CONTACT.

register. There was nothing to suggest they'd double back into town, but B.M.V. put the description of the car on the "hot sheet" as a matter of routine.[6] I called in when I found it and Cen-Con'll have relayed the word to the Sheriff's Office. That's why I thought *you'd* come, you being a deputy.'

'That I am,' the red head admitted wryly. 'Damn it! Some days it doesn't pay to get out of bed. *Why* didn't I go with Brad to El Paso?' After her rhetorical question had brought smiles of sympathy to the faces of her audience, she went on, 'Can I use your car's radio to check in with the Office, please?'

'Feel free,' O'Malley assented.

'Ian Grantley and Dave Bulpin are on their way here,' the red head announced after having made the call. 'But, when he heard what you'd said about the chance of those yoyos being at the Stenhart's place, Mac McCall kindly *asked* me to handle things until they arrive.'

'I wonder if he took his hat off when he *asked* you?' O'Malley drawled dryly, referring to First Deputy Angus "Mac" McCall's habit of so rarely removing his head-dress there was a legend among the local peace officers that he slept with it on. 'What do you want doing, ma'am?'

'Just who are *they*, Andy?' Alice inquired, instead of replying to the patrolman's question.

'Four real *fine* specimens of "liberal" humanity who'd be the heroes of almost every television movie,' Wilson replied. 'Martin Young, Bernard Grant, Peter Hill and Paul Donovan. They were draft dodgers who went to Canada claiming their beliefs wouldn't allow them to take another human being's life and, like others of their kind, spent enough of their time on Trudeau's Turf at one of the training camps for urban guerillas that were set up there to have learned how to handle firearms and kill people with

6. *'B.M.V.': the Gusher City Police Department's Bureau of Motor Vehicles.*

bombs. Although we haven't had any reports to prove they've done anything *active* along those lines since they came back after the amnesty, they've been on the fringes of several incidents and know enough for us to consider it might be informative to get our hands on them. Word got to us that they were coming from San Francisco to Houston to take part in a big Gay Rights parade and we've been looking for them ever since.'

'Are they queers?' O'Malley asked, sounding as if he was expecting an answer in the affirmative.

'As a three dollar bill,' Wilson replied. 'All of them.'

'Then, if all they're going to do is join a Gay Rights parade, why the hell would they want all the fire-power?' the patrolman queried, anticipating the point Alice was about to raise. 'Decent folks might not take kind' to them marching the streets, but not bad enough for them to figure they'll need a Uzi and a riot gun for protection. It's only their kind's use violence to try to stop folks doing things they don't agree with.'

'I'll go along with you on that,' Wilson affirmed. 'But I'm damned if I can guess the answer. Our informant never mentioned anything about them being armed, but having the guns along explains why they're travelling by car instead of flying.'

'You warned the Sheriff and Chief Hogan they were on their way?' Alice remarked, but—in spite of the repeated suggestions made on numerous television "cop" shows that the F.B.I. adopted a policy of non-cooperation when dealing with local peace officers—the words were a statement and not a question.

'We passed word that they *might* come through Gusher City as Grant used to live here and asked for a watch to be kept and us to be informed if they were seen,' Wilson replied. 'Nothing had been said about them having the guns, so that was all we felt was needed. As far as we *know*, despite rumours that they've kept up their training with firearms, they've *never* done anything heavy until now. The worst they've had is a few busts for possession and creating a disturbance while under the influence of narcotics. That's how we got hold of their mug sheets and, although they've shortened their hair and got rid of their beards according to the witness, I was able to identify them by their fingerprints when Buck sent samples from the diner. B.M.V. called me when you checked in about the car, Mr. O'Malley, so I came straight over to let you know what you might be up against.'

'We heard they'd used a Uzi and sawed off riot gun at the diner, as well as a couple of handguns, and the fry cook reckoned they looked like they could've been high on something stronger than just grass,' the patrolman stated. 'But we're obliged for the warning. How do we play it, Miss Fayde?'

'*Carefully*,' Alice answered, setting her memory to work to recollect the lie of the land. A glance had already informed her that none of the vehicles could be seen from the house, due to the curve which had given Lombard Crescent its name. 'You've got the back covered from Adrian Street?'

'That I have,' O'Malley confirmed, gratified by noticing the inquiry was made more in the fashion of a statement from one who felt sure he would have taken the precaution. 'And, should they try to go out through the back of the Stenhart's and the garden of the house behind, they'll meet up with a Dobermann dog that's been trained real good for guard work. How much more back-up are you figuring on calling in?'

'I don't know yet,' Alice admitted, then looked along the street. 'Anyways, it's out of *my* hands now. Ian and Dave are here. They'll decide after they've had a chance to eye-ball the situation.'

'Maybe you'll get your day off watch after all,' O'Malley commented, also glancing in the direction of an approaching official vehicle which had the colour scheme and insignia of the Sheriff's Office.

'*Maybe*,' the red head answered. 'But I wouldn't want to take a bet on it.'

*   *   *

'Why hello, my dear,' greeted the woman whose professional name had been "Emmy-Mae Stenhart", opening the front door of 1820 Lombard Crescent in answer to the ring on the bell. 'It's *Hazel Holiday* from over on Mulberry Drive, isn't it?'

'Yes,' Woman Deputy Alice Fayde lied. She was alert to the possibility that, if the men responsible for the multiple homicides at Sergeant Dan's Diner were present, her name and official status might be known to the one who had lived in the Evans Hill District. Between deep breaths, she continued, 'I hope that you don't mind me dropping by, but I'm jogging and shouldn't have had that second cup of coffee with my breakfast. I know it's an imposition, but will you let me use your bathroom?'

The arrival of Deputy Sheriffs Ian Grantley and David Bulpin had not ended the red head's participation in the affair to which she had inadvertantly become involved!

Nor, despite her earlier comments about being off watch, had Alice any genuine wish to leave the scene!

Taking charge because he was the senior local peace officer on the scene, having served longer with the Sheriff's Office than Alice, Grantley had wasted no time in acquainting himself with the situation. The first thing he had declared was, regardless of what 'Miz Emmy-Mae' had told Patrolman O'Malley, they must act upon the assumption that the four men were on the premises. All the peace officers had realized that an answer in the affirmative would mean their troubles were only beginning. Should the men be there, they knew the ideal solution would be to get some of their number inside the house without their arrival being detected. There was, O'Malley had warned, one major barrier to this. The owner of the property behind 1820 Lombard Crescent would have been willing to prevent his Dobermann pinscher dog from raising the alarm while they were approaching from the rear. However, there was a window on that side of the sitting-room through which the officers might be seen. Even if this did not happen, it might prove impossible to effect a

187

sufficiently silent entry to prevent putting the lives of the three women in dire jeopardy. A few months earlier, during a series of burglaries in which violence was frequently used against the victims, the sisters had acted upon his advice by having installed a very efficient alarm system covering every door and window.

Commenting with a wry grin at the grizzled patrolman that *some* people did not make life any easier, Grantley had agreed with Alice when she claimed her sex, the way in which she was dressed, and her earlier acquaintance with the Stenhart Sisters made her the most suitable person present to visit them in the hope of discovering whether they were being compelled to supply a hiding place for the quartet. He had known she was fully aware of the dangers entailed by the plan she proposed, but he could not think of anything offering a better chance of success and he felt confident of her ability to cope with whatever situation might arise.

Silently thanking the circumstances which had caused her to be dressed in a fashion offering a reason for gaining admittance, the red head had made preparations for what she and all the men knew could prove a hazardous assignment. Aware that the longer the delay, the greater chance of something happening to alert the quartet to the danger of discovery, they had decided against waiting for the Bureau of Communications to deliver a suitably small battery operated microphone which could have been hidden on her person and allow whatever was said in her presence to be heard by the other officers. However, although she would be leaving behind her Pete Ludwig shoulder bag, she was not going on the assignment unarmed. She had tucked the Colt Commander automatic pistol into the waistband at the rear of her trousers so it was concealed beneath the loose fitting sweater and had taken other measures to prevent her purpose being suspected.

By the time Alice reached the two storey house owned by the Stenhart Sisters, she presented a sight which gave credence to the explanation for her visit. In addition to sucking in breaths as if from the exertion of exercise, her hair and face were suitably damp. Only the latter had happened while she was coming along the street from where she had left her companions. Wanting to give the impression of having covered a greater distance, her sweater was darkened by what appeared to be perspiration. However, as was the case with her red locks, the effect had been produced by the judicious application of water.

Having made her approach on the sidewalk as if doing nothing more than jogging, Alice had turned through the gate in the white picket fence. While going along the short path, she had given the four windows at the front of the building a very careful examination. The boy had claimed to have seen the masculine faces at the right side window on the ground floor. Nevertheless, she subjected those upstairs to a scrutiny without detecting anything to suggest a watch was being kept from them. Returning her gaze to the ground floor, she found her view inside was restricted in each case by the Venetian blinds with which they were fitted being closed. However, while her own vision was restricted, she could not detect any sign of the horizontal flaps of either being parted sufficiently to allow anybody to be looking out and she felt sure she had arrived without being seen.

There had been a delay before Emmy-Mae had opened the front door in response to Alice ringing its bell, but it was not of a sufficient duration to be proof of anything. Nor did the woman's appearance on coming into view provide any indication of whether all was well. About an inch shorter than the red head, she had greyish-blonde curly hair and was slender. As had always been the case when they met, she looked, dressed and spoke much like the late Billie Burke, a comedienne who had also made a speciality in potraying one possessed of a fluttery and less than intelligent nature.

'Well, I don't kn—!' Emmy-Mae began, glancing to the

right across the entrance hall towards the double doors of what the visitor remembered was the main sitting-room that stretched from the front to the rear of the house.

'It is quite *urgent*,' Alice claimed, giving a good impersonation of one who had need to make use of the facility she had mentioned without delay. 'And I don't know anybody else around here to ask.'

'Then you *must* come in, dear,' the woman assented. Closing the door after having allowed the red head to enter, she led the way along the hall. 'But I do hope you won't be *too* long. My sisters have already left for *St. Xavier's* and *Father Donoghue* gets so *cross* if I'm late.'

'I'll be as quick as I can,' Alice promised.

Following the slender woman along the hall, the red head continued to study her surroundings without making her scrutiny noticeable. Everything was as she recollected from the visits she and her cousin had paid in their 'teens. As she was passing, she noticed that the double doors of the sitting-room were open about an inch. Although she could not see anybody through the gap, she had the sensation of being watched. However, she decided against making any attempt to discover whether the feeling was justified. Because the Venetian blind had been drawn at the rear window as well as the front and the lights were not on, the large room was poorly illuminated. Therefore, most of its interior and the staircase she knew led to the second floor at the back side were beyond her range of vision and, if the men were there, they would almost certainly be scattered around it. Therefore, remembering the lessons she had learned while taking instruction in how to deal with combat situations, she realized that trying to enter without knowing what was inside could prove fatal for herself and the Sisters if her supposition was correct.

'Let me make sure everything is *tidy*, dear,' Emmy-Mae suggested on arriving at the entrance to the bathroom. Going in, she emerged after a couple of seconds. 'There. It's all ready for you.'

Entering the bathroom, Alice pushed the door closed.

Glancing around, at first sight, she saw nothing to suggest there was a genuine need for her visit. She had hoped, if there was some form of duress being applied to prevent her being informed verbally, Emmy-Mae would take the opportunity to write a message while inside. However, no such information was supplied and, apart from a couple of cigarette butts which had been stubbed out by grinding them with a foot against the floor, everything was neat and tidy. On the point of leaving, as there was some truth in the reason she had given to gain admittance, she decided to take advantage of the opportunity to relieve herself. Reaching towards the raised lid of the toilet, even as her hand touched it, she was struck by a thought.

Not only had the cover been lifted back, presumably by whoever used the toilet last, but the seat was also raised!

Removing the Colt from her waistband and laying it on the side of the bath without making a sound, Alice did what was necessary to make use of the toilet. While doing so, she gave consideration to the position in which she had found the seat. Unless it had been left that way when it was being cleaned, there was no other reason for a *woman* to raise it. Yet Emmy-Mae had told O'Malley there were no men on the premises.

Replacing the seat and sitting down, the red head carried out the secondary reason for the visit. However, instead of standing up at the conclusion, she bent and retrieved the cigarette butts. One sniff informed her that the contents of both was not tobacco. Even without the way in which they had been discarded, instead of being placed in the ashtray on top of the cistern, she would have known they had not been smoked by any of the Sisters. Although they had been in show business since they were children, none had ever used *marijuana*. In fact, she remembered how all three had stressed their repugnance for the habit and warned Hazel and herself of the dangers of indulging on several occasions.

Much of modern law enforcement work was a matter of receiving information from 'stool pigeons', awaiting reports of the findings made by technicians such as pathologists, fingerprint specialists and other experts, or checking files held by various agencies. Nevertheless, there were still occasions when there was a need for deductive reasoning by the officer conducting the investigation. Being aware of this, Jack Tragg insisted upon all his deputies—especially those who worked out of the Sheriff's Office in Gusher City—possessing a flair for remembering conservations and relating them to what had been, or was being seen. One of the reasons Alice had gained promotion was that she had the requisite trait and now she began to put it to use.

Starting from what she had seen while approaching the house, the red head concluded the condition of the Venetian blinds could be significant. Although this could have been nothing more than a measure taken to prevent the sun shining into the front rooms, she felt sure O'Malley would have commented if they had been closed when he paid his visit. That Emmy-Mae should have mistaken her for her cousin would not have struck most people as being out of character. Not only was Hazel's picture used on the advertizement for her gymnasium in the local newspapers, but Alice had appeared in television news items several times and this might have led to the confusion. Yet she recollected the noticeable emphasis put upon the name. There had been a similar accentuation when the woman was explaining the absence of her 'sisters'. St. Xavier's was a Catholic church and, even if they had changed from the Episcopalian beliefs they—like herself— had followed when she was living in the area, she remembered that Father Donoghue had died a few weeks before in a traffic accident.

Many people would have considered the confusion was to be expected from Emmy-Mae, but Alice was not amongst their number!

Having portrayed the fluttery, vague and unintelligent role for so many years, it had become ingrained in the slender woman's everyday behaviour. Being better informed, the red head knew it was far from being her true nature. In real life, appearances not withstanding, Emmy-Mae was shrewd and perceptive. Sufficiently so, in fact, for Alice to believe that, having been identified correctly and the real purpose of her visit surmised, the 'mistaken identity' and other emphasised discrepancies were made deliberately to alert her to the presence of the men.

Standing up and adjusting her attire, Alice returned the black automatic pistol to its place of concealment. Then, having washed and dried her hands, she returned to the hall. Still there was no visible evidence to support her suppositions. However, she gave a slight nod and, just as briefly, opened her left hand to display the two cigarette butts she had picked up. Nothing showed on Emmy-Mae's face, but she made what appeared to be a fluttery gesture in the course of which her right forefinger pointed towards the patrially open double doors. At the same time, she bent her left thumb across her palm and spread the fingers open.

Nothing showed on Alice's face, but she drew an unpleasant conclusion from what she saw and deduced!

'Thank you, Miss Emmy-Mae,' the red head said, trying successfully to prevent any of her thoughts from being reflected in the timbre of her voice. Walking along the passage accompanied by the woman, without giving so much as a glance at the entrance to the sitting-room, she continued, 'If *Father Donoghue* gets annoyed, blame me for making you late and say I'll apologise in person at Evening Mass.'

'I will, dear, I will,' the slender woman promised, but her manner gave no indication of whether or not she had reached the desired conclusion from the suggestion. However, coming to a halt at the front entrance, she turned the knob of its Yale lock. Then, after a quick glance behind her, she pressed down the stud which prevented it from operating when the door was closed. 'And, as we have so *few* visitors, you will be sure to come to see us again before long, won't you?'

'You can count on *that*, Miss Emmy-Mae,' Alice promised, concluding from there being no reaction that the way in which the lock was being manipulated had not been seen by the men in the sitting-room. Then, glancing at the grandfather clock at the side of the door, she went on, 'Mercy, is *that* the time?'

'Yes,' the woman confirmed. 'Old Grandpappy is *never* wrong.'

'Then it's later than I thought,' the red head declared. 'Could I go out the back and cut through your garden on to Adrian Street, please? That way I can get home quicker.'

'I'm sorry, dear,' Emmy-Mae answered, sounding at her most flustered and bewildered. 'But Mildred has put on the alarm system and, although I know how to turn off the warning bell for the front door, she's *never* been able to teach me what to do with the rest of it.'

'Very well,' Alice said with a sigh, having elicited information regarding the state of the alarm system which she would rather have been otherwise. 'I'll just have to go the long way and hope my gentleman friend waits for me. Goodbye, Miss Emmy-Mae, and thank you.'

Leaving the house and listening to the door being closed behind her, the red head let out a long breath. There was no longer any doubt in her mind that the newsboy had been correct when claiming he had seen men inside. The problem which now had to be faced was how to bring about their removal without endangering the lives of the three female occupants.

Although Alice had never been actively involved in a situation involving the holding of hostages,[7] she was well versed in the theory for dealing with such an eventuality. Before leaving her companions, a basic contingency plan had been formulated. Being convinced that the quartet were on the premises, it now fell upon her to put the

7. *An occasion when such a situation arose is recorded in*: Case One, 'Hostages', THE LAWMEN OF ROCKABYE COUNTY.

scheme into operation. The first thing was for her to notify the other officers of what she had discovered.

What came next was likely to prove harder and vastly more dangerous for the red head and the Stenhart Sisters!

Furthermore, the success or failure of the rescue operation rested mainly upon the apparently vague and far from intelligent 'Miss Emmy-Mae'!

* * *   * * *

'She's gone,' Emmy-Mae Stenhart announced, returning to the sitting-room. Her normal fluttery demeanour was enhanced by a tone which implied fright and pleading as she went on in a louder voice than usual, 'I had to let her come in.'

'Who was she?' Bernard Grant demanded in his somewhat whining Mid-West accent, switching on the lights and following the slender woman as she went to the table. It was he who had stood, holding the Uzi submachine gun, against the slightly open double doors keeping watch on the entrance hall. 'And why the hell did she pick *here* to come for a piss?'

'Her name's Hazel Holiday,' Emmy-Mae replied. 'She and that *blonde haired* cousin of hers often used to come here selling girl scout cookies, didn't they, Mildred?'

'They did,' confirmed the woman to whom the question was directed, standing covered by the revolver in the hand of Paul Donovan in the far side front corner of the room where they were beyond the range of vision of anybody passing the doors.

Regardless of how they had been billed in the theatre, it seemed unlikely that there was a close family tie between the Stenhart Sisters!

Tallest of the three, 'Mildred Stenhart' had been the 'talking woman'—the female equivalent of the 'straight man' of a male comedy team—in the verbal portion of their act. Although her black hair was streaked with grey, her bulky frame gave signs of being firmly fleshed beneath the blouse and slacks she had on and she still moved

195

almost as lightly on her feet as when she had performed in their spectacular comedy adagio routines. Her good looking face had a grimly forbidding expression which was far from being her true nature, but neither it nor her deep contralto voice gave any sign of whether she had drawn the required inference from what she had heard since the arrival of the visitor.

Seated at the top of the staircase watched over by Martin Young—who was also armed with a revolver— from a few steps below, time had dealt kindly with 'Amelia Stenhart' and there was still sufficient evidence of why Patrolman O'Malley had developed 'the hots' for her when he was a newly inducted recruit in World War II. Of the three, she alone took measures to conceal any grey patches in her brunette hair. The judicious application of makeup ensured her beautiful features showed few traces of her age, and her figure, in a stylish dress, was still sufficiently well endowed and curvaceous to be worthy of masculine admiration. In the act, she had been a counter-balance between the zany behaviour of Emmy-Mae and Mildred's apparent efforts to bring sense and dignity to the performance.

None of the invaders of 1820 Lombard Crescent were related in any way, but—especially as they had had their hitherto shoulder long brownish hair and beards removed—there was a marked likeness about their appearance. All were tallish, lean and had sallow faces with hollow cheeks and sunken eyes indicative of the addication to narcotics which had led to their need to hide instead of continuing their journey to Houston. Having antagonized a couple of very prominent 'liberals' and being ordered to carry out an assignment by people they were in no position to refuse, they had obeyed their instructions to discard the 'hippy' attire they had worn in Canada and at San Francisco and now had on range style hats, open necked shirts, leather vests, Levi pants and sharp toed Western style boots. It was attire worn by a section of the community for which they felt a close to paranoic hatred and was selected as being most suited for their purpose.

Grant, who had trimmed the growth on his upper lip until it was in the fashion attributed to Emiliano Zapata,[8] had been responsible for the position in which the quartet now found themselves. It had been at his instigation that they had followed a route eastwards which entailed passing through Rockabye County. He had also suggested they stop for a meal at Sergeant Dan's Diner. Although the others had realized they must acquire some other means of transport, due to the tyres of their own being worn almost through, they had decided to do so at a lonely portion of the road where the theft would not be discovered for some time after it had taken place. Therefore, none of them had realized he had an ulterior motive for the selection and insistence upon taking with them the firearms issued for the assignment when they left their vehicle.

Nor was Grant recognized by the owner as one of three hippies he had given a thrashing to when they tried to assault him as he was returning alone to collect his car from a parking lot after he had been a leading speaker at a rally giving support to the American presence in Vietnam. However, the recipient had neither forgotten nor forgiven the painful treatment he had suffered. Although he had been no more enamoured than the others of the task they were being compelled to perform in Houston, knowing it was far more risky than anything else they had done, he had seen how he might turn it to his advantage.

Putting to use his remembrance of how Sergeant Dan thought on certain subjects, Grant had deliberately steered the conversation at their table in a way which he felt sure would supply him with an excuse for what he meant to do. Nor, particularly as he had heard them speaking with the accents of Texans, was he turned from his purpose by the sight of the woman and her children.

8. *Emiliano Zapata; Mexican revolutionary leader between 1911–16, much respected by 'liberals' for his beliefs.*

Instead, he had considered their presence would be even more certain to provoke the response he required from the owner. He had not doubted that his companions would follow his lead when they discovered they were in the presence of one who—having won the supreme award for gallantry given by the United States during the Korean War and, as was proved by the insignia of the National Rifle Association prominently displayed, obviously supported the continuation of private ownership of firearms—was anathema to their beliefs. What was more, in addition to having kept 'high' himself on the supply of cocaine they had brought with them, he had made certain the others were in a similar condition.

Although Young and Donovan had had their revolvers concealed in the back of the waistbands of their trousers, Grant and Peter Hill carried the more potent weapons they had received in small knapsacks. When Sergeant Dan had taken exception to their foul mouthed conservation, it only needed Grant to produce and start firing the Uzi to induce the others to follow his lead. Nor, in their narcotic inflamed state, had they needed his command to kill the other occupants of the room to avoid leaving witnesses. With their victims down and the offending picture and poster marked by bullets, none of them had thought to check if there was anybody else in the building. Instead, after Grant had looted the till, they had left.

Boarding the car in which the woman and her children had arrived from Gusher City, they had covered a couple of miles before Grant realized the driver, Donovan, had set of in the direction its hood was pointing and they were almost at the county line. Turning back, they had passed the Diner when they had seen the flashing red lights of two official vehicles speeding towards them. Fortunately for them, they had been driving without lights and, by turning along a small side road through a patch of scrub oaks, had avoided being seen by the deputy sheriffs hurrying in response to the telephone call from the fry-cook they had not known was in the building.

Concluding that the authorities had been informed of what they had done, as they could not think of any other reason for the use of red lights, wailing sirens and the speed at which the vehicles were travelling in the direction of the Diner, there had been an acrimonious discussion between the quartet. Being unaware that there was a living and uninjured witness, each of them was determined not to accept the blame for the failure to make sure all their victims were dead before leaving. However, having taken into account that Grant was nursing his Uzi had prevented the other three from pointing out he had provoked the incident and was the first to open fire. Having been just as disinclined to have the matter mentioned, he had turned the debate to what they should do next.

Although Donovan had suggested they should use what they had done as an excuse not to go to Houston, he found no support from his companions. They were all of the opinion that, should it prove necessary for them to seek refuge in a country with a sympathetic government which would refuse a request for their extradition, they could only count upon the assistance of the influential 'liberals' who had given them their instructions if those instructions had been carried out. The next point facing them was the safest route to their destination. Remembering how they had set off the wrong way on their departure from the Diner, Grant had suggested any search would be made in the direction of the county line. However, while this had proved to be the case, it had been decided unanimously to remain in their place of concealment until the following morning when there would be more traffic on the road.

Having stayed where they were through the hours of darkness without interference, the four men had remained unchallenged on the drive to the Evans Hill District of Gusher City. When the car had run out of petrol, despite believing the police did not suspect they were in the vicinity, they had felt it would be most inadvisable for them to try and steal a replacement in such a residential location during daylight. Nor had they been any better enamoured of the prospect of walking the streets, particularly as Grant and Hill had left behind the knapsacks which would otherwise have served to hide their weapons. However, fortune still seemed to be favouring them. Having lived in the area prior to becoming a draft dodger, Grant had recognized his surroundings and, remembering who lived at 1820 Lombard Cresent, he claimed they would find a safe refuge there until night came.

Keeping the Uzi and sawed-off pump action shotgun concealed as best they could and taking the rest of their belongings with them, the quartet had not seen anybody as they walked the short distance from the abandoned vehicle to their destination. They had gained admittance when Emmy-Mae had come to the door in the belief that its bell was being rung by the boy who delivered the newspapers and often called on Sunday morning to discuss the forthcoming week's activities at the club she and her 'sisters' ran for the local children. Grant and Donovan had not been aware that they had allowed themselves to be seen at the front window by the youngster as he was passing, instead of paying the expected call, because he had started late and been in a hurry to finish his work as his father was taking him on a trip.

On the arrival of Patrolman O'Malley, being convinced by her behaviour that Emmy-Mae would be too frightened and not sufficiently intelligent to betray them, Grant had sent her to find out the reason for the unwelcome visit. He had warned her that each of her 'sisters' would be covered by a weapon and made to move so far apart there would be no way their lives could be saved if the peace officer insisted upon entering and inspecting the dining-room. Although his companions had not been enamoured of the way in which he acted without consulting them, having their kind's resentment towards anybody who gave them even sensible orders, they had done as he said before she set off to carry out the instructions. Discovering their presence was at least suspected by the patrolman was most disconcerting for the four men, but they had been convinced he accepted the statement that only she and her 'sisters' were on the premises made by Emma-Mae. Nevertheless, after he had gone away, they had taken what they had considered to be the sensible precaution of drawing down and closing the Venetian blinds in all the first floor rooms. None of them had realized that, while doing so prevented them from being seen even accidentally by anybody passing the house, their range of vision outside was equally limited.

When the doorbell had rung again, the quartet had adopted similar tactics without attempting to ascertain who the latest arrival might be. Despite the second caller having been allowed access to carry out what they had heard was the purpose of the visit, they were satisfied that she was just a chance passer-by and had gone away without knowing they were on the premises.

'Why'd you take so long to come back?' Donovan demanded, spicing his words with profanities—a habit he shared with all his companions—but he was motivated less by suspicion than feeling it was time he did something to show he did not accept Grant was in sole control of the situation.

'I w—watched Miss Holiday until she was going along the sidewalk,' Emmy-Mae replied, still speaking louder than was absolutely necessary. 'I thought you would want me to, they always do in the movies.'

'What is she?' Hill asked, throwing aside the *marijuana* cigarette—which he and his companions smoked as a cheaper, albeit less effective, supplement for their addiction to sniffing cocaine—he was about to light and speaking for the same reason Donovan had asked the previous question.

'Who?' Emmy-Mae inquired.

'That Southern whore you let in, you god-damned stupid bitch!' Hill explained, raising his voice in asperity over the apparent simplicity of the slender woman.

'Sh—She owns a gymnasium,' Emmy-Mae replied.

'What the hell are *you* doing?' Grant demanded, swinging his gaze to where Donovan had walked away

201

from Mildred and was starting to part two of the vertical slats on the front window's Venetian blind.

'I'm going to see if everything's all right,' the recipient of the question answered sullenly, sharing his companions' resentment over the way in which his interrogator had been behaving as if in command of them.

'I said no—!' Grant began.

'There're two fellers coming along the sidewalk,' Donovan interrupted. 'And they look like pigs to me!'

'Let me see!' Grant spat out. Hurrying across the room, he elongated and peered through the gap. He had no difficulty in recognizing Deputy Sheriff David Bulpin, who had arrested two of his homosexual friends for possession of *marijuana* and, as he had deserted them just in time to avoid the same fate, had been responsible for his decision to leave Gusher City. After letting out a hiss of rage, he went on, 'They *are* pigs!'

'*What*?' Donovan gasped, only having made the suggestion in an attempt to justify his behaviour.

'I said they *are* pigs!' Grant bellowed. 'And, judging by the way they're eye-balling this place, that god-damned harness bull didn't believe her and's got them here.'

'Wh—What do we do?' Young yelped, turning his back on Amelia.

'We let them know we're holding these three old bitches as hostages!' Grant declared, before either of the other two men could speak. 'Get back and stick your piece in the gut of that fat whore and, if they turn in here, I'll tell them you're set to blow her away if they don't come up with *everything* we ask for!'

'*You* tipped off the pigs!' Hill snarled. His sallow face was working in fury that was three parts fear as he made the accusation. Glaring at and starting to raise the sawed-off riot gun with the intention of striking Emmy-Mae with its butt, he continued with even greater heat, 'God-damn you, I'll smash your stupid head in!'

*　　*　　*

202

Hearing what was being said in the dining-room, Woman Deputy Alice Fayde knew she must play the most dangerous part of her assignment!

After Emmy-Mae Stenhart had closed the front door behind her, the red head had gone along the path to the gate in the picket fence. A glance in each direction had informed her that rest of the plan made by herself and Deputy Sheriff Ian Grantley was progressing satisfactorily. Being clad in civilian clothing suitable for the neighbourhood, he and Deputy Sheriff David Bulpin were approaching openly along the sidewalk. Although neither Bernard Grant nor Paul Donovan noticed, they were followed at a short distance by Special Agent Andrew Wilson of the Federal Bureau of Investigation and two detectives from the Evans Hill Division who had arrived while the arrangements were being made. Nor was this all the assistance which would be available. Converging from both ends of the street, the uniformed patrolmen from Gusher City Police Department—half of whom were armed with more potent weapons such as riot guns, carried as standard equipment in their 'black and whites', to supplement the basically defensive handguns of the others—were passing across the gardens in front of the intervening houses.

In some parts of the city, particularly those occupied by 'trendy' middle class-middle management 'liberals', such an 'invasion of privacy' on the part of peace officers—no matter how justified by circumstances—would have aroused protests which might have been heard by the men responsible for it to be considered necessary. Being possessed of a firm belief in the maintenance of law and order, a simple statement that the officers were engaged upon official business was sufficient to induce silence on the part of the residents of Lombard Crescent whose property was being traversed. Nor, having a similar respect for members of the G.C.P.D., did the people on the other side of the street who saw what was happening offer to satisfy their curiosity by coming from their homes to either look closer or call questions.

Having made sure help to effect the rescue was at hand, Alice had raised and flexed her arms. It looked like the kind of limbering up exercise a jogger might perform, but was the pre-arranged signal to notify the male peace officers that she had ascertained the men were on the premises. As a precaution in case any of the quartet should be watching between the slats of the dining-room's closed Venetian blinds, she went out of the gate. Then, turning in the direction from which she had approached the building, she began to jog until satisfied she would no longer be within sight of a lookout's restricted range of vision. However, instead of waiting for the others to arrive, she had vaulted the picket fence and darted swiftly across the lawn. Keeping close to the front of the building, taking the precaution of crouching below the level of the sill while passing the kitchen window, even though she did not believe any of the men would be watching through it, she had reached and gained admission through the unlocked door.

On entering, holding her Colt Commander automatic pistol in both hands, with the safety catch in the firing position and right forefinger curled through the trigger-guard, the red head once again had been silently blessing the way in which she was dressed. The thick rubber bottoms of her jogging shoes allowed her to move in a silence which few other styles of footwear would have permitted and she had advanced along the hallway until she was standing outside the double doors to the dining-room without hearing anything to suggest her arrival had been detected. Showing the presence of mind which she had hoped for, Emmy-Mae had not closed them on returning from having seen her off the premises. Although she had not taken the chance of trying to look inside, she could hear the voices of some of its occupants clearly enough to have been able to form an idea of roughly where they were positioned.

If the rest of the plan for the operation had gone as was envisaged, Alice was to wait until the male peace officers had taken up their positions. Then, as soon as the two male deputies had joined her, the others would have literally burst into the house through its doors and windows, counting upon the commotion to confuse the four men for long enough to prevent them from taking cover behind and using the 'sisters' as shields. She was only to take action before Grantley and Bulpin arrived if their approach was detected, or something else which could not be foreseen was to happen. From what she had just heard, the need for her intervention had come. Accepting the inevitable, she drew a measure of consolation from two things. The first was the very thorough training in combat shooting given to all its officers by the Rockabye County Department of Public Safety and in which she was a qualified 'Expert'. Secondly and of equal importance was the knowledge she had of the three women being held hostage.

While she had confidence in her own ability, the red head was all too aware that the outcome of the affair depended in a great part upon whether the Stenhart Sisters justified her beliefs where they were concerned!

Stepping swiftly across the threshold of the dining-room, Alice brought her automatic to shoulder level and at arms' length. However, advantageous as it might have been for her to start shooting the moment she came into view, she knew she must not do so. Training and departmental regulations, produced to meet the standards of conduct required by a country whose government was imbued with a belief in the 'rights of the individual'—not excluding those who had failed to show a similar respect for the 'rights' of others—demanded that she gave the men an opportunity to surrender even, if by doing so, she forfeited the element of surprise and put her own life at risk.

'Peace officer here!' the red head shouted. '*Freeze*!'

While speaking, Alice was instinctively following the routine instilled during numerous lessons in dealing with multiple combatant situations she had received. Swinging her gaze swiftly from one to the other occupant, although she was unable to identify the men by their respective names, she was thinking as swiftly as she could of the order of precedence in which she must deal with them. She realized that drawing the correct conclusions could spell the difference between life and death for herself and three women.

One glance informed the red head that, even without having been compelled to announce herself in such a fashion, there was no chance of her entrance going unnoticed by all the men. Nor, as she had already deduced from hearing their voices, were they close enough together for her to be able to cover them in such a fashion that each would feel himself sufficiently threatened to the extent that they would surrender rather than risk being the selected target. The nearest was by the table in the centre of the room, with a sawed-off riot gun raised to carry out the threat he had made to Emmy-Mae. On the stairs, another of the quartet was armed with a revolver which he was starting to bring into alignment. Closest together were the pair by the window. The one armed with a revolver was already moving towards Mildred Stenhart, but the second held a Uzi submachine gun and was staring towards the doorway. What was more, regardless of the obvious surprise he had received, he began to raise his weapon in a way suggestive of possessing skill in its use.

The latter point warned Alice which man she must make her first objective!

Unfortunately, despite giving evidence of being equally startled, the other three were displaying signs of responding quickly to the danger posed by the arrival of the red head!

There was, Alice realized, no possible way she could render all four men *hors de combat* swiftly enough to prevent some of them from being able to open fire upon her!

The red head knew her only hope of salvation lay in the Stenhart Sisters justifying her confidence in them!

Forcing herself to maintain an icy calm and following

the dictates of her trained reflexes, Alice swung the Colt Commander in the direction of the man who she had concluded was the greatest peril. She was holding it in the way which, as developed and perfected by master combat pistol handler, Sheriff Jack Weaver of Lancaster, California, allowed much greater accuracy and control to be attained than when only a single hand was employed. What was more, when purchasing it as a present for her,[9] Brad Counter had had it 'accurized' by the Pachmyr Gun Works of Los Angeles to increase its already considerable potential as a basically defensive weapon. Aligning the barrel—equipped with sights superior to those with which it left the factory—upon the centre of the moustached man's chest, she squeezed at the 'trigger shoe' fitted to give the impression of a lighter 'pull' for the forefinger without reducing the safety margin offered by the four pounds' pressure required to release the sear and permit the hammer to perform its function.[10]

How effectively the red head had acquired skill at handling the powerful pistol showed when it roared once, then—the recoil kick having been counteracted while the cocking slide was carrying out the recharging of the chamber—a second time in *very* quick succession. Flying as they were directed, the two .45 calibre bullets took Bernard Grant where they were aimed before he could turn the Uzi into its desired alignment and he was slammed backwards against the wall by the impact. It also caused him to tilt the weapon upwards involuntarily. As he rebounded helplessly from the unyielding surface, although he had continued to squeeze the trigger and the mechanism was set for automatic fire, the contents of the magazine which were discharged before it fell from his hands went harmlessly into the ceiling.

9. *Why the present was given is told in*: THE 1/4 SECOND DRAW.
10. *A more detailed description of what is entailed by the 'accurizing' process can be found in*: Footnote Six *of the* Appendix *giving information concerning Deputy Sheriff Bradford 'Brad' Counter in various volumes of the* Rockabye County *series.*

Swiftly though the red head had removed the threat posed by the moustached man, the others were already responding in a way which could create an equal peril. Each of them was beginning to turn his weapon in her direction and, as she was starting to redirect the Colt to the one who she considered was now the most immediate danger, the only consolation she might have drawn was from realizing she had at least diverted them from their hostages. However, the thought was nullified by her realizing this might only be a temporary state of affairs. Given an opportunity, which would arise should she be shot before they were all prevented from doing so, the survivors would quickly cover the women they were momentarily ignoring. What was more, with their narcotic-inflamed tempers aroused, they might forget the sisters were to be used as hostages and shoot all three when the deputies, who would by this time be near the front door, changed direction and broke the window as being the quickest way to intervene.

Fortunately for Alice, unlike her, the three men were failing to take one very important factor into account!

Since the invasion of their home, the Stenhart Sisters had behaved in a completely passive and compliant fashion. They had not attempted to alert Patrolman O'Malley to the true state of affairs when he paid his visit. Nor had Mildred and Amelia done anything which might have informed the female caller that Emmy-Mae had lied when claiming the quartet were not on the premises. However, although the invaders had not appreciated the fact, their behaviour was caused by good sense rather than fear. It was intended to lull the men into a sense of false security which might offer an opportunity to turn the tables on them. What was more, they were equipped physically as well as mentally to do so should the chance be presented. While they might not be as fit as in the days when their act was regularly described by critics as 'offering the most agile and vigorous knockabout comedy adagio routine we have seen for many years', they still kept themselves in good condition. Therefore, they were far from being the meek and defenceless victims envisaged by their captors.

208

Without the need for discussion or advice, the entrance of Alice struck each of the Sisters as being the moment they had awaited!

Thrusting herself from the wall, Mildred knotted and swung her big right fist. It was a punch many a man would have been pleased to deliver, driven with force and precision by the full weight of a heavy and powerful body. Caught on the temple, Paul Donovan was knocked unconscious before he was aware any such action was contemplated. As the revolver slipped unheeded from his grasp, he hurtled sideways to collide with Grant's rebounding body and they went to the floor together.

Although Amelia lacked the size and strength of her larger 'sister', she proved just as adequate in supplying the assistance so badly needed by their rescuer. Instead of taking the time to stand up, raising both feet, she placed them in the centre of Martin Young's back and the thrust she gave with her shapely legs was powered by well developed muscles. A wail of alarm burst from Young as he was propelled forward from where he was standing on the stairs. He lost his hold on the revolver he had been aiming at the red head, but gave the matter no thought. There was nothing he could do to save himself plummeting downwards and he arrived head first on the floor. The sickening crunch of his descent and the limp way in which his body subsided indicated he would be taking no further interest in what was going on.

Of the captives, Emmy-Mae had been the one who the men had considered would give them least trouble. Everything about her had suggested that, even if she had not been terrified, she lacked the intelligence needed to take any action against them. The way in which she had behaved during the two visits had strengthened the impression she had deliberately sought to enhance. Therefore, Peter Hill did not give her so much as a thought when he forgot his intention of striking her and swung around. He learned how seriously he had been mistaken when he received a push which sent him staggering a few paces.

Having delivered the shove, Emmy-Mae continued to

prove she had a very good grasp of the situation. While she had diverted Hill, she knew her action was not sufficient to prevent him from resuming hostilities when he regained control over his movements and, as she lacked the strength to have dealt with him more effectively, this would happen very soon. She also realized she was standing on the line in which Alice was swinging the Colt. Concluding she would be an impediment to the red head's freedom to start shooting if she remained where she was, she twisted around and threw herself to the floor in the kind of rolling dive which had been a feature of her part in the Stenhart Sisters' act. Despite giving a squeak of pain, caused by discovering she had lost some of the agility which once allowed her to alight on even the boards of a stage without being hurt, she was satisfied that she had achieved her purpose.

Coming to a stop, Hill glared around. Much as he wished to avenge himself upon the slender woman, a sentiment increased by the unexpected push she had given him, he realized there was a far more pressing matter before he could do so. Snarling a sound more bestial than human, he tried to bring the riot gun into alignment upon the red head. Before he could quite achieve his purpose, the big automatic pistol was pointing his way. Accepting that no verbal persuasion would dissuade him from making an attempt to kill her, Alice responded in the only way which would save her life.

Once again, held rock steady in its new alignment, the Colt dispatched a bullet!

This time, however, the point of aim was different!

Knowing her own life and probably those of the three women would be forfeit if she failed, the red head lined the Colt's sights to attain an instantaneous kill. She achieved her purpose. Sent through the centre of his forehead, the truncated cone of lead was driven—as were all the rounds she had put into the magazine—by the increased charge of powder hand-loaded to achieve an even greater propulsive power than offered by the standard number of grains. It destroyed his brain and brought an immediate end to the automative processes which could otherwise have allowed him to fire the riot gun if he had been hit almost anywhere else. As it was, the weapon fell undischarged and he was flung against the table. Falling backwards on to it, he slid over to drop lifeless to the floor.

Before any of the women could speak, heavy footsteps thudded in the entrance hall!

However, the two male deputies who burst into the sitting-room found there was no need for the revolvers they held ready for use!

Grant and Hill were already dead, testimony to the skill with which Alice had handled her Colt automatic under extremely dangerous and worrying circumstances. Although Young was still alive, he expired as a result of his injuries before medical assistance arrived. Nor would he have survived if such help had been at hand immediately. On being revived, if Donovan had not had other things on his mind, he might have counted himself fortunate that he had suffered nothing worse than the blow which knocked him insensible.

'I'd like to say I'm sorry things turned out the way they did,' Alice remarked a few minutes after having fired the final shot of the rescue. Having left Grantley to deal with the situation in the sitting-room, she was seated at the kitchen table with the Stenhart Sisters. Like herself, they were all pale faced. However, being sensible and practical, they too were accepting that they had done what was necessary to save themselves from being killed and they suffered no remorse at having been compelled to help cause three men to die. 'But I can't, knowing what they did at Sergeant Dan's.'

'You did what you had to do,' Mildred asserted. 'And, if you hadn't killed those two, they'd have killed you and, most probably, us as well.'

'They deserved to die!' Emmy-Mae went on, with a most uncharacteristic firmness and vehemence. Gingerly rubbing at her right hip, which still throbbed from its contact with the floor at the conclusion of the dive, she continued, 'They boasted to us how they'd killed Sergeant Dan, that poor woman and her children and the one Mildred hit said they'd be doing some more killing when they got away.'

'Did he tell you where that would be?' Alice inquired, remembering what she had been told by the Agent Andrew Wilson about the destination for which the men were heading.

'No, the one with the moustache told him to shut his mouth, but not in those *exact* words, the foul-mouthed *beast*,' Emmy-Mae replied.[11] 'By the way, my dear, I'm sorry there wasn't time while I was in the bathroom for me to write on the mirror with soap and tell you they were here, the way I saw it done in a Jimmy Cagney movie.'[12]

'That's all right,' the red head answered and managed a smile at the way in which the slender woman had reverted to her usual demeanour. 'Even before I found the butts of grass they'd stamped out on the floor, I saw one of them had left the toilet seat up and knew you'd got men in the house.'

'I *hoped* it would make you realize we had,' Emmy-Mae declared, once more looking at her most vague and unintelligent. 'That's why I lifted it while I was in there.'

11. *Being questioned about his comment and finding himself the sole survivor, Paul Donovan sought to reduce the consequences of his part in the killings at Sergeant Dan's Diner by telling why he and his companions were going to Houston. Although they would have been willing to be participants in the Gay Rights parade, their purpose was nothing so innocuous. It was permitted by the authorities on the condition that it kept to a proscribed route. Agitators were to be present and cause a deviation from the agreed line of march. When the police intervened, Donovan and his three companions, dressed in a fashion which would give the impression they were 'rednecks' taking violent exception to the parade, were to start shooting from a hiding place nearby and provoke the officers into opening fire on the marchers in return. The motive behind the scheme was a combination of causing civil strife, debasing the image of the law enforcement officers who were allowed to carry arms, deriding the United States throughout the rest of the Free World and giving strength to the efforts of 'liberals' to have the private ownership of firearms abolished. Being warned, the authorities in Houston were able to prevent a replacement group from carrying out the plan.*

12. *The movie was* WHITE HEAT, *made in 1949, starring James Cagney, Virginia Mayo and Edmund O'Brien.*

THE END

APPENDIX ONE

Always something of a tomboy, with the full approval of her parents, Dawn Drummond-Clayton had duplicated the lessons in martial arts, use of weapons[1] and wilderness survival that her inseparable companion, James Allenvale 'Bunduki' Gunn was receiving.[2] Even during her formal and conventional education, which had not been neglected, she had contrived to keep up her training and did not forget what she had been taught. In addition, while attending Roedean,[3] she had taken part in every permissible sporting

---

1. *According to many acknowledged authorities—including master cutler William D. 'Bo' Randall, of Randall-Made Knives, ORLANDO, Florida, 32802, U.S.A.—Dawn's father, Sir Armond John Drummond-Clayton is the world's foremost exponent of fighting with a knife an other edged weapons. His definitive work on the subject,* KNIFE FIGHTING THROUGHOUT THE WORLD, *like an equally comprehensive work on unarmed combat, by Commander James Bond, seconded from the Royal Navy to the British Secret Service—its preparation is described by his biographer, Ian Fleming in:* DOCTOR NO—*was published only by Her Majesty's Stationary Office. Being classified 'Top Secret', neither volume is recorded in that department's records and the only copies of both works are in the possession of Britain's M.I.5 and America's Central Intelligence Agency.*

2. *Further details regarding James Allenvale 'Bunduki' Gunn are given in the* Bunduki *series. His sobriquet is derived from the Swahili word for a hand held firearm of any kind and permitted the horrible pun that, when a baby, he was,* toto ya bunduki, *'son of a gun'.*

3. *Although Dawn's parents, Lady Hazel and Sir Armond John Drummond-Clayton served with the owner and headmistress in the little publicised branch of British Military Intelligence code-named, 'Group Thirteen', their family background did not meet with the special qualifications required to allow her to be a pupil at Benkinsop's Academy For The Daughters Of Gentlefolk.*

and athletic activity, excelling in them all. However, like Bunduki, she had become completely disenchanted by the blatantly one-sided political bias and hypocrisy of the international sporting bodies and authorities, who banned South Africa from competition while welcoming with open arms far more viciously repressive left wing regimes. Therefore, despite being a world class athlete, gymnast, swimmer and fenced with sabre or epee, she refused to enter their events. For all that, she *always* kept herself in the peak of physical condition.

As was the case with Bunduki, much of Dawn's perfect health stemmed from being allowed to share in the longevity pills obtained by his adoptive parents.[4] Specimens had been presented to Dr. Clark 'Doc' Savage, Jr., for analysis and reproduction.[5] He had discovered that, in addition to slowing down the ageing process in

---

3a. Miss Amelia Penelope Diana 'Benkers' Benkinsop, George Medal—Britain's civilian equivalent of the Victoria Cross, highest military honour for valour—M.A., B. Sc. (Oxon), Honorary Member, Holloway Old Girls' Association (granted after having shared a cell at that prison with a member of a combined Communist-Nazi spy ring during 1940, while Russia was still enjoying the benefits of a non-aggression pact with Germany, to obtain information which broke it up) belongs to a family with a long established prominence in international criminal circles. Some of her history is recorded in: BLONDE GENIUS and Part One, 'Fifteen The Hard Way', J.T.'S LADIES.

3c. An earlier Miss Amelia Penelope Diana 'Benkers' Benkinsop—by tradition the eldest daughter always bore the same name and sobriquet, no matter who her father had been—paid a visit to the United States of America during the mid-1870's, some details of which are described in: BEGUINAGE IS DEAD!; Part Three, 'Birds Of A Feather'; WANTED! BELLE STARR and Part Five, 'The Butcher's Fiery End', J.T.'S LADIES.

4. For reasons which we explain in: Part Twelve, 'The Mchawi's Powers', J.T.'S HUNDREDTH, we can no longer disclose the identity of Bunduki's adoptive parents.

5. Details of Doctor Clark 'Doc' Savage, Jr.'s life and adventures are recorded in Kenneth Robeson's extensive series of Doc Savage biographies and in: DOC SAVAGE, His Apocalyptic Life, by Philip Jose Farmer. The latter also elaborates upon the original source of the longevity pills.

human beings—granting those taking the tablets what amounted to immortality, barring accidental death, suicide, or murder—they also gave complete immunity from every tropical disease and destroyed all such harmful internal parasites such as the various *nematode* worms (commonly called 'hookworms') of the genera *Nacator* which might be ingested while eating the raw flesh of wild animals. This was to become a matter of some importance when, shortly after the events recorded in this volume, she and Bunduki were to be transported by super intelligent beings known as the 'Suppliers' to the primitive planet of Zillikian. There, she had need of all her training and skills in order to survive.

5a. *Unfortunately, Doc Savage was unable to isolate the immunity from disease element so that the tablets could be reproduced without the added effect of increasing the life expectancy of the recipient. The latter factor, taken with the ever multiplying birthrate of human beings, would have led to the world becoming over-populated. Therefore, it was considered the pills were unsuitable for general use and they were never released to the public.*

APPENDIX TWO

Unlike her partner, Deputy Sheriff Bradford 'Brad' Counter,[1] Woman Deputy Alice Fayde entered the Rockabye County Sheriff's Office by conventional means. Prior to the appointment, she had served seven years on the Gusher City Police Department's Bureau Of Women Officers,[2] rising through the ranks from walking a beat to becoming a sergeant in the Detective Bureau. She had worked in such diverse Divisions as Evans Park—the slum area known as the 'Bad Bit'—and high-rent Upton Heights. In addition, she had spent time in various specialist Squads, such as Traffic, Juvenile and Narcotics. All of which had combined to give her a very thorough knowledge of law enforcement duties. Furthermore, she had become an expert shot with a handgun, or *offensive* weapons such a telescopic sighted 'sniper's' rifle and a 'trench', or 'riot' gun.[2] Her training had also instilled a

1. *Details regarding the career and family background of Deputy Sheriff Bradford 'Brad' Counter are given in the various volumes of the* Rockabye County *series.*

2. *'Riot gun': a single barrelled, twelve gauge, five shot, generally pump action, shotgun used by law enforcement agencies. One of the earliest examples was the Winchester Model of 1897 as modified for use in the trench warfare of World War 1 by having the barrel reduced to twenty inches—'sporting' versions being at least four inches longer—given a radiating cooling sleeve to permit sustained rapid fire and equipped to take a bayonet.*

2a. *The 'trench gun', as such weapons—they are no longer classed as sporting guns—came to be known proved to be an exceptionally effective device for use at close, or in confined, quarters, especially when charged with nine .32 calibre buckshot balls. One purpose to which it was put was to deflect 'stick' hand grenades thrown by the enemy.*

sound working knowledge of unarmed combat, which she had been compelled to put to use when in contention against dangerous female criminals on more than one occasion.[3] As a deputy, she had a rank equivalent to a lieutenant in the G.C.P.D.'s Patrol Bureau, or a detective sergeant.

In addition to their other duties, the Sheriff's Office were responsible for the investigation throughout the whole of Rockabye County of homicide and twenty-two other legal infractions—such as arson, wife-beating, bigamy, assault and train wrecking—which might end in murder. The idea behind handling the subsidiary crimes was so that, if death should result through their commission, the officers in charge would already have knowledge of the facts leading up to it.

The Sheriff's Office based in the Gusher City Department Of Public Safety Building worked a two-watch rota.

2b. *After trench guns had been employed to play a major part in breaking up a mass infantry attack, the Germans—who had already delivered assaults with poison gas, including the vicious 'mustard' variety; an early version of which was responsible for some of the events recorded in* A MATTER OF HONOUR—*complained such use was an 'inhumane and barbaric way of waging war'. Their threat to execute any member of the American Expeditionary Force captured with a trench gun in his possession was countered by a reminder from the United States that a number of German prisoners of war were being held and Congress would know what action to take by way of reprisals.*

2c. *Between World War 1 and 2, peace officers adopted the trench gun format as an offensive weapon—handguns being primarily issued for defensive purposes-and these were given the name, 'riot guns'. However, during the early 1970's, the management of the Remington Arms Company considered the term 'riot gun' was inaccurate and had an undesirable connotation as such weapons were not confined to coping with civic disorders. The correct purpose, they claimed with complete justification, was to supplement the* defensive *armament of peace officers in all types of law enforcement combat situations. Therefore, the Company designated such firearms of the kind which they manufacture 'police guns'.*

3. *Occasions when Woman Deputy Alice Fayde was compelled to defend herself with bare hands against another woman are recorded in*: THE PROFESSIONAL KILLERS, THE DEPUTIES *and* BAD HOMBRE.

The Day watch commenced at eight in the morning and ended at four in the afternoon, with the Night Watch continuing from four until midnight. If deputies were required between midnight and eight in the morning, the G.C.P.D.'s permanently manned 'Business Office' would call them from their homes.

APPENDIX THREE

In every democracy, the laws framed for the protection of the innocent have loopholes which can be exploited for the benefit of the undeniably guilty—and frequently are!

Although accepting that such a state of affairs must exist in a free society, the serving Governor of Texas grew very concerned over the ever increasing wave of lawlessness which had followed in the wake of the well meant—albeit unpopular, ill advised and difficult to enforce—ratification of the so called 'Volstead Act'.[1] He concluded that only unconventional methods could cope with malefactors who slipped through the meshes of the legal system. Ordinary peace officers, being severely restricted by Federal, State, county and municipal regulations, were unable to take the necessary action in circumstances of this nature.[2]

1. 'Volstead Act', the colloquial name for the Eighteenth (Prohibition) Amendment to the Constitution of the United States of America. This defined intoxicating liquors as those containing more than one half of one percent alcohol and made illegal the manufacture, transportation and sale of such liquors for beverage purposes. Introduced by Representative Andrew J. Volstead of Minnesota, the act was ratified—over the veto of President Woodrow Wilson—on October the 18th, 1919. By the time it was repealed in 1933, it had inadvertently helped finance and pave the way for the rise of 'organized crime'.
2. The jurisdictional authority of a town marshal or police department was restricted to the municipality by whom they were hired, and a sheriff's office within the boundaries of the county to which its personnel were elected. As was suggested by the title of the latter, Arizona and Texas Rangers and State Police were restricted to their specific States.

While pondering upon the problem, the Governor met three prominent European criminologists who were touring the United States and giving a series of lectures on this subject to the heads of major law enforcement agencies. Acting upon the unconventional suggestions of George Manfred, Leon Gonzales and Raymond Poiccart,[3] he had instructed the State Attorney General to select a special group of Texas Rangers who would form—without any mention of it being made public—a new Company given the identifying letter 'Z' and put under the command of Major Benson Tragg. Every man was picked for his courage, skill with weapons and bare handed combat, integrity, specialized knowledge and devotion to the cause of justice. Their purpose was to deal with such criminals as could not be touched by conventional methods, even if the means they employed to do so might be considered as stepping beyond the legal boundaries of the law.[4]

Having met Sergeant Alvin Dustine Fog and the other members of Company 'Z' while they were engaged in trapping a crooked financier who could not be extradited from Mexico, and while she was trying to take revenge upon him for causing the death of her parents, Rita Yarborough was made an 'official unofficial' member of the group.[5] She proved herself very useful, particularly when there was a need to deal with other women in the course of Company 'Z's' specialized type of duties.[6]

Except for Company 'Z' when on 'official unofficial' assignments, in general Rangers were expected to wait until invited by county or municipal agencies before being able to participate in either's investigations. United States' Marshals, their deputies, the Federal Bureau of Investigation and Prohibition agents had country-wide jurisdiction. However, the first three were responsible only for handling 'Federal' crimes such as robbery of the mails and kidnapping.

2a. During the late 1870's, the Governor of Arizona formed a similar force to cope with law breaking in his State. A similar decision was taken by a later Governor and the Arizona Rangers were brought back into being. Why it was considered necessary to organize the first force, how it operated and was finally disbanded is recorded in the Waco *series.*

2b. The Texas Rangers were to all practical intents and purposes abolished—their functions being taken over by the more prosaic Department Of Public Safety at Austin and the Highway Patrol—on October the 17th, 1935. This was almost one hundred years to the day after their formation. Although their first purpose was to act as militia, or what in present day terms would be called a 'para-military' organization, to help fend off marauding Indians, they became increasingly responsible for supporting the local authorities in the enforcement of law and order.

3. George Manfred, Leon Gonzales and Raymond Poiccart were the surving members of the 'Four Just Men' crime fighting organization, the fourth having been killed before their first recorded adventure was published. Although none of the following volumes cover their lecture tour of the United States, see chronologically: THE FOUR JUST MEN, THE COUNCIL OF JUSTICE, THE LAW OF THE FOUR JUST MEN, AGAIN THE THREE *and* THE THREE JUST MEN. *by Edgar Wallace.*

5. Told in: RAPIDO CLINT.

6. An example of how Rita Yarborough dealt with another woman in the course of an assignment is given in: THE RETURN OF RAPIDO CLINT AND MR. J.G. REEDER.

OTHER FINE NOVELS AVAILABLE BY
J.T. EDSON

The prices shown below were correct at the time of going to press. However Transworld Publishers reserve the right to show new retail prices on covers which may differ from those previously advertised in the text or elsewhere.

ORDER FORM

All these books are available at your book shop or newsagent, or can be ordered direct from the publisher. Just tick the titles you want and fill in the form below.

Transworld Publishers, Cash Sales Department,
61-63 Uxbridge Road, Ealing, London, W5 5SA

Please send cheque or postal order, not cash. All cheques and postal orders must be in £ sterling and made payable to Transworld Publishers Ltd.

Please allow cost of book(s) plus the following for postage and packing:

U.K./Republic of Ireland Customers:
Orders in excess of £5; no charge
Orders under £5; add 50p

Overseas Customers:
All orders; add £1.50

NAME (Block Letters) ....

ADDRESS ....

....